The Bold Choices of a Devoted Lady

(Book 3 in the Nouveau Riche Series)

By Ramona Elmes

www.ramonaelmes.com

For my mom.

You may not be an avid romance reader anymore, but my love of this genre started by stealing your books. Thank you for always being so encouraging, blunt, and helpful.

Contents

The Bold Choices of a Devoted Lady

Chapter 1	1
Chapter 2	14
Chapter 3	29
Chapter 4	39
Chapter 5	52
Chapter 6	64
Chapter 7	73
Chapter 8	84
Chapter 9	94
Chapter 10	106
Chapter 11	116
Chapter 12	126
Chapter 13	137
Chapter 14	147
Chapter 15	158
Chapter 16	168
Chapter 17	176
Chapter 18	187
Chapter 19	200
Chapter 20	209

Chapter 21 219
Chapter 22 229
Chapter 23 241
Chapter 24 253
Chapter 25 263
Chapter 26 273
Chapter 27 281
Chapter 28 290
Chapter 29 302
Chapter 30 312
Chapter 31 321
Thank You for Reading! 331
About the Author 333
Acknowledgements 335

Prologue

Philadelphia - 1831

Annie Kincaide threw herself on her bed and let out an exaggerated sigh. She despised the girls she was forced to spend time with now that her adoptive parents had built a home on Philadelphia's prestigious Chestnut Street. Since they'd moved, everyone in their new social circle eyed them with curiosity and disdain.

These new girls acted as if the streets the Kincaides came from were a shocking embarrassment. Annie rolled her eyes. Only Chestnut Street, Walnut Street, and Mulberry Street were acceptable places to live. Her parents smiled through similar pointed statements or ignored them all together. Annie couldn't fathom why Maggie and Joseph would want to move them to such a neighborhood.

The girls who just left her house, with their uncontrollable giggles and flouncy dresses, only enhanced Annie's irritation of the family's new home. Annie smacked at the ruffles on her own dress in disgust. She looked around at her expansive bedroom filled with endless luxuries. Most nights, she snuck into Sophia's room, uncomfortable with the space and not wanting to be alone.

Annie vividly remembered the day Maggie and Joseph took them to see the plot where their current home would be built. Her siblings Sam, Jack, and Sophia had smiled in delight, but Annie had frowned, unable to hide her alarm. She didn't want to move and didn't understand why Joseph and Maggie did.

She loved their small townhouse that was close to where Joseph and Maggie's shipping company was located in Southwark. The sounds of the docks, watching the men and women coming and going from their jobs, and even the smell wafting off the water, was a great comfort to her. It was their home. Well, it was their home until Maggie and Joseph changed everything.

The increase in riots and crime in Southwark ultimately spurred their move and Annie could logically understand their concerns, but her heart belonged to their old neighborhood. Not the fashionable streets that they now promenaded along with other well-to-do families, who either insisted on showing off their new wealth or highlighting their family name.

For the people of Southwark, money was used for survival. The girls she knew there were either working or training in their trade. Happiness existed, but it came with a large dose of realism. The bubbly girls of Chestnut Street, Walnut Street, and Mulberry Street likely had never seen anything beyond their fancy streets. She snorted, thinking about how ridiculous they acted. Their greatest concerns centered on who was wearing the most stylish dress and who would dazzle society during their coming out.

"Annie, I was wondering where you disappeared to. You dashed away so quickly after your friends left," Maggie said.

Annie jutted her chin out. "Those girls are not my friends. They only tolerate us because of our money. They whisper awful things when they think no one is listening."

A sigh was the only response Annie received, but she felt the bed shift as Maggie came to sit next to her on the bed. She rolled over and sat up, pulling her knees to her chest. Her governess would likely be upset at her unladylike position, but Annie didn't care.

"Give them time. They can't all be bad."

Annie glanced at her in disbelief and Maggie smiled at her. "We want you all to have the very best. That is why we have spent so much time on your education since you came to live with us. To give you back a little of what you lost."

Guilt clouded her mother's face. Annie knew she was remembering the fateful decision they made all those years ago to leave Annie and Jack at the orphanage. A decision that resulted in Jack and Annie enduring hellish years, where survival was based on the headmistress Mrs. Seawald's whims. They barely escaped and only did so because of Annie's horrific accident. Annie instinctively ran her thumb across the scars on her opposite arm. Scars that would stay with her forever.

Unlike Jack, Annie didn't remember their real parents, so she couldn't miss what she'd never had. Life at the orphanage and with Maggie and Joseph was all she knew. Yes, the orphanage had been awful, but without that part of her life she wouldn't have met her brother Sam or be here now with her family. Even if she hated Chestnut Street, she loved her family.

"You could have never known what it would be like under Mrs. Seawald's care," Annie said, hating seeing her mother upset.

Maggie leaned in and squeezed her hand. "You don't need to do that. It was the worst choice and I regret it. Even more now that you are mine to love."

Annie squeezed her hand back, knowing no words would suffice. She suspected this house and acquainting them with the elite of Philadelphia was Maggie and Joseph's way of making amends for the life that was taken from her and Jack. Still, she didn't and couldn't miss a life she never had.

"What if I can never be like them?" Annie whispered, revealing her self-doubt.

Annie didn't know how to be lighthearted. She didn't know how to giggle at silly things. She was happy at times, but never in the silly way those girls behaved. Not in the way her younger sister Sophia acted. They were girls who had never endured anything.

"You will find your way among them," Maggie reassured.

"I am not like Sophia. I am not a silly person who carries silly books around. Someone who thinks fairy tales exist. Such nonsense," she scoffed.

A thump of something hitting the elegant carpet in the hallway drew both of their eyes to the door. The patter of feet and the shutting of the door caused Annie's brows to rise in alarm.

"Was that Sophia? Did she hear me?" Annie asked, horrified.

"You will make amends," Maggie said, with the confidence only a mother had.

When Annie and her brothers came to live with Maggie and Joseph, she had been skeptical of them. It was Sophia, their daughter, that eventually wore down her defenses. She had only been nine at the time and unaware of Jack and Annie's previous connection to her parents. Sophia had ignored Annie's hostile looks and followed her everywhere until Annie finally started to look forward to spending time with her always-happy sister.

Someday they would all have to tell Sophia the whole truth about how Annie, Jack, and Sam came to be in their lives, but Maggie and Joseph wanted to wait until she was older. She didn't blame them. If it was Annie's choice, she would never tell her, but the rest of her family was adamant she would be told.

Annie's mind wandered back to the current dilemma, dealing with the girls of the elite. How she wished she didn't have to. She buried her face in her knees. Maggie rubbed her back and said, "The thing is, you don't have to be like them, but you have to let them be who they are too. You can still accept them without wanting to be them."

"What if they don't like who I am?" Annie said, lifting her head, revealing more of her fears.

Maggie grabbed her by the chin and smiled at her. "Witty. Brilliant. Loyal. Who wouldn't want a friend like you?"

Annie smiled back at her, encouraged by her words.

"What are my girls doing in here?" Joseph said, bounding into the room.

Maggie released her chin. "Just chatting."

"Did you have a grand time with your new friends?" Joseph asked earnestly.

Her mother rose and patted him on the chest. "She is still figuring it out."

"In a couple years, those will be the girls you will have your coming out with. You have plenty of time to discover who is to be a friend or foe."

Annie scowled. "I do not care if I have a coming out. I do not care if I ever marry."

Joseph chuckled, and Annie stared at him mutinously. "I do not care."

Her father sobered, realizing how serious she was. He shrugged and said, "You will have a coming out. Still, we won't force you to marry. That will be your choice. You will be set for life, regardless."

Annie looked at him, surprised, expecting a fight. She nodded in acceptance. He winked at her. "But keep in mind, Maggie also said she would never marry before she set her eyes on me."

Maggie rolled her eyes and swatted at him.

Later that night, Annie made her way quietly into Sophia's

room. The fire was still going, and she saw a lump in the center of the bed move slightly. She pushed at it. "Move over."

The lump said nothing, and Annie pushed at it again.

The covers flew back, and Sophia glared at her. "Why? I am just a silly girl. Why would you want to spend time with me?"

Annie rolled her eyes at her thirteen-year-old sister's theatrics. Still, she hated to see Sophia so upset. Maggie was right. She could accept silliness and grow to love it, even if it wasn't who she was. Her love for Sophia proved that.

"I am sorry my words hurt your feelings. It was unkind," Annie stated.

Sophia's eyes flashed. "Yes, it was. I don't go about complaining about how serious you are. You know why? Because I accept you for who you are."

Annie nodded. "I am sorry. Why don't you read me some of the novelette you have hiding under the blankets?"

Sophia's chin tilted stubbornly. "Why? You don't believe in fairy tales."

It was true, but she very much wanted her sister to keep believing in them. She would never ever want Sophia to know or endure any of the hardships she had in her life.

"Perhaps with the right story, I will change my mind," Annie said.

Sophia still sat there silently until Annie nudged her over and slid under the blankets with her. "Now, what is this story about?"

Her sister, unable to stay angry at anyone, gave in. "It is about a knight who rescues a princess from an ogre, but then it turns out the knight is the true villain, and you will never guess."

"What?" Annie said, amused at her excitement.

"The ogre becomes the hero and wins the princess's hand in marriage," Sophia exclaimed.

Annie stopped herself from snorting. "Well, read me some."

Sophia opened the book but turned to Annie. "I love you, Annie. I hope you get your own fairy tale someday, silliness and all."

"Perhaps. Now start reading."

Annie didn't have it in her heart to tell her sister that she didn't believe in such things. Still, she secretly hoped for her sister's sake they could be true. At least true for girls who believed in silly things and looked at the world with giddiness. For Annie, that part of her was long gone, if it ever existed.

Her sister whispered softly, "You don't have to believe because I believe for you."

Annie laid her head on her sister's shoulder as Sophia introduced the ogre turned hero of the novelette.

Chapter 1

The Gentlemen's Club, the Den, London, May 1842

The Duke of Peyton's sister, Lady Annabelle Kincaide, or just Annie to her friends and family, stood in the perplexing cottage that looked like a woodsman's hut. Well, besides the tree jutting out of the middle of it. Why would someone build a cottage around a tree? The structure was utterly ridiculous but equally fascinating.

She ran her fingers along the tree trunk in somewhat disbelief before pacing nervously. She smiled, amused. Somehow it suited Simon Miller. This was Miller's home. The place he spent his time when not seeing to his duties at the gentlemen's club he was a partner in.

The gentlemen's club, the Den, was only a few hundred yards away from the cottage. Tonight, music and laughter echoed through the lush gardens that, alongside Simon's dwelling, were sprinkled with cottages designed to represent famous sites from all over the world. Rumors were rampant about the liaisons that took place in the cottages, even reaching the innocent ears of the *ton*. A decadent place filled with gambling, dancing, and drinking that allowed the elite of London to play without any censorship.

Perhaps more shocking, twice a year the club planned to host scandalous balls, opening its doors to the elite, both women and men, so they could freely find lovers and companions without gossip. Tonight, was the second ball the Den hosted this year. The invitation called it the Ball of Sin.

What happened at the balls was said to remain at the balls. Any gossip or sharing of who attended was fiercely guarded, and those who spread gossip could be removed or banned from the premises. Innocents were banned altogether.

She chuckled to herself. That was why when she arrived at the Den tonight, the butler Donahue's eyes shot up in alarm. Annie insisted that she attend the Ball of Sin, but the butler followed protocol and made her stay in the carriage. She demanded to see Miller, refusing to leave. The butler, flustered, joined her in the carriage and then ushered her to Miller's cottage.

Annie supposed even with the mask Donahue would know her. The Den had been owned by her family for a brief time. Back then, the lush grounds and building were known as the Merry estate. The poor butler had cared for the place through more than one improper owner. Prior to her own family, the estate was owned by the young Marquess of Merry, whose reputation was almost as notorious as his predecessor.

She took her cloak and mask off before glancing down at her scandalous dress. Likely not as risqué as some, but the midnight blue dress dropped daringly low and swathed her arms in black lace, making her appear more courtesan than young lady. She chuckled, thinking about Donahue's expression when he identified who she was. To be honest, she'd been shocked to see him and assumed turning the estate into a gentlemen's club would have caused him to seek employment elsewhere.

She clutched her small purse that held what she came to give Miller. The purse contained a letter and a portrait of herself. Tonight, she was here to tell Miller her true feelings about him. That she cared for him. She blushed at the thought. Her lips lifted in an amused smirk, thinking she was seeking the fairy tale Sophia was always trying to force on her. Her smirk turned to a frown; nervous because she hadn't seen Miller in quite some time.

She did her best to push the doubt away, remembering the kiss they'd shared prior to her and her family moving to

England. Before the kiss, she cared for Miller but only as a dear friend. He was her confidant. Someone she never worried about offending and could be her true self with. They had been laughing, and he kissed her. A brief kiss, but one that seemed to open a door that wasn't there before.

He left for England shortly afterwards, and since she and her family arrived, had been distant. His distance made Annie's actions tonight risky and was why she couldn't completely keep her nerves calm. Regardless, she would have her answer tonight. Annie couldn't wait any longer; she needed to know how he felt.

Still, she was being reckless. She could be ruined if she was found at the Den, destroying her and Sophia's chance for proper matches. She smiled. Her love-obsessed sister would be all for her actions.

No more guessing. Tonight, she would know if Miller reciprocated her feelings.

"Annie? What are you wearing and what are you doing here? Jack and Sam would be livid if they knew about this," Miller said, entering the cottage.

She turned to see him standing at the door. Her eyes swept over him, and she sucked in her breath. Why was it before the kiss she'd never noticed how handsome he was? She always considered Miller impressive, but in the last few years there was a physical connection between them that intensified whenever they were near one another.

Perhaps it was the physical transformation Miller had undergone in the last few years. He was larger and more imposing. Her eyes roamed over his wide shoulders and across his hard chest. He had only been twenty-four when he joined her family's employ and appeared to be closer to a boy than a man. She gulped. But now he seemed like a man.

She flushed, embarrassed at her thoughts and the sensations coursing through her. Still, her feelings stemmed from so much more than his appearance. Miller was respectful, but more than that, he treated her as his equal. A quality that Annie knew was rare in a man. If she didn't have such an aversion to marriage, she probably would have realized long ago how much Miller meant to her.

"Annie?"

Her gaze snapped back to his brown eyes, studying her intently.

"I have something to say to you," she began, pulling the letter and portrait from her purse.

Annie was never good with words and her nerves caused her hands to shake. Miller frowned at her.

"Perhaps I could visit you tomorrow, and we can talk?" he said, grabbing her cloak.

"I care for you," Annie blurted out.

Her light flush darkened across her skin, and she hated herself for it. She never blushed. Miller placed the cloak down, turning away from her. He paused, and Annie wondered what he was thinking.

Finally, he turned around. "Annie, I think you're confused. If this is about the kiss in Philadelphia, I apologize. It shouldn't have happened."

"I'm not looking for an apology. I care for you," she stated matter-of-factly.

He walked towards her and smiled, but it wasn't his normal smile. The one he used when only they knew each other's thoughts. Instead, he smiled at her as if she was some young impetuous child or girl. "Annie, you think you care for me.

Your family has been through so much in the last few years. I promise, what you are feeling is nothing more than a fanciful crush."

Her eyes widened in shock at both his smirk and condescending tone. Why was he talking to her like that? Miller never talked to anyone in such a patronizing way, least of all women. Their friendship started because of how different he was from other men in that regard. Most men only spoke to women, but Miller, even beyond her, took the time to listen to the women in his acquaintance as he would any man.

"I promise you a kiss by your future husband will be far better than what we shared," Miller added.

She turned cold, shocked by his words. "And our friendship?"

"We will always be friends, but Annie be reasonable. You are a lady. I was your family's man-of-affairs and with that comes a certain level of camaraderie with my employer," he said, pragmatically.

The cold turned to hurt. Also, confusion, that he was insinuating their friendship was based on his employment. "You kissed me."

Her eyes pierced his, demanding he say something. His brown eyes narrowed, and he clenched his jaw before looking away. Why was he angry?

"So you are saying it was nothing, and our friendship was merely part of being employed by my family?"

He still wasn't looking at her. "Look at me," she demanded.

Simon lifted his eyes to hers. "We are friends, but perhaps you have interpreted my actions to be more than they are."

For the last five years, Miller had never been far from her side. Almost every day at her family home in Philadelphia, he joined her for walks in the garden or kept her company in the sitting room. Confusion clouded her memories of their time together.

The hurt in her intensified. Her lips trembled, and she hated that she couldn't hide her reaction. She took a deep breath to calm her emotions.

Was this why she hadn't seen Miller in so long?

Their conversations had been just a way to keep her family happy. For a brief moment, his eyes filled with concern, but then it was gone. He smiled at her again and said, "We are in different places. I am the owner of a gentlemen's club, and you are a lady. I want what is best for you and your whole family, but nothing more. Your carriage is outside. Let's get you home before anyone notices you are gone."

He grabbed her cloak and walked to the door of the cottage, waiting for her. As Annie got closer to him, the hurt subsided, but fury built within her. At him, but more so at herself for thinking something actually existed between them.

And the kiss. Did he kiss all women he knew that way? He swung the door open as she reached him, and he smiled down at her condescendingly.

Annie probably would have said nothing, but his smile inflamed the fury she felt. The letter and portrait were still in her hands. In a fit of anger, she ripped them in half mere inches from his face and tossed the pieces to the floor.

She glared at him. "Perhaps you shouldn't kiss your employers."

The smile disappeared from his face, and he attempted to pick up the discarded papers. Annie pushed past him, out the door to the carriage. She remembered her cloak at the last moment and spun on her heels. She collided into him. He had followed her out. Her cloak fell to the ground as he grabbed her forearms to steady her. Their bodies, so intimately touching, disconcerted Annie. She wanted to revel in it, but his words echoed through her mind. She pushed against his chest. "Let me go."

Miller released her instantly and ran his hands through his brown hair. "Annie—"

She grabbed her cloak from the ground and held her hand up. "No. You have said all that is needed. Do not worry, Mr. Miller, I will no longer be a bother to you. You don't have to pretend to enjoy yourself when you are around me. It is quite clear we are and have only been acquaintances."

Annie rushed to the carriage and ignored the coachman who helped her in. She normally wasn't so rude, but she needed to be alone and to not look back at Miller standing just a few feet away. He made his way to the carriage window as if to say something to her. Annie tapped on the side of the carriage, needing to be anywhere but in front of Miller's cottage. The carriage started moving, and he stepped back.

The first tear slid down her cheek, and she swiped at it. Annie wouldn't cry. She had endured worse things than being told by Simon Miller he didn't care for her the way she cared for him. Hell, she survived the death of her parents, spent most of her life in an orphanage, and endured a horrific injury before being taken in by Maggie and Joseph.

She let her head fall back against the cushioned seats in the carriage. Then why did it hurt so much? Not only was she hurt, but embarrassed. She didn't want to feel this way. She never wanted love. That was Sophia's desire, not hers.

Their kiss in the sitting room at the Kincaide's family estate in Philadelphia flashed in her mind.

"You should have heard him out at least," Miller said, watching Annie's suitor depart from the sitting-room window.

Annie snorted and walked to the window to stare with him. "Nonsense. Any man who starts his proposal by listing off why he is the best to make choices for me is not a consideration. Morley can barely remember what he said five minutes ago. I'm not sure why he thought I would consider it. Oh, that's right, I'm a spinster."

Simon smiled down at her with a twinkle in his eyes. "You are twenty-four. Spinsterhood is not upon you."

She rolled her eyes and said, "It certainly is, and I embrace it."

He laughed. "Don't embrace it too quickly."

"You see my options. Men only see me as a wealthy heiress without a thought in my head. Most probably would prefer me thoughtless."

"Not all men want that. There are plenty of men who would delight in conversing with you," he said.

Something in his tone changed. His brown eyes flared with something she hadn't seen in them before, desire. At the time, Annie didn't realize how close they were standing until one of his hands cupped the back of her head. Her stomach dropped right before Simon's lips grazed hers so delicately and light. She gasped and was drawn to taste his lips again, but just as fast he stepped away and smiled at her. "I shouldn't have done that."

Perhaps he shouldn't have, but Annie wanted him to do it again.

"Yet you did," she said, slightly breathless.

He smiled sheepishly at her, and Annie blurted out. "What if I want you to do it again?"

Miller wrapped his arms around her waist and drew her close. The intense desire that swam in his eyes wasn't that of a man about to provide a chaste kiss. The front door slammed shut, and they sprang apart. He took a deep breath.

Footsteps rapidly approached the sitting room and Sophia flounced in. "Miller! I thought you were in London."

He smiled warmly at Sophia. "I leave tomorrow morning, but I should go. I have much to prepare."

He headed to the door but stopped and looked back at Annie with a smile. A connection passed between them, and Annie smiled back at him, seeing them as something different for the first time.

Annie scowled at the memory. He had smiled at her then as if they had shared something special, unlike the condescending smile he had given her this evening. The arrogant ass, she thought. She frowned. What changed? Since arriving in London, Miller had been distant. Did Annie read too much into the simple kiss and his reaction? Perhaps it had really been the smallest of kisses. But why kiss her at all?

She hated him. She stared out the window, knowing that wasn't true, but a way for her to easily explain the ache in her chest.

~

Simon Miller stood, watching the carriage carrying Annie Kincaide move down the bridleway. He didn't turn his gaze away until it rounded a corner and was out of sight. His heart hammered as he stalked back into his cottage. He slammed the door so hard the wood holding the cottage together rattled around him. Her hurt face appeared in his mind. What he had done to her was reprehensible, but it was for her own good.

He moved to the sideboard and poured himself a glass of brandy, trying to compose his thoughts. And where did she obtain such a scandalous dress? He felt himself go hard as he conjured another vision of her in his mind. His beautiful Annie, so scantily dressed, threw his senses in disarray. He yearned to touch her, to shake her thick black hair free from the pins containing it. But the dress was what almost brought him to his knees.

Annie was often more covered up than other women. She had suffered a horrible incident that left scars down one side of her body. Her arms had still been covered in a translucent lace, but the front of the dress had electrified his senses. The neckline scooped down far beyond what was acceptable for an unwed lady, presenting her bosom as if they were a feast for him alone. The dress had cinched at her waist before swirling around her in more black lace and midnight blue fabric.

She looked beautiful, hell she looked like temptation come alive. From the moment he walked into the cottage, he yearned to kiss her and not in the gentle kiss he gave her in Philadelphia,
but a hard, searing kiss that would leave her breathless.

As he drank his brandy, his eyes landed on the papers Annie had ripped up and thrown at him. Simon placed his glass on a table and slowly walked over to where they laid, scattered. He told himself he should throw them in the fireplace. Whatever Annie's words were, they were not for him. He had told her as much. He grabbed the papers in one hand and crossed the room. As he considered throwing them in the fire, he glanced down.

The top paper was the upper half of a portrait of Annie. One her family commissioned for her season in London. In her anger, she had torn the portrait in half at her waist. He stared down at the woman that appeared in his dreams every night. She stared out of the portrait with more of a smirk than a smile. The artist had captured the wry humor that emanated from Annie. Most people thought she was arrogant or unfriendly, but it was simply that Annie refused, or possibly didn't even have it in her, to be a giggling, simpering lady.

Most men would be put off by her temperament, but for Simon

it only fueled his desire for her. He strode back to the table, tossing the papers on its surface. He grabbed his drink and stared into the fire.

The damn kiss, no matter how chaste it was, had been constantly on his mind. Afterwards, he left for London filled with happiness and optimism that a courtship between him and Annie was imminent.

Then he saw Tobias Walker at Devons' tavern. He scowled, thinking of the man. The man whose actions sent his father to prison and ultimately his death. His obsession to exact justice against Walker had started to diminish during his time in Philadelphia. He had grown to not just care for Annie, but the rest of the Kincaide family as well. But the moment he saw Walker in London, it all came roaring back.

When he wasn't preparing for the Kincaides move to London, he had practically stalked the man. His fury only grew as he watched Walker mingle among the *ton.* He had not only survived in London but thrived. It strengthened Miller's resolve to prove his father's innocence and destroy Walker. By the time Annie arrived in London, he knew that he could never have a life with her. She had endured so much already. He would not let his obsession overwhelm her life like it had his.

Miller did his best to keep her at a distance, but every one of her smiles beckoned him, and he yearned to talk to her. More than that, he craved to touch her. When Devons and his business partner, the Marquess of Derry, made him an offer to be partners in the Den, he jumped at the chance. He resigned as the Kincaides man-of-affairs, hoping that Annie would move on, not because he didn't want her, but because he wanted more for her than what he could offer.

He glanced down at the letter, sliding the two pieces together. His eyes drank in her words from the paper. Once he was finished, in a fit of rage, he hurled his glass into the fireplace.

No, Annie needed to forget him. Walker was now a wealthy man and married to a lady whose family were power players among the *ton*. Justice wouldn't come easy and was potentially dangerous if all the information he gathered about Walker was true.

A knock on his door took him away from his thoughts, and he slid the papers into a drawer.

"Come in."

Sebastian Devons, one of his partners in the club, strolled in. He was dressed in his best evening finery. Simon didn't know another man who delighted playing host as much as Devons did. This evening was the first annual Ball of Sin, and he had no doubt the who's who of the *ton* would be back next year. "Is everything all right?"

"Fine," Miller stated.

"Donahue mentioned there was a young lady who demanded to see you. He was worried you may debauch her."

Simon snorted. "Donahue has worked for you for at least a year now, and he is worried about me debauching an innocent?"

Devons ignored the jab. "I think he was specifically worried about who the lady was."

His partner knew that Annie was here. Simon glowered at him. "Leave it alone. Nothing happened. I sent her home."

"Very bold for her to pay you a visit here. Is there something going on?"

"Devons," Simon warned.

Devons lifted a black brow in surprise. "It's my duty to protect my friends and their family."

"It was my duty before it was ever yours," Simon snapped,

unable to control his emotions.

Devons studied him, silently, but finally said, "Well, good. There has been enough Kincaide drama this evening. Sam Kincaide just showed up and hauled his wife away to one of the cottages."

"Really?"

Devons chuckled. "Threatened Connolly if he touched his wife. That is why marriage is not for me. It makes men irrational. Still, you have always seemed like more of a marriage-minded man. Your visitor wouldn't be a bad choice."

He couldn't consider a life with her. "Not something I am looking for."

"Then let's make sure our attendees are having fun at the Ball of Sin. I am sure there is a woman just waiting for you to appear. They all find your proper business-only traits a challenge. Well at least to my rakish reputation."

Simon shook his head at his partner. His reputation was one of the blackest in all of London. It should deter women from him, but they flocked to him. "We both know that's a lie."

Devons chuckled and Simon followed him out of the cottage. He needed to forget Annie Kincaide. She was not for him and never would be.

Chapter 2

A few weeks later, Annie sat with her sister Sophia in the sitting room waiting for her brother Jack and his wife Mercy, so they could attend the theater. Sophia practically bounced up and down with excitement. Viscount Landers would be joining them in their box this evening. Annie couldn't understand what her sister saw in the foppish man, but he made her giddy.

She sighed as Sophia jumped up, pacing back and forth. She was a vision in her lavender gown with her red hair trailing down her back in large curls. Annie ran her hands over her own green gown. She knew it accentuated her coloring and gave her a sophisticated look. Her own mane would usually trail down her back like Sophia's but tonight her maid styled the mass of thick hair in a stylish updo that was more age appropriate for her twenty-six years.

"Would you please relax? You are making me dizzy with all of your energy."

Sophia beamed at her. "I can't help it. I'm so delighted that Landers will be joining us. I know you don't like him, but he is everything I want in a suitor."

Annie did her best to smile at her sister, reminding herself that more than anything she wanted her to be happy. After her debacle with Miller, she promised herself she wouldn't pass judgement on anyone's wants and desires. How could she? She had been certain that Miller shared her feelings, but it was apparent she was lacking in her own perception of people's emotions.

"Do you think Sam and Clara will join us?" Sophia asked, taking her away from her thoughts.

Annie didn't know. Her brother's relationship with his new wife appeared strained. What a mess she and her siblings were. Jack had deceived Mercy into marrying him, Sam had all but deserted his wife once they were married, Sophia was mooning over a man who seemed to have only the slightest interest in her, and well, she had professed her feelings to a man who at one point worked for her family. Yes, a mess.

She shrugged. "I think they are still trying to get used to one another."

"He loves her," Sophia smiled dreamily.

Annie's lips quirked into a smile at Sophia's expression. How her sister loved the idea of romance. Seeing their brothers fall so hard had only strengthened Sophia's desire to find a love match. Still, their steps to marriage and love had not been easy. She wasn't even sure Sam and his wife Clara were beyond their troubles yet.

"Perhaps but our two brothers have made quite a mess of their marriages," Annie pointed out.

"They say the best husbands are rakes and scoundrels. They certainly started with that reputation. Look at Jack and how devoted he is to Mercy."

Yes, their brother was fiercely devoted to his wife. Of all four of them, Annie never expected him to fall so hard, but she was happy for him.

"We just need to find the perfect husband for you," Sophia said.

Annie frowned at her, uninterested in discussing any potential suitors. Sophia clapped her hands. "I know who is perfect for you."

Please don't say his name, she thought pleadingly. Annie shook her head, hoping to end the conversation. Sophia's eyes darted around the room as if to see if anyone could hear her, even though they were alone. She sat on the sofa and smiled. “Simon Miller.”

Just his name intensified the ache that felt permanently lodged in her chest. Yes, she was moving on from her silly thoughts, but it didn’t mean the feelings she felt weren’t real.

“He adores you and I have a sneaking suspicion you adore him as well,” Sophia said with a wink.

Annie forced herself to use her usual smirk and rolled her eyes. “Don’t push your fantasies on me. You’re wrong.”

Sophia studied her. Annie looked away as a blush started to crawl up her neck.

“So you're telling me that you have no feelings for Miller? Look at me,” Sophia said.

Annie turned back, her face the color of a strawberry. “Miller is a family acquaintance, nothing more.”

“And the kiss?” Sophia whispered.

The blush covering Annie’s face went from the shade of a strawberry to a bright red apple. Why did she ever tell Sophia about the damn kiss?

She scowled at Sophia. “It was nothing. The smallest of kisses, actually.”

Her sister's brows drew together in puzzlement. “I know you better than anyone. You would have never mentioned the event if it didn’t mean something. Why are you acting this way? He is mad for you.”

“You are wrong,” Annie stated flatly.

“I don’t believe that. I will ask him,” Sophia said, shaking her head.

"Don't you dare," Annie snapped.

"He could be the one. You can't give up on him without pursuing it," Sophia said, glaring at her in annoyance.

Sophia thought she was simply ignoring Miller's feelings. The mortification from the night of the Ball of Sin was still with her. She normally told Sophia everything but just thinking about explaining her rash actions to her, horrified Annie.

Annie shook her head and Sophia sighed. "I will not let you sabotage your chance of happily ever after."

Annie stood and walked to the window. "Where are Jack and Mercy?"

"Don't change the subject."

Annie spun around. "I don't need to tell him anything. I've already revealed my feelings to him, and he didn't feel the same way."

Sophia's mouth dropped open in shock. She stared at Annie as if she couldn't comprehend what she said.

"Sorry you have been waiting on us so long," Mercy said entering the room, with Jack following behind her.

Annie smiled at her sister-in-law, happy for the reprieve. Jack stood behind her looking displeased. She smiled at him. He was the masculine version of herself. Dark hair, blue eyes, and a haughty face that left people either in awe of him or terrified.

"You look almost as thrilled to attend the theater as I am," she said to him.

"You need to find a husband," he said, bluntly.

Mercy rolled her eyes. She looked lovely next to Annie's broody brother. Her curvy figure was wrapped in a pale pink dress as her curls sat on top of her head, spiraling down her back.

Unlike her husband, she appeared delighted to be attending the theater.

"Even if Sophia and Annie find husbands this season, we would still attend the theater," Mercy pointed out.

Jack snorted before turning to Sophia. "Why are you standing there silently?"

She glanced one more time at Annie before turning back to Jack with a bright smile. "Nothing. Just lost in thought."

"Hopefully not thinking about Landers. I don't know how I will tolerate him for the evening," Jack grumbled.

Mercy wrapped her arm in his. "Stop. There is nothing wrong with Landers."

"He's young," Annie stated.

Sophia rolled her eyes and wrapped her arm in Annie's. "I'm young as well."

They made their way out of the house into the Peyton carriage. Sophia sat across from Annie as they rode through the London streets. Annie avoided looking at her sister, hoping that by the time they were alone again their conversation would be forgotten. The theater was only a short ride, and everyone seemed content with the silence.

Annie stared out the window, her mind scattered with thoughts of Miller. Why did Sophia have to say he adored her? She had convinced herself it was in her head but to hear someone else say it only made her wonder what if.

Why was she wondering this? He had said in his own words that he was nothing more than a family friend. She knew why. Besides the kiss they shared, she and Miller had been close. He could deny it or write it off as nothing, but it wasn't a farce. He knew everything about her, even the parts she didn't share with anyone.

Or at least it had been real for her. Annie swallowed, a lump forming in her throat. Over the last few weeks Annie realized even though Miller knew so much about her, she knew nothing about him. It was as if he didn't exist before he became her family's man-of-affairs and that was the one thing that convinced her perhaps she had thought too much of their friendship. What she imagined as closeness was rather one-sided. She blushed, knowing that proved Miller's pragmatic point about their friendship being part of his employment.

The carriage came to a stop, and she pushed the thoughts from her mind. She needed to let any thoughts about Miller go. It didn't matter anymore. She followed her family to their box and settled herself in one of the chairs. Her eyes flitted around the elegantly ordained Covent Garden Theater. She clasped her hands tightly together in her lap, overwhelmed by the opulence. She shouldn't be.

It had been many years since she, Jack, and Sam cuddled together to ward off the cold in the orphanage in Philadelphia. Still, as she glanced around at the boxes containing ladies dripping with jewels and draped in the finest silk, she couldn't shake the feeling of being an outsider. Her blood was noble but years of living outside the noble class made her relate more to the self-made men and women she grew up with.

"You're quiet tonight," Jack said, sitting next to her.

She rolled her eyes. "I am always quiet."

"True but you seem different."

Why were her siblings so perceptive? "I am perfectly fine. More than fine actually. Tired of being dragged around to events but until you give up on marrying me off, I will suffer through them."

He snorted. "You will find someone in your own time."

"We are nothing like them, and they know it."

Jack frowned at her. "Your blood is just as noble as any of the lords and ladies that frequent this place."

"I don't care about noble blood. And I know for a fact neither do you. Yet, here we are trying to find me a lord."

Jack was quiet for a moment. "You know I only want your happiness. If you don't wish to marry a lord, I don't care. I want you to have these opportunities because being the wife of a gentleman will give you more freedom. But more than marrying for a title, I would have you marry for love."

Annie sighed. She adored Mercy, but she had turned Jack into a love-sick fool.

A bell chimed and Mercy, Sophia and Landers sat, joining them. Annie tried to focus on the play but quickly lost interest. She looked over at Mercy and Sophia who were enraptured by the action on the stage and then glanced at Jack and Landers, who both appeared half asleep.

Her gaze wandered over the other boxes. The boxes were almost like their own shows with everyone on display. She didn't focus on anyone in particular until her gaze fell on a box with Sebastian Devons. Her stomach fluttered, knowing he was Miller's partner at the Den. She looked closer and spied Miller seated in the far corner of the box with Lady Hawley or as Annie knew her, Addie. She was a recent new friend that her family had met through Sam's new wife.

Annie liked her. She was a lady who flouted convention but as she watched her with Miller jealousy bloomed in her chest. They were seated close together. Annie frowned as Miller leaned in and whispered something in Addie's ear. She turned to him and laughed a breath away from his mouth. He grinned down at her. Annie stood unable to watch any more of their flirtatious display.

Her family glanced at her startled, and she whispered, "I need some air."

She left the box and strode into the hallway holding her sides. She told herself it was better that she saw him with someone else and Addie was lovely. Still, it hurt so much.

"Annie? What's wrong?" Sophia asked, having followed her into the hallway.

Annie, not able to keep that night at the Den to herself any longer turned and said, "I know Miller doesn't care for me like you insinuated earlier because he told me so. He said I would find someone else. That we were too different."

Sophia's eyes widened in shock. She was speechless as if she didn't understand what Annie was saying.

Annie laughed at the absurdity of the situation. "Do you know he is here tonight? He is sitting in a box with Addie. A lady, we both like. They are a breath away from kissing."

Sophia frowned. "We may like her, but she's married."

Annie scoffed. "You and I both know that marriage is nothing to the *ton*. My point is I'm not his choice. He made that absolutely clear."

Sophia's frown deepened and Annie knew her vulnerability was shining through. She was always ready with a witty remark or sarcastic comment but tonight she couldn't form one.

Sophia took a deep breath and smiled. She walked over to Annie. "Forget him."

Annie smiled sadly. "I'm not sure I can."

"You can and you will," Sophia insisted.

Annie smiled at her sister, loving her support. Her smile started to tremble, and a tear hit her cheek. Sophia rushed to her and wrapped her arms around her. The loud sob Annie tried to keep contained escaped.

"You will get through this, Annie," she insisted.

~

Simon stumbled into his cottage at the Den with his arms wrapped around the ravishing Lady Hawley. She giggled as he propelled her backwards. He cupped the back of her head and kissed her. She was perhaps one of the most sinfully attractive women in London. Beyond that, she was someone Simon really enjoyed spending time with. They had both joined Devons in his box at the theater and spent the evening laughing and drinking.

He kissed her deeply and a nibble of guilt sprung up within him. She was the perfect distraction from the woman he was trying to forget. Annie flashed in his mind. He noticed her the moment she entered her brother's box tonight. Even though he hadn't seen her in weeks, his want for her came rushing back.

She had been a vision in an emerald gown that highlighted her black lush hair and accentuated a figure that he had fantasized about many times. He had drunk in the sight of her normal smirk and perceptive eyes that perused the lords and ladies gossiping. In another time or place he would have been with the Kincaides in their box, and she would have leaned in to whisper to him.

Lady Hawley laughed and cupped his face. "Where did you go? Are you in there, Miller?"

He smiled down at her, "Sorry, my lady."

She pulled herself from his arms. “Call me Addie. How about you pour me some brandy?”

Simon pushed his thoughts of Annie from his mind, reminding himself it was he who said she needed to move on. “Call me Simon.”

She smiled at him as he stumbled his way to the sideboard. Throwing back brandy all evening perhaps wasn’t the best idea. Yet it helped him from looking over at Annie at the theater. He poured brandy into two glasses and told himself to embrace having fun.

He turned and Addie was walking around the cottage, unsteadily with a bemused expression on her face. “Why do you think the Marquess of Merry would want a cottage designed to be a huntsman’s lodge in his gardens?”

“Why did he want one that looks like a Grecian temple or a grotto that looks like where Neptune kept his harem of mermaids?”

Addie’s eyes widened in delight, and she smiled wickedly at him. She was truly a beautiful woman. Dark haired and more curves than most women were comfortable showing. She walked towards him on her unsteady feet and took one of the glasses from his hand. She raised the glass to her vibrant red lips. “Perhaps, Simon, one evening we could go for a swim in Neptune's grotto. That sounds delightful.”

He smiled at her. “I would enjoy that.”

She sat down on his bed and patted the place next to him. “Join me.”

Simon placed his glass down and removed his jacket. He pulled his cravat free, and Addie’s eyes roamed over him in admiration.

He sat down next to her as she placed her glass on a small table next to the bed. "I was surprised that you invited me back here. For the owner of a gentlemen's club you are fairly reserved, Simon."

Her hands played with the front of his shirt. Simon's eyes traveled down to where her bosom spilled out of her top. The lords were all mad for her, constantly seeking her favor. She looked up at him, her red lips formed in a wicked smile.

"I'm not that reserved."

She laughed. "You have no idea how many ladies would love to hear you say those words while sitting with you in this cottage."

Simon felt his neck heat.

"Are you blushing? Goodness, it just adds to your charm," she exclaimed.

He didn't bother responding but pulled her to him, and they fell back against the bed with her on top of him. She gasped as he brought her lips to his. He kissed her hungrily, wanting to get lost in the moment. He almost did, and then he shook the pins from her hair. Black curls cascaded down her back and his mind went to Annie.

Simon wondered how it would feel to run his fingers through her hair. To feel her slender curves pushed up against his. He attempted to focus on the present and the delectable form pressed against his body, but it left him empty. The kiss that started so amorous a moment ago turned flat. Addie pulled back and studied him. She sighed before rolling onto her back.

"Who is she?"

Addie sat up and grabbed her drink, appearing unfazed at the turn of events. "Grab your brandy and tell me who is the delightful lady that is ruining my evening?"

He started to speak, and Addie shook her head, pointing to his glass. His lips twitched upwards. He did really like her, just not in the right way.

Simon grabbed his glass and joined her back on the bed. She lifted a brow at him. "So, who is she?"

It must have been the brandy, but Simon really wanted to tell her. Ultimately, he didn't. "An old friend."

She lounged back on the bed with her back against the massive wooden headboard. She was a sight with her black curls spilling everywhere and her red lips swollen from their attempt at passionate kissing. Simon was mad to refuse such a tryst but the lady in question seemed unconcerned about their current predicament.

"You came over with the Kincaides from Philadelphia. A lady you can't forget from America, perhaps?" she mused.

"It doesn't matter."

She studied him. "Perhaps one of the Kincaide ladies?"

He frowned at her. She smiled at him in triumph. "Maybe Sophia?" She shook her head. "No, she isn't your type."

He laughed. "Do you think you know me so well?"

Bemused, she smiled. "I can be very perceptive when it comes to men. I don't expect loyalty or love from my partners, but I do expect all of their attention when we are together."

Guilt surged through him. He didn't want her to think he had intentionally toyed with her.

"Addie—" he began.

She shook her head and laughed loudly. Her laugh made Simon

grin as she was notoriously known for how boisterous and distracting it could be. It was as if her laughter erupted from her.

"Goodness. My heart isn't broken. Maybe my pride but now I am more fascinated to know who this lady is, but I think I know. Is it Lady Annabelle or as her friends know her, Annie?"

He stayed silent. She threw back the last bit of her brandy. "Thank goodness, we didn't begin anything. She is a little prickly, but I adore her."

"She isn't prickly. She's just different."

"Ahh...so I was right."

Addie stood and walked over to the sideboard, pouring herself some more brandy. "Why not pursue her?"

"I have other things I am focused on. She is a dear friend of mine. I care for her greatly, but she isn't for me."

She sat back down next to him. "Why is everything with the Kincaides so bloody complicated? They are constantly engaged in over-the-top dramatics."

Simon laughed. "Complicated, yes, but some of the most loyal and caring people I have ever known."

Addie smiled at his defense of them. There was a kindness exuding from Addie that Simon hadn't noticed before. He wondered if she intentionally kept it hidden. In all their encounters she was fun, lively, and flirtatious but the Addie he was drinking with was different from that lady.

"What?" she said, swatting him.

"You are kinder than you let on," he stated.

Addie, the seductress of the *ton,* blushed.

"Goodness Simon, such words will go to my head. Now enough about me. You should reconsider pursuing her. You and Annie would be wonderful together."

Addie leaned back on one arm, sipping on her drink, looking like the temptress she portrayed to the world. He had to admit he admired her. She was one of the few women he'd ever met who did exactly as she pleased. Her husband, Lord Hawley, was a scholar and spent more time abroad than in England but Simon met him once. He wondered why they were separated.

"What of your situation?"

She smiled. "What about it?"

"You are married. I met your husband once—"

She rolled her eyes. "I know what you are going to say, he is quite a likable sort. Everyone tells me that."

He said nothing. She became lost in thought but finally said, "Our past isn't so simple. We hurt each other quite a bit in the beginning of our marriage. So, we did our best to avoid each other and then one day I realized I hadn't seen him in over a year."

"Perhaps time will eventually mend old wounds," Simon said, realizing that Addie likely didn't share even this much about her husband with anyone.

"Some things can never be fixed."

Simon said nothing, sensing any conversation about Lord Hawley was over. She finished her drink and hopped up. She wobbled over to the sideboard again, grabbing his glass on the way. She poured a rather large amount of brandy into each glass and spun around.

"Well, there is only one thing we can do if becoming lovers is not an option," she declared with a mischievous smile.

"What?" he said, grinning back at her.

"Well, get bloody lushy, of course!"

Chapter 3

The next morning, Annie sat eating breakfast when Sophia flounced into the room with her normal enthusiasm. She stopped when her eyes connected with Annie's. Annie almost groaned out loud knowing more questions would likely be directed her way. After the ride home from the theater last night, she hurried to her bedroom and told her maid she wished to not be disturbed.

Sophia's eyes narrowed as she studied her. Clearly, her reprieve was over. Annie braced for a barrage of questions, but her sister surprised her. She looked away and walked to the sideboard quietly. She continued to say nothing as she filled her plate before sitting across from her. The room had a disturbing stillness as Sophia nibbled on her food. Annie didn't know what was more torturous, waiting for Sophia to ask her questions or having to answer them.

Finally, as if unable to stay silent any longer, Sophia asked, "So we didn't go into details last night about Miller, but how do you know he doesn't care for you?"

Annie placed her cutlery on the table and looked at her sister. She should make something up, but Sophia would know. Her sister could read her so well. "I snuck away to the Ball of Sin to speak with him and confessed my feelings. He didn't reciprocate."

Her sister's eyes widened in shock. "I don't believe it."

Annie shrugged one of her slender shoulders. "It was awful. I made a fool out of myself."

"Not that." A slow smile spread across Sophia's face. "That you would do something so romantic. Now if it was me, no one would be surprised."

Heat rushed to Annie's cheeks. Sophia was right about that. Annie was always ready with a sarcastic remark or a practical answer but never fanciful actions. Her actions would be perfect for one of Sophia's romance novelettes. Well, if it had ended differently. Annie smiled wryly at her sister. "It can only be romantic, or as you like to say a happily ever after if both parties feel the same."

"What did he say?"

Annie shook her head. "It doesn't matter. I can't believe I went to visit him. My attempt at a romantic declaration fell horribly flat."

Sophia just stared at her, patiently waiting for her to explain. They were so different. Sophia was an open book, unable to contain her thoughts and emotions. Annie struggled to open up about anything. Of course, there was a list of reasons why she was that way. Life hadn't always been easy. She instinctively rubbed at the fabric covering her scars. Her eyes connected with Sophia's, and she smiled, still waiting.

Annie sighed. "I dressed up for the ball and somehow the butler knew I shouldn't be in attendance. I demanded to meet with Miller. He ushered me off to his cottage on the grounds."

"Which one?" Sophia asked, amused.

The Kincaides for a brief time lived at the estate that eventually became the Den. Sophia had spent plenty of time exploring the little cottages littered throughout the vast gardens.

"The Huntsman's Lodge," Annie said.

Sophia smiled as if happy with Miller's choice. "Continue."

She hated explaining this. "When he arrived, I told him I had feelings for him, and he said I would find someone else. That he was friendly with me because he worked for our family."

"That's a damn lie!"

Annie's mouth quirked up at her sister's incredibly unladylike use of profanity. A habit they both had picked up from their brothers. Now, Jack and Sam did their best to discourage such improper talk, but when it was just Annie and Sophia they did as they pleased.

"That's what he said and then sent me on my way. Well, not before in anger, I ripped up a note and portrait I brought him and threw them at his feet."

Sophia nodded in approval. "Good for you!"

Annie smiled at her sheepishly. "My temper flared a bit."

Sophia drummed her fingers on the table, thinking, before she said, "He's lying."

How Annie wished that, but nothing about that night from his words to his actions indicated he wasn't telling the truth. "He was very adamant. It was so embarrassing. I don't know how I will ever face him again."

She hoped the ache and mortification of that night would magically disappear. Sophia scowled with anger flashing in her eyes. "If I see him, I will tell him he isn't welcome."

"You will do no such thing. Perhaps I read too much into our friendship."

"He kissed you," Sophia pointed out.

Annie wouldn't and couldn't analyze the kiss. Miller said it was nothing. "It doesn't matter. I think what I am most upset about is I felt like he was the one man who liked me for me. He understood me. I know I can be difficult."

Sophia rolled her eyes. "We all have our faults."

True, but most people hadn't endured what Annie had. A vision of the orphanage's headmistress Mrs. Seawald flashed in her mind. She unconsciously ran her hand along the sleeve that hid her scars. She jerked her hand away. For some reason, when she was nervous or conflicted, she would rub them. She frowned. Sometimes she wondered who she would be if that one event hadn't taken place. Would she be as carefree as Sophia?

"Stop it! There is nothing wrong with you. I can see it in your face. You aren't damaged. You are a survivor, and more than that you are the most loyal and devoted person I know," Sophia said, frowning at her.

Annie sighed. "I'm fine."

"He is nothing special. Dozens of men just like Simon Miller would gladly woo you. Better men, actually."

A smirk filled Annie's face at Sophia's declaration. Her sister was an awful liar, and her expressive face betrayed her real thoughts. They both knew Miller too well to really believe he wasn't a good man. Part of her heart ached because she knew how wonderful he was, even if he didn't care for her in the way she wanted. Polite, charming, and present was what exuded from him no matter who he was speaking with.

"Deep down we both know Miller has an exemplary character."

They sat silently for a moment until Sophia slapped her hand on the table.

"Forget him," she insisted. "Spend the rest of the season meeting new men. Different men."

That was the last thing on Annie's mind. "It is not about

meeting more men."

Her sister winked at her. "Why not? What better way is there to forget your feelings for Miller?"

Maybe Sophia was right. She held too many gentlemen at arms' length, not even giving them a chance. She'd been wrong about Miller. Was she wrong about the gentlemen who attempted to court and pursue her?

Still, marriage wasn't her focus. Her perceptive sister added, "I'm not saying you have to marry, but what does it hurt to at least be more open to potential suitors? Instead of begrudgingly participating in the season, embrace it."

Her sister was right. She had spent most of her time hiding out as they navigated their seasons, while Sophia had embraced every ball, tea, and other social events. She would never be giddy like her sister, but maybe it was time to immerse herself in it, instead of mocking it.

"Just 'til the season is over," Annie told her sister.

Sophia smiled in excitement. "We will have so much fun!"

Heaven help her, Annie thought, but she nodded.

~

Simon sat in one of the over-the-top opulent chairs that Devons insisted were perfect for the cardroom at the Den. The wingback chairs were vibrant with deep blues, purples, and greens. Every time Simon saw them, he thought he was staring at a room full of peacocks. He smirked. The nobs loved them. It was like his business partner had a sixth sense about what would appeal to the *ton*. The gaudier, the better.

A booming laugh from across the room caused him to turn his gaze in the direction of a table full of lords playing cards. Well, mostly lords but one man. Simon's eyes narrowed as he watched the lone untitled gentleman. He was older than Simon, in his late forties and oozed wealth but not the type of wealth that came from family, but the kind that came from new money.

In that regard, he wasn't much different from Simon. But unlike Simon's newly accumulated money, the man he watched had stolen his. Specifically stolen from a bank in New York City. The largest sum of money taken from a bank, or at least that is what the newspapers liked to say. Simon wasn't sure that was true, or if it made for a splashier headline to sell papers.

Simon's hand tightened around his glass as he clenched his jaw, his thoughts going dark. The fortune the man had stolen was from the very bank his father had worked at for most of his life. Well, until he was carted off to the prison on Blackwell Island.

The thief, Tobias Walker, tossed a coin at a pretty serving girl who winked back at him. Simon had to admit he was a charming man. He was well liked by the nobs he spent time with. As he should be, he was married to an earl's daughter. Simon relaxed his hand, knowing that his anger would only be detrimental to proving Walker's guilt. Guilt for a crime his father had been locked up for.

How he wanted to walk over and slam his fist into the man's face, but right now Simon needed to stay focused on gathering information about him. He convinced a maid, Miss Markam, in Walker's home to work with him. Miss Markam was fiercely loyal to Walker's wife and detested the man.

From all that Simon learned, Walker had arrived in London shortly after his father's sentencing. With his newfound wealth and charm, he was able to woo his wife speedily into marriage. The marriage had been trumpeted as a love match, but from everything Simon discovered it quickly turned into a bleak arrangement. Walker openly engaged in numerous affairs while his wife turned a blind eye.

Devons sat at the table. "I'm surprised you are out mingling."

Simon ripped his gaze away from Walker. "I thought showing my face would be good."

His business partner's eyes flitted from Walker back to Simon. He lifted a black brow. "What holds your interest at that table?"

Simon cursed how observant Devons was. Laughter erupted from the table, and Lord Deveroe smacked Walker on the back as they stood. Simon was tempted to tell Devons but held back. Not only was it his secret, but he now had Miss Markam to think about.

"Nothing in particular."

Devons snorted. Walker and Lord Deveroe made their way across the room. The men were dressed in over-the-top waistcoats that were almost as gaudy as the cardroom chairs. As they passed Simon and Devons, Lord Deveroe came to a stop. He staggered slightly, revealing how inebriated he was. Walker slung his arm around him to help steady him.

"Walker, you should meet Miller. He is one of you."

Walker laughed. "And what do you mean by that?"

The drunk lord said, "Well, he is an American."

The amusement faded from Walker's eyes, and his gaze pierced Simon. Finally, he grinned. "Ahh...another American. We must stick together. What's your name again?"

Simon forced himself to smile back. "Simon Miller."

"He's Derry's and my partner in the Den," Devons added.

Walker was still smiling, but his eyes drilled into Simon as if trying to determine if he knew him. Simon felt fortunate that until arriving in London, he was confident their paths had never crossed.

“Where are you from, Mr. Miller?”

The fury in Simon bubbled and swirled. Simon couldn't confront him yet. He didn’t have all the answers he needed. “Here and there but most recently from Philadelphia.”

“I know some Millers from New York City. Any relations there by any chance?”

Simon tilted his head and studied Walker. Shocked, Walker would even acknowledge knowing anyone with that name.

“None that I can think of,” Simon said.

Simon didn’t lie often, but this situation seemed to require it. He needed to find evidence of Walker’s crimes before he revealed his connection to his father.

“Well, I think I will help Lord Deveroe home, but perhaps we can play a game of cards next time I am at the Den. We Americans must stick together.”

Bile burned Simon’s throat, but he kept it down. “I would like that.”

Walker and Lord Deveroe stumbled on to the door. Simon turned back to see Devons staring at him questioningly. Simon raised a brow in response.

“Didn’t you say you were originally from New York City?” Devons asked.

Simon shrugged, and it seemed as if Devons wanted to say more but was prevented from asking when another lord pulled him away. Ever the accommodating host, he shifted his attention to the gentleman.

Simon rose and made his way out to his cottage in the gardens.

Once he entered, he removed his cravat and waistcoat. He moved to the room he used for sparring and jabbed at the bag hanging in the corner. He hit the bag over and over again, letting his mind drift away to a conversation from long ago.

Simon followed one of the guards down the stone hallway of the prison. Every sound echoed off the hard surface, designed likely to make escape harder. Not that escaping Blackwell Island was remotely possible. Large waves smashed against the island rocks along the coastline. Only desperation would drive a man to attempt the swim. The island his father now called home was considered inescapable.

In Simon's most desperate moments, he plotted in his mind how he would break his father out of the prison. Unfortunately, it always ended with him concluding that it was impossible. His thoughts were interrupted by the guard unlocking a metal door and jerking his head for Simon to enter.

Shortly after, another guard escorted his father into the room. His normally neatly attired father staggered into the room, and Simon had to force himself to keep his expression blank. Once a strapping man, his father looked frail, and his previously perfectly trimmed hair hung almost to his shoulders.

His father could read him so easily and immediately said, "I'm fine. Don't worry."

How could Simon not worry? His father, once a teller at one of the most prestigious banks in New York City, now was locked up for a crime he didn't commit.

"Tell me who you think could have done this?"

His father frowned at him. "I can't imagine anyone setting me up. Why? It's all a misunderstanding. I will not place blame on anyone."

Simon, in any other situation, would have appreciated his father's good-hearted nature but not at this moment.

"Who else would have access to the vault?"

His father looked at him, pleadingly. "Do not spend your time fretting about this. I want you to live a full happy life."

Simon, all of twenty-four years old, laughed darkly. "I will never allow you to stay here."

A coughing fit took over his father, and Simon frowned at him with concern, knowing he couldn't survive much longer.

"Tell me something, anything."

After recovering from the fit, he said, "I am the only one who had access to the vaults."

"Who else worked that day?"

His father sighed. "Several tellers."

"But who worked closely with you?" Simon demanded.

"Tobias Walker, but he didn't have access to the vaults. Only I did."

Tobias Walker, Sam said in his mind. Who was he?

"Don't focus on this."

Simon shook his head, "I will get you out of here."

Simon's fist connected to the bag as he came back to the present. He needed to prove Walker's guilt. He needed to make sure the man paid for his crimes. Simon hit the bag harder, remembering how sick his father was at the end of his life. How he likely took his last breath alone. Again, he hit the bag. He'd failed in getting his father off Blackwell Island, but he wouldn't fail in proving his innocence.

Chapter 4

The Duke of Peyton's Country Estate - February 1843

Annie looked around at her family, mingling with guests in the drawing room. Mercy stood next to her while Sam and Clara sat by a window, not doing a very good job of mingling but more lost in each other. Her gaze flitted to where Sophia stood with her new husband, Landers, listening to Lord Connolly tell an incredibly dry story. Sophia's husband sighed in boredom. Jack was not far from them, glowering at the man. Her gaze darted back to Sam and Clara as her sister-in-law laughed and swatted her brother. At least they were happy. They deserved to be.

The last ten months had been difficult. First Clara had been kidnapped and just when the family was recovering, Sophia eloped with Landers to Gretna Green. The family was still unsure of him. Sure, everyone was attempting to embrace him, but he certainly didn't try to impress any of them, including Sophia. Annie frowned.

"I didn't think Jack would go through with this," Mercy said, taking her frown as something else entirely.

Yes, her brother was on a mission to see her wed. Annie had taken Sophia's advice and embraced the rest of last season, gaining many suitors. This year's season was in full swing, and Jack had decided to hold a house party, inviting who he deemed as her most worthy suitors.

Her eyes roamed over the gentlemen in question; there was Lord Henley, who'd arrived with his mother and his sister; Lord Connolly, teller of dry stories and land neighbor, who'd brought his elderly aunt; Lord Sutton and his very stern father; and lastly Lord Bromley who'd arrived alone.

"I can't believe they actually made the trip out here. I hope we don't all get snowed in together. I don't think I could tolerate it. I will need to fake an illness and sneak off."

Mercy giggled. "Our winter has been pretty mild for February, and we are only a few hours' ride from London."

"Thank goodness," Annie said, dryly.

Mercy wrapped her arm in Annie's. "Walk around the room with me, please."

Annie happily obliged. She adored Mercy and was glad her rude behavior to her in the beginning of her and Jack's relationship hadn't prevented them from forming a bond.

"Are we escaping?"

Mercy giggled again. "Jack told me you gave final approval on whom he invited."

"I did, but you know Jack, I didn't really have a choice."

"Liar. You and your brother are far too similar for me to believe we would still be hosting this party, if you didn't want us to."

She was right. Annie had agreed and deep-down she didn't mind any of the gentlemen in the room. Actually, some she enjoyed spending time with. Her gaze flitted to Bromley, and her lips tilted upwards as he wiggled his eyebrows at Henley's sister. The young lady blushed a deep rose color in response.

Of all her suitors, he was the one she had the most fun with. He was flamboyant and loud. Traits Annie didn't normally like. Still, somehow, they became friends. It didn't hurt that he was sinfully handsome. Even now, attired in an obnoxious pink waistcoat, he attracted female stares.

"You don't have to choose any of them. You know that."

Annie tore her eyes away from Bromley and laughed. "Jack

knows he could never force me to do anything. He can try all he wants, but if I want to marry, I will when I'm ready. It definitely won't be because Jack rounded up all my suitors in one place."

Mercy snickered and gave Annie's arm a squeeze. "I tried to tell him that."

How her moody, bossy brother ended up with such a lovely wife, Annie still didn't know. Mercy was very dear to Annie. Both of her sisters-in-law were. Her heart twisted as she glanced back at Sophia and Landers. Her sister waved her hands dramatically while talking to Landers who appeared completely uninterested. Annie wanted to whack him across the head.

Not that she could judge their relationship. Perhaps he was different when they were alone. She blushed slightly, remembering how badly she'd misjudged things with Miller. She rarely saw him anymore, but the ache and embarrassment were still ever present in her chest. Maybe not as strong but it had never gone away.

He would be here this week. Nerves filled Annie's stomach. She pushed them away. This wouldn't be the first time she'd seen Miller since the Ball of Sin. They had attended many of the same events since that night. Still, it upset her that Jack would invite him to something that was so blatantly about getting her wed.

She demanded he uninvite him, so he wouldn't think she thought he was a suitor. Jack had been shocked by her request but said he wouldn't. He explained he invited both Miller and Derry, so he and Sam had someone to talk with that they liked. Derry declined due to another engagement.

Annie frowned at the memory. Jack had acted like she was being irrational.

Curiosity, getting the better of her, she asked, "Did Miller arrive?"

Mercy shook her head. "Not yet, but I was told I'm not to consider him a suitor."

Annie flushed. Mercy glanced at her, curiously. "I was quite surprised by that. You seemed close."

Annie looked straight ahead as they walked. "Not at all."

She didn't want to glance at Mercy. She had no doubt her face would be filled with disbelief. She wouldn't get all wrapped up in questioning Miller's feelings. She already had his answer.

A few hours later, Annie sat at dinner. Bromley and Connolly were seated next to her but neither kept her attention as much as the man seated farther down next to Sophia. Simon Miller laughed as Sophia excitedly explained a tale that Annie had no doubt Miller had probably heard a dozen times.

She studied him. His light brown hair and brown eyes filled with mirth. When she'd first caught sight of him in the drawing room while waiting for dinner to start, her eyes had flared with shock. Miller had always been fit but since she saw him in December, he'd added solid pounds to his frame.

He glanced her way, and the laughter in his eyes died. A flutter in her stomach warned her to look away, and she yanked her gaze back to Bromley who watched her with an amused expression.

She blushed furiously.

"I didn't realize I had competition," he whispered but appeared unconcerned.

"Nothing of the sort."

He smiled down at her. "You are ravishing tonight."

The man was certainly charming, regardless of how loud his

clothes were. He had a dimple on his cheek that Annie had no doubt made ladies' hearts flutter. He preened, jokingly.

"Don't try your charm with me," she said dryly.

"You wound me. I want nothing more than to charm you and only you," he said, discreetly squeezing her hand.

She flushed and thought perhaps she could be charmed by Bromley. "I would say competition," he murmured.

Annie pulled her gaze away from him, and her eyes connected with Miller's. His brown eyes flashed with anger. He clenched his jaw as he stared back at her. Her eyes widened in surprise. The room was filled with laughter and chatter, but it all slipped away as she looked back at him.

Bromley nudged her, and she jerked her gaze away. Her sister stared at her expectantly. Annie smiled. "Sorry, I didn't hear you."

Sophia glanced between Miller and her. She seemed amused by their exchange. Annie hoped no one else noticed.

"Miller and I were just laughing about the time in Philadelphia that Mr. Olsteen fell in the pond," Sophia said.

Annie smirked, remembering the incident.

"What happened?" Bromley asked.

"It was nothing. He was saying something inappropriate, and the world didn't like it. As we walked, he happened to tumble into a pond."

Her eyes connected with Miller's again, and a memory passed between them. The memory of Annie telling him how she slid her parasol under Olsteen's feet, and he tumbled into the pond. His mouth twitched, and Annie knew he was trying not to smile.

"Did you push him?" Lord Henley's mother asked, outraged.

Sophia gasped. "My lady, what would make you think Lady Annabelle is capable of such things?"

Because she was, Annie thought. The older woman blushed and shook her head.

"Of course not," Annie said, demurely.

She glanced back at Miller, and his gaze roamed over her slowly. Her heart thumped wildly in her chest. She cursed her reaction, reminding herself that this blasted connection she'd thought she had with him wasn't real. It was going to be a long few days.

~

Everyone in the dining room rose and made their way out of the room. The men went left towards Jack's study, and the women made their way back to the drawing room. Simon stopped, watching the ladies laugh as they meandered down the expansive hallway of the estate home.

His eyes lingered over Annie's slender frame. Her hair was twisted up high on her head in an artful pile of curls that highlighted her elegant neck. An escaped single curl trailed down her back. His body stirred in response. He cursed his damn reaction to her.

Still, he couldn't look away. His eyes watched the sway of her hips as she walked. He had seen Annie sporadically over the last few months but only for short amounts of time, and even in those moments, he never allowed himself to really take her in. He'd falsely convinced himself that his infatuation with Annie was over, even though he was living like a damn monk. But watching her over dinner, he knew that was a lie.

"She is quite lovely," Bromley said, and Henley nodded in

agreement.

She was so much more than lovely, Simon thought. He didn't say anything but turned and made his way into Jack's study.

Sam clapped Simon on the back as he entered. He leaned in. "I am so glad you are here. I don't think I could tolerate these nobs if it was just me and Jack."

Simon smiled and accepted a glass of brandy from Jack. He crossed the expansive room and stood by the fireplace. Jack's study was larger than some families' homes, well at least the families who were not part of the upper echelons of London society. Simon sipped his brandy, shockingly at ease among these men of the *ton*.

If anyone would have told him as a young boy in New York City that he would be drinking with lords as an adult, he would have laughed and laughed. Still, he would trade all of this and his wealth to have his father back.

Further away from his location, Jack and Sam reluctantly joined Lord Sutton and his father in the sitting area of the study. The son, excited to converse with them, leaned forward and said, "Rumor has it you will choose a husband for your sister this season."

Sam scowled at the man causing him to recoil into his chair. "Our sister will have the option of choosing someone."

The Kincaides fierce loyalty to one another always left Simon in awe. Most prominent men or peers would choose their sister's husband, but the Kincaides were a different lot. It would ultimately be Annie's choice. Simon looked away from the discussion and glowered for a moment, looking around at Annie's other potential suitors, unimpressed.

Henley was likely pursuing Annie because his mother approved. Connolly was doubtlessly here because marrying a neighboring landowner's sister would be useful. He had also been at the Kincaides' Christmas festivities last year. He was an annoying man, but Simon doubted Annie really saw him as a potential suitor. Simon suspected that Sutton did really admire Annie, but they wouldn't suit. Annie would destroy him with her bluntness. Then there was Bromley, Simon thought as his eyes narrowed in on the man in question.

He was a ridiculously over the top lord who Annie seemed to delight in speaking with. He was financially secure. Perhaps a bit of a rake, but he did seem to truly be interested in Annie. Simon wanted to write him off immediately, but he knew it was jealousy that made him feel that way. He should hope Annie ended up with Bromley. As if the man knew his thoughts, he looked at him and raised his brandy glass. Simon raised his in return, smirking at him.

Jealousy festered in Simon. He wanted to pound in Bromley's face. He needed to calm down. He wasn't a man who solved things with his fist. He found it to be the least suitable option to solve a problem. No, Simon wouldn't stand in the way if Bromley was Annie's choice. The rest of them were not worth her time.

The man who irked him decided at that moment to make his way over to him, smiling. Simon flattened his mouth into a straight line. He may be the best option for Annie, but he didn't have to spend time with him.

"Miller, I don't think we have really had a chance to talk," Bromley said.

"I am not sure we have much to discuss," Simon said.

Bromley laughed. "You are a close family friend of the Kincaides. You will have to tell me how I can win them over in pursuit of Lady Annabelle."

Simon studied him, hoping to catch some form of insincerity

but even with all Bromley's flashy clothes and over the top cheeriness, he seemed sincere.

"Win her over and you will win her family over. She seems to like you," Simon said, begrudgingly.

Bromley nodded. "What is she to you?"

"The Kincaides are close family friends."

Bromley smirked at him. "I didn't ask what the family meant to you but what she meant to you."

She meant everything to him, Simon screamed in his head. Well, almost everything. Justice for his father was what drove him in his life, but without that it would have been Annie, but he couldn't say that aloud.

"I won't get in your way," Simon bit out, knowing what he was giving up.

"You watch her."

Simon was too startled by Bromley's bluntness to say anything at first. Finally, he said, "She deserves the best. That is what I can say as a family friend."

Connolly sauntered over. "Bromley, have you been back to Plymouth recently? Mrs. Walker just arrived back in London from an extended visit to her family home there."

Bromley stiffened. "It has been many years since I have seen Mrs. Walker."

Simon's mind swirled with questions. He hadn't expected Walker's name to come up in conversation. How was he connected to Bromley? If they were friends, he would do everything in his power to keep Annie from him.

Simon kept himself calm. "Are you a friend of the Walkers?"

Bromley clenched his jaw before rolling his shoulders back

in an attempt to relax. “No. Mine and Mrs. Walker’s family properties border each other. We were friends when I was younger, but it’s been many years. I’m not fond of her husband.”

Connolly shook his head and snickered. “He scuffled with Walker prior to the Walkers getting married.”

“Enough Connolly,” Bromley snapped.

“I don’t understand why you don’t like him. He is one of my favorite people to head to the clubs with.”

“Perhaps I think he spends too much time at his clubs,” Bromley bit out.

Simon's gaze flew back and forth between the men. Not only did he have a connection to Walker, but he didn’t like him.

Bromley, as if realizing he was acting out of sorts, chuckled and smacked Connolly on the back. “It’s old news.”

Simon, unable to help himself, said, “I heard their marriage was a love match. I’ve never heard of a fight.”

“Oh, it was quickly forgotten as people focused on the wedding. Bromley was written off as having a tendre for Mrs. Walker. Not sure what you or Walker saw in her. She is rather mousy.”

“Connolly—” Bromley started.

“Should we join the ladies?” Jack asked, interrupting the conversation.

Simon walked beside Bromley. “What didn't you like about Walker?”

Bromley stopped in the hallway, and Simon did the same. “My actions against Mr. Walker were not because of a tendre as Connolly states, but because I was close to Mrs. Walker’s family.

I doubted his sincerity."

"And now that has proven true."

Bromley frowned and nodded. "I don't want you to think that what Connolly said is an accurate depiction of my feelings for Mrs. Walker. We are simply old friends. I am here with the best of intentions to court Lady Annabelle."

Simon again realized he was sincere. He raised his hands and shook his head. "It has nothing to do with me."

Bromley did smile slightly then. "Funny, I have a feeling it does."

He continued, and Simon followed behind him. They made their way to the drawing room where the ladies sat. His eyes connected with Annie's, and she yanked her gaze away. He cursed the connection between them knowing she felt it too. A connection filled with desire but more than that a closeness that couldn't be hidden.

As Simon settled himself against a wall, Annie stood, making her way to the terrace doors that were open thanks to the mild weather. She stood at the railing, and his eyes swept over her. Her dress, made of the deepest orange, seemed to glow against the darkness outside. He moved to join her, telling himself he just wanted to know she was well.

He stood a few feet from her staring out at the dark gardens, partially visible because of the full moon. Their actions were perfectly acceptable as the rest of the party could easily join them or see them from where they stood on the terrace.

"It's a lovely night, especially for February," Simon said.

She turned to him slightly and pursed her lips. "What do you want?"

That was his Annie, never one to mince words. What did he

want? He wanted a hell of a lot but right now he just wanted this strain between them to disappear. "A truce. I would like us to be friends again."

He was surprised at his own words, but it was true.

She scoffed at what he said. "This from the man who told me he was only friends with me because he was in my family's employ."

"I didn't explain myself clearly. I miss our friendship, but I need you to understand it can never be more than that. I didn't want to mislead you."

She looked at him then and her eyes flashed. "Don't speak to me like I am some naive miss. You could have simply said it wasn't going to happen. Instead, you acted as if you merely tolerated me while employed by my family."

He loved the fire in her.

"I apologize. You're right. Can we start over or go back to how it was before you shared your feelings with me?"

A light pink blush covered Annie. She was quiet for a moment but glanced at him wryly. "As long as we never talk about that night again. Most ridiculous thing I have ever done."

"Not ridiculous had it been a better man with you that night."

She said nothing, and Simon wondered what she was thinking.

Finally, she quietly said, "I will likely become betrothed this season."

Simon forced the words out he needed to say. "I am happy for you. Who is it to be?"

She smiled sadly. "I'm unsure, but I agree I don't want us tiptoeing around each other anymore. I can't do it."

"So, let's start over. Friends."

She nodded, not looking at him. What was he doing? He had intentionally kept her at arms-length, and now here he was asking for her friendship again. He could be friends with Annie Kincaide and it be nothing more, he told himself. They both stared out at the gardens, quiet.

Chapter 5

Annie walked to the breakfast room, feeling much better than she had in a long time. She was happy she and Miller had talked. Their relationship would never be the same, but if some of the tension and awkwardness disappeared, perhaps they could have a real friendship or at least be cordial with each other.

As she entered, both Bromley and Miller rose. Bromley ran an appreciative gaze over her, and Annie's cheeks pinkened in response. Miller's face turned stony at his stare, but he said nothing.

She smiled at both of them. Bromley grinned at her. "You look beautiful, Lady Annabelle."

Bromley did make her feel beautiful in her sage green day dress. She smoothed her hands over her skirt, happy with her selection for the day.

"Isn't she lovely, Miller?"

Annie's eyes darted to Miller, horrified that Bromley had presented him with such a question. He glared openly at Bromley, and the man grinned back at him. They all stood awkwardly staring at one another.

Finally, Miller folded his newspaper. "Well, if you will excuse me, I have some paperwork I need to read through."

Annie watched him as he made his way around the table, passing her. The awkwardness still hung between them. She chided herself. It hadn't even been a day since they spoke.

As if sensing he was making a mess of his departure, Miller stopped in front of her and smiled. "Bromley, you are correct.

She is a vision. Excuse my behavior. Perhaps when I'm finished with my paperwork, I will be more fun to be around."

She warmed at his words, knowing he was making an effort. "Hopefully you will get through it quickly, and we will see you soon."

"You shall."

Annie made her way to her seat and was quiet while one of the servants placed a plate of her favorites in front of her. She glanced at Bromley who was sitting back in his chair with an amused expression on his face.

"I'm not sure what to make of you and Miller. There seems to be a level of oddness between the two of you," he said.

Annie scoffed, hoping her lie wasn't evident. "He is a close family friend."

"That's how he explained it as well."

Annie's eyes widened. "You spoke to Miller about me?"

"Just a bit. A man likes to know what he is up against," he said, softly.

Annie rolled her eyes. "You are being absurd. Miller and I have known each other for years."

Bromley rose and sat down next to her. He placed his hand over Annie's and gently ran his thumb across her skin. She stared at him, knowing a woman could easily look at his face for all of her life. Perhaps Bromley was the one. His thumb moved closer to the edge of the sleeve sitting at her wrist, and she self-consciously pulled her hand back.

He cleared his throat. "If I was too forward, I apologize. I lost myself for a moment."

He rose and made his way back to his seat. She frowned,

hating what really made her pull her hand back. How she hated her scars, and that they made her embarrassed. She shook her head. "It isn't that. I probably should have explained this before. As children Jack, Sam, and I lived in an orphanage for quite a few years."

Bromley nodded. "I've heard the rumors."

Yep, the Kincaides were still notorious in London after all this time, she thought. Annie took a deep breath. "During that time, I was hurt, leaving scars up my arm and along the side of my body."

Bromley's brows drew together in concern. "Do they still bother you?"

"No, it was so long ago, but that is why I always wear long sleeves."

He was quiet for a moment. "You are by far one of the most beautiful women I have ever known and now I know the most courageous. I am honored you shared this with me."

Annie didn't know what she expected but not the adoration shining in Bromley's eyes. For all his pomp, he was truly a good man and also perhaps one Annie could see spending her life with.

"You are too kind," she said.

He winked at her. "It isn't kindness I'm feeling right now, my lady."

Annie rolled her eyes again. "Back to being charming."

He shrugged, grinning at her. "I don't want to disappoint you."

A few hours later, Annie wandered through the maze at the Peyton estate. It was a brisk day but nothing her coat couldn't keep her warm from. When Jack took over the estate, the maze had been long forgotten and grown over. Mercy made it her duty to restore it to its former glory. Annie loved walking through the pathways. No one would describe her as whimsical, including herself, but being in the maze felt magical to her.

As she walked, she pondered Bromley's reaction to the revelation of her scars. She knew he wouldn't be rude, but his lack of concern for them startled her. Could he be her future husband? All his actions pointed to the fact he would be a wonderful partner but yet, she hesitated.

Annie sighed. She didn't discuss her scars with anyone outside of her family and only a few people had ever seen her in a dress that revealed them. And only one man, Miller. As a family friend, he often stayed with her family and on hot sweltering days at home Annie would forgo her long sleeves. Simon never pushed her to explain them.

The one time they came up, it was she who mentioned them with a snarky comment. He'd taken his hand and run it along her scarred forearm and said, "You are beautiful, and this can never take away from that."

Those words had meant so much to her. Lord Bromley and Simon Miller. Two good men. She shook her head. Why was she thinking of Miller at all? He was not a contender for her hand.

She turned the corner and stumbled into the man she was trying to forget. Annie fell against his hard chest and gasped. He grabbed her arms and steadied her on her feet. He stood in his trousers with his shirt sleeves rolled up to his forearms. The heat of his muscular chest against her fingers sent a tremor through her. She stumbled back, and he held her so she wouldn't tip over.

"I'm fine. You can release me," she said.

He rolled his sleeves down and slid his waistcoat back on.

"What are you doing?"

He finished buttoning his coat. "Training."

Without a thought about improperness, she asked, "Is that why you are so large now?"

He stilled for a moment shocked by her words and then threw his head back, laughing.

She shook her head, horrified by her own bluntness. Some things she could never change about herself. Annie smirked. "Not appropriate, I know."

Miller smiled at her, looking more boyish than his twenty-nine years. "Perhaps not appropriate but very much you. It's good your newfound zest for the London season hasn't changed you much. I would hate that."

She smiled back at him, mischievously. For a brief moment, Annie did feel like she had her old friend back.

"Why?" she asked.

He seemed reluctant to share more but finally said, "I want to make sure I'm able to handle any problems at the Den."

Annie tilted her head and studied him. Something was amiss. What was he hiding? He changed the subject and said flatly, "So Bromley seems like a strong contender for your hand."

She spotted a bench and sat, shifting her skirts so Miller could join her, but he decided to stay standing. She wished he would sit. Her gaze flew over him, taking in his hard chest her fingers were just pressed up against and his thighs... She pushed the decadent thoughts from her mind, swallowing.

"He makes me laugh."

He pursed his lips as if contemplating her words. He smiled at her. "I'm sure it doesn't hurt that he is an attractive sort."

Her gaze flew to his eyes, but she didn't see any anger or jealousy. She shrugged. "He is, but that isn't why I would pick him. He makes me happy."

A silence fell between them. Annie wondered what he was thinking. He kicked at the ground with his boot. The connection between them swirled in the air. Would it ever go away? If she wed Bromley, would she have that with him someday? She hoped so.

He sat down next to her. "If he makes you happy, I think you should accept his offer."

Bromley did make her happy and made her laugh in ridiculous fits, but she felt a sharp pain at Miller's words. And she hated herself for it. She was tempted to ask him what it was about her that made him not want her. She wouldn't! Annie had made a fool of herself enough around Miller. Instead, she kept the conversation focused on Bromley.

"I told him about my scars today," she said.

"What did he say?" Simon asked, frowning as if he was ready to rip Bromley apart.

"He didn't care," she said.

"As he shouldn't. Your scars don't matter."

She shifted so she could see his face. He had gone all stony again. She wanted to keep the camaraderie they had just forged last night. She nudged him, playfully. "What about you? No women you are planning to woo?"

She wouldn't fall apart at his answer, no matter what. She could be friends with Miller, she told herself determinedly.

He shifted, so he was facing her, and his gaze roamed over her face.

Her heart ached a little. Again, she was tempted to ask him what it was about her that made him not have romantic feelings for her. As they studied each other, she knew even though she didn't say the question aloud, it was written all over her face. His face filled with sadness and Annie didn't understand why. He wasn't the one who had been hurt in the situation.

Shockingly, he cupped her face in his hands. "I have other plans, and no, they don't involve other women."

She placed her hands over his and for a mad moment she thought he would kiss her. Where did the thought come from? He had bluntly told her he didn't feel that way about her.

She started to speak, but he released her from his grasp and shook his head. "Accept Bromley if he offers. I need to return to the house."

He stood and strode down the pathway. She stared at his retreating form, puzzled. Her heart hammered. What other plans did he have?

~

Simon stomped toward the house, needing distance from Annie. Fury overwhelmed him. He needed to focus on Walker, but he couldn't stop thinking about her. Being so close to her made him want to forget about all of his plans. Temptation to forget them and pursue her roared within him.

Still, Simon knew if he did, his anger that Walker walked free and his father died in prison would always be in the back of his mind. Annie had been through too much in her own life. He would not burden her with more heartache and anger. He wanted her to be happy.

As it was, he was playing a dangerous cat-and-mouse game with Tobias Walker. Since they'd met at the Den, they played cards together every week, not by Simon's request but by Walker's. Simon knew Walker sensed something was amiss. During the games, he peppered him with constant questions about Philadelphia and New York City. Simon was always careful to not reveal his past in New York City, but the more time they spent together the more difficult it was becoming.

He re-entered the house through the terrace doors leading into the drawing room. The opulent room was quiet. Simon rolled his eyes. Likely all the house guests were just starting their day. At parties like this, events went well into the night, and everyone slept late. He entered the foyer and was stopped by the duke's butler.

"Mr. Miller, a letter has arrived for you today."

Simon looked at him startled, not expecting anyone to reach out to him. Devons and Derry, his partners in the club, he knew had everything well-in-hand. That only left Miss Markam. Dread filled him. He took the letter and practically raced up to his room. Once inside, he opened it.

Mr. Miller,

I did not send this letter to you to raise concern but to inform you I believe I have identified where the bars may be located. I also was able to learn from a coachman that Walker travels to Blackpool a couple times a year to visit another American named Allen Lemming. I would recommend you travel there to find out more.

When you are back in London, we should meet to discuss the possible location of the bars. I'm unsure if they can be accessed without revealing to Mr. Walker that someone is looking for them. As I have told you before, I want to make sure Mrs. Walker is adequately protected. I fear for her in all of this. I have not shared with her that I am assisting you. Mr. Walker can be quite ruthless to those who betray him.

Miss Markam

Shock clouded his face. Simon hadn't expected to hear from Miss Markam and certainly hadn't expected her to so quickly find the location of the bars. They were Walker's only link to the theft at the bank his father worked at. In total, the items in the vault that was broken into had been valued at five hundred thousand dollars, but it wasn't all money. Fifty thousand of it was stamped gold bars. Unlike money, they were not as easy to get rid of. Simon had a hunch Walker was still holding on to them. He just didn't know where.

And who was Allen Lemming? He pulled his leather notepad from his pocket and scribbled the name and town on to the paper. Simon frowned, concerned about Miss Markam. He worried she was asking too many questions and putting herself in danger. He placed his notepad on a table by the bed and grabbed stationary from a small desk. He quickly scribbled out a note for her.

Miss Markam,

This is great news. Please refrain from doing anything else until I return.

Miller

Everything in him wanted to rush back to London, but it was a reckless thought. They needed to tread carefully. Walker wasn't a fool. He rose and made his way back down the corridor to the foyer stairs. His eyes lingered on a portrait of the previous Duke and Duchess of Peyton. Annie looked like her father, a softer version, but she had his eyes, hair, and coloring.

Perhaps it was this house. Her essence seemed to be everywhere. He made his way down the stairs and stopped in the foyer, dropping his letter with the rest that would be sent out. The risk was too great for him to send it directly to Miss Markam; instead, it would be delivered to a shop where she could pick it up.

He strode to Jack's study and briskly knocked on the door. The rest of this elite party may not be up yet, but he had no doubt Jack and Sam would be up.

The door opened and Sam grinned at him.

"Miller! Join us. We are the only ones who seem to be awake."

The man had always been cheerful, but since he'd fixed things with his wife, he was downright joyful. A sliver of envy snaked through Miller, but he pushed it away.

Simon smiled. "Still getting used to living like gentlemen."

A snort was his response from Sam. Even though he was not a gentleman, he was far wealthier than most of the *ton.*

Jack sat behind his massive, intricately carved mahogany desk. His boots were propped up on the desk as he leaned back in his chair. He frowned. "It's almost noon. Is no one really up yet?"

Simon laughed and sat in one of the chairs. "They are up. One could argue that the two of you are simply avoiding them."

Jack chuckled. "True."

Simon stared at the two men sitting in the room and realized he trusted no one more than the Kincaides. He would trust Annie and Sophia just as much. He was tempted to explain everything to them but stopped himself. It wasn't their fight. In the last few years, the Kincaide family endured its fair share of tragedy and danger. He would not add more to that when they all seemed to just be settling into genteel life.

Still, he needed to put his affairs in order. He took a deep breath, and both of the men looked at him with concern.

"What is it?" Sam asked.

"I need to make you aware of something," Simon said. "I have drawn up a will. In my will I bequeathed my share of the Den to your family."

"Is there a reason why you are telling us this now?" Jack asked.

Simon shook his head. "I just need you to know my wishes if something happens."

Jack and Sam looked at each other before turning back to him.

"What's going on? Devons said you spend all day training in your cottage and if you're not doing that you're away. He thinks you are hiding something," Jack stated.

Simon scowled. "Devons needs to mind his own business."

Jack rose and poured all of them a brandy. His request had changed the air in the room. There was a sense of foreboding. Simon hadn't intended that. Jack handed him the drink.

"We are here for you if you need us. That is the only point we are trying to make," Jack clarified.

Simon nodded and in an attempt to change the subject and lighten the mood, said, "Brandy so early. I promise it isn't that serious."

"What should we think when you announce you are going to leave us a damn fortune?" Sam pointed out.

"What do you want us to do with it?" Jack asked.

Simon wanted to say give it to Annie, but that would have been highly improper. "Sell it to Devons and Derry and do something good with it."

His response seemed to alarm them more. They all sipped their brandy quietly. Finally, Jack said, "We'll follow your wishes. Again, if we can help, let us know."

Sam nodded in agreement. He couldn't drag the Kincaides into his plans. He wasn't sure how everything would end. Walker could go to prison or Simon may be required to exact justice on his own. He couldn't let the Kincaides help because he didn't want to endanger them but also he didn't want them to get in his way. Simon forced a smile. "Not necessary."

Chapter 6

Annie glanced around at the normally stuffy Peyton estate ballroom with amusement. The immense room was draped in variations of blues and whites. Crystals hung randomly throughout the room. She felt like she was sitting in the middle of a winter wonderland. Mercy and Jack had definitely outdone themselves.

She shouldn't be surprised. They were quickly becoming known in high society circles for throwing stunning balls. The Kincaides may still be considered scandalous but very few declined their invites.

Sophia in a shimmering white and silver gown twirled around the ballroom with her husband. Perhaps, they would be okay. For most of the estate party he had seemed closed off from Sophia, but tonight they appeared happy. She gave a silent thank you. She needed Sophia to have her happily ever after.

She ran her hand over her own silvery gown, feeling like a snowy enchantress. The majority of her hair hung down her back in thick black curls. Only the sides were swept up in a knot wrapped in crystals.

Her eyes darted around the ballroom taking in all the attendees there. It was the main event of the house party. Lords and ladies residing near the Peyton estate had also been invited. The room was filled with people swathed in silvers, golds, blues, and whites.

"Goodness, it may be February, but this room is certainly warm," Clara said, joining her.

She fanned herself. Annie smiled at her. She was a vision in a light blue dress. Annie searched for Sam, surprised he was not within arm's reach. Clara had been kidnapped at the end of the last season, and Sam was never far from her since.

"I convinced him to fetch me some punch. Your brother worries too much."

Annie nodded in agreement. "He does, but it is only because of how much he cares for you."

Clara glowed at Annie's words. "Would you like to come sit with me?"

Annie shook her head. "You go. I'm sure Sam will be along soon with your punch."

Squeezing her hand, Clara whispered, "You look stunning by the way."

She smiled at the compliment. Her eyes roamed through the crowd, and she stopped herself. She was looking for Miller. A surge of anger rushed through her. Annie had spent the better part of the afternoon analyzing Miller's words in the maze. She needed to stop. Over the past few months, she had done so well on not focusing on him.

And he was right! Bromley was an exceptional catch. Her focus should and would be him. She hadn't planned on marrying before her feelings for Miller had appeared. Now that she opened the door to other options, perhaps she would marry.

Her gaze found Bromley who was charming a group of people. Life assuredly wouldn't be dull with him. He must have felt her eyes on him because he looked her way and winked. Tonight, he wore a lemon-colored waistcoat that should have been obnoxious with his blond hair, but it worked for him. Her lips quirked at his glaringly out-of-place wardrobe compared to the wintery outfits in the room.

Bromley did as he pleased, and Annie loved that about him. He excused himself from the group and made his way to Annie.

He bowed formally and looked at her mischievously. "Lady Annabelle, would you care to join me for a stroll around the room?"

She smiled and rose, taking his arm. "Of course, Lord Bromley."

They walked, and Annie knew everyone was watching them. As they made a turn, she noticed Miller enter the ballroom. Her body tingled. He was dressed in pants that hugged his legs and a midnight blue waistcoat.

"Silver suits you," Bromley said.

Annie blushed, tearing her gaze away from where Miller stopped to chat with a few lords.

"Thank you," she murmured.

He leaned in and whispered, "I would like to spend some time with you privately."

Her brows shot together in surprise. A lady couldn't very well be alone with a gentleman. Sensing her shock, he said, "I believe I have made my intentions quite clear."

Intrigued, Annie asked, "How do you propose we meet privately in the middle of a ball?"

"Wait a few minutes after I depart and meet me in the library."

The appropriate response was no, but instead, she nodded. Bromley smiled at her and bowed before departing. She waited a few minutes and then made her way out of the ballroom to the foyer, quickly walking to the library. She opened the door and found Bromley standing by the fireplace.

He turned toward her, and she was struck by how truly handsome he was. He spent most of his time joking and playing to the crowd. Distinguished was the word that came to mind as he stood quietly in the elegant Peyton estate library. She rocked on her feet nervously, not used to this solemn

Bromley in front of her.

"I am glad you joined me," he said.

"You are so serious. You're making me nervous."

He grinned and held out his hand. She slowly walked over to him, curious what he was up to.

"I imagine you are wondering why I asked you to join me. You must know that my intentions towards you are honorable."

Annie's stomach dropped. Was he going to propose to her? She wasn't sure she was prepared for a proposal. Her gaze flicked to the door, irrationally planning her escape. Please don't ask, she thought.

"If you are—" she started.

He pulled her close, cutting her off. Her big blue eyes peered up at him in confusion. He leaned closer to her and whispered, "I want to kiss you. May I do that, Lady Annabelle?"

He was going to kiss her! Why was she relieved it was that and not a proposal? Annie should refuse but she didn't. She was tempted to see what a kiss with him would be like. She hated herself for thinking it, but she wondered how it would compare to Miller's brief kiss.

He leaned down and brushed his warm lips across hers. It was the briefest kiss, not unlike Miller's. He did it again, but this time deepened the kiss. His tongue teased her mouth, and she curiously opened her lips. There was nothing unpleasant about Bromley's kiss, but something was missing.

Frustrated, she threw herself into the kiss, sparring with his tongue. She needed this kiss to mean more than the fleeting kiss she had with Miller. Annoyance flashed through her. They both stepped back. Bromley smiled at her. "You know I would propose to you right now if I thought you would say yes."

She bit her lip, nervous that he sensed something amiss with their kiss. "What makes you think I wouldn't?"

"I think someone else has your attention," he said, watching her intensely.

Damn it! She started to speak, and he shook his head, "Don't. All I ask is that you spend the next few days thinking about how we could grow together. I think we would be a great match."

He was right, they would be well suited. Still, something held her back. Someone, she thought, annoyed.

"Return to the ballroom and in a few minutes, I will follow," he said, interrupting her conflicting thoughts.

She made her way back to the festivities. Her mind filled with thoughts surrounding her encounter with Bromley. She sat and her eyes connected with Miller's. He swiftly made his way over to her. She pursed her lips and looked away.

"Where have you been?" he demanded in a hushed tone.

"That isn't your concern."

"Were you alone with Bromley?"

She stood and pasted a smile on her face. She didn't particularly feel like smiling but dumping a glass of punch on his head wasn't an option unless she wanted to cause a scene. "Excuse me, Mr. Miller. I think I'm wanted elsewhere."

"Annie!" he quietly seethed.

She leaned in and whispered furiously, "Don't you dare question me. You have no right! Again, excuse me."

Annie didn't look back. She stomped in the direction of the refreshments. Who was he to question her?

~

Simon cursed the anger that filled him as he stalked through the Peyton maze the next morning. He tried to tell himself logically that if Annie welcomed Bromley's suit, it was for the best, but it did nothing to curb his fury. The moment he noticed both Annie and Bromley were missing from the ballroom the night before, he knew they had left to meet somewhere privately.

As he conversed and chatted, his rage had simmered thinking about Bromley kissing her. Touching her! A private meeting was bordering on scandalous, but only if a betrothal wasn't imminent.

He scowled as his pace quickened. Simon rounded a corner and stopped in his tracks. Annie was sedately walking through the maze without a care in the world. His eyes ran over her figure in her periwinkle frock. It cinched at her waist and his heart constricted as he thought of Bromley's hands running over her body.

She stiffened as if sensing someone was behind her. She turned and her eyes widened in surprise. Simon's eyes took in her large blue eyes and full plump lips. Lips that Bromley likely tasted. He suppressed his fury, knowing he had no right.

"It's you," she snapped.

This woman! He threw his hands wide. "How lucky am I to encounter you here, Annie," he said sarcastically.

She spun on her heel and continued on, increasing her pace. Fine by him, Simon thought. He slowed down, not wanting to continue whatever this moment was they were having.

He came to an intersection and took the path towards the center of the maze. Annie stood with her hands on her hips, fixing him with a glare.

He shook his head. “Annie, I’m not in the mood.”

“Whoever gave you permission to use my first name?”

“It won’t happen again, my lady,” he bit out.

She marched up to him, poking him in the chest. “You’re a nuisance.”

Her blue eyes blazed, and part of her hair had tumbled down her back. He should leave. He should be angry with her haughty tone, but all he could think about was how damn gorgeous she was.

She was the spitting image of all the refined ladies that covered the Peyton estate walls, but it was this fire and bite that was irresistible to Simon. No, Annie Kincaide didn’t shrink from a fight and by god she would speak her mind, no matter the cost.

Bromley wasn’t good enough for her, Simon decided. He didn’t know who was, but it wasn’t him. “Did he kiss you?”

She smirked at him. “It isn’t any of your concern.”

His brown eyes pierced her as he stepped closer to her. “Annie, tell me.”

She took a deep breath at his closeness, her chest heaving up and down. The dark side of him took a certain grim satisfaction that he could throw her off kilter. What was he doing?

“He did kiss me. He is quite thorough.”

He didn’t care what he was doing. “You shouldn’t be alone with him.”

She stepped back, attempting to put space between them. “We are alone now. You are a hypocrite, Simon Miller. You think you can judge me for a kiss but you're frolicking with women all the time.”

"Annie, you need to think of your reputation."

She scoffed. "You didn't care about that when you kissed me. I think I shall kiss whoever I want. I rather liked kissing Bromley."

Jealousy flared within him. She was goading him, but logic had escaped Simon. "Was it more than a kiss?"

"What does it matter?" she asked, not looking at him.

"It matters."

"It was just the thing to get over your rather little kiss," she said, savagely.

Simon knew she was provoking him, but he couldn't resist stepping closer. "Oh, really."

Annie glared at him. "Yes! Thanks to Bromley, I have been thoroughly kissed. Nothing else could compare."

He looped his arm around her waist. The air filled with a tension that was barely tolerable. "You wouldn't," she screeched.

He grinned maddeningly at her. "You would be wrong."

With that he firmly pressed his lips to hers. She gasped, and he plunged his tongue into her mouth. He wanted to consume her the way she consumed him. She looped her arms around his neck, and his mouth tilted up in satisfaction. He broke their kiss, to trail additional kisses down her neck and across her bosom. She moaned.

He pulled her closer to him, against his manhood. Her eyes flew to his. Simon whispered into her ear. "Can't compare, huh?"

Simon kissed her again, deeply as their bodies melded into each other. She clutched his waistcoat and whimpered, pushing into him. They were wild, plunging their tongues into each other's mouths.

He groaned and teased her bottom lip before sparring with her delectable tongue again. His cock throbbed against his pants. She moaned, and he gloated with satisfaction. Annie pushed deeper into him, pressing the apex of her thighs against his manhood. How he wanted this woman.

A sound coming from the beginning of the maze caused him to quickly release Annie. They stumbled apart. Annie was flushed and breathing deeply. Simon wasn't sure he had ever seen a lovelier sight.

Sophia rounded the bend and stopped in her tracks. She looked from Simon to Annie and her eyes widened in surprise. An awkward silence hung in the air.

"What is it, Soph?" Annie asked, breathless.

She looked back and forth between them, but finally said, "An urgent letter has arrived for Miller."

Sophia placed the letter in his own shaky hands. He opened it up.

Mr. Miller,

It is urgent you return to London at once. There is another item of interest besides the gold bars. I don't want to say more.

Miss Markam

He lifted his head and locked eyes with Annie. She frowned at him, still breathless. Damn it. There was no rationalizing the kiss that just took place between them.

"I must leave," he said.

Annie's eyes flashed with anger. He turned and walked away.

Chapter 7

Annie's gaze followed Miller as he fled down the pathway. A million questions swirled in her mind. The first one being why the man who had just kissed her so passionately, left. Once the sound of his footsteps disappeared, Sophia spun around. "What are you doing out here with Miller?"

She touched her lips, still bruised from his intense kiss. A blush rushed over Annie. "I came out for a walk, and Miller had the same idea. It isn't what it seems."

Her sister snorted, shaking her head. Annie glanced at her sideways. Sophia raised a questioning brow. "Is there still nothing between you and Miller?"

Annie took a deep breath. Her body still tingled from his touch. What could she say? Her sister was adept at reading her and would catch on if she flat out denied something was amiss. Annie smoothed her light purple frock, trying to formulate a response. Finally, she said tersely, "I can't talk about this."

"Bromley is ready to ask for you. He is meeting with Jack right now while you are out here getting ravished by Miller," Sophia exclaimed, seemingly torn between giddiness and horror.

Annie frowned at her sister, not liking the conclusion she jumped to even if it was correct. Bromley, her potential betrothed, was meeting with Jack. He had told her to think about what she wanted. Why would he do that? She needed time.

Her mind swirled with Miller's actions and Bromley's intentions. She should say yes, but she couldn't until she spoke with Miller. She needed to understand why he had kissed her. He had said that they could never be. What she should do is accept what he told her and forget about the kiss, or ravishment as Sophia called it.

Instead, she said, "I need to go back to the house."

She needed to see him before he left. Sophia grabbed her arm. Annie looked back at her, impatiently. Her sister smiled at her softly, "Take a moment."

"For what?"

Sophia's beautiful doll-like face turned serious. "Take time to think about what you are about to do. You told me Miller said that you two would never be together. Whatever happened out here may not change that."

Annie attempted to speak, but Sophia interrupted her. "I know what it is like to choose someone you want so badly and find out it is rather one-sided. I want you to have more. You deserve more, Annie."

So many emotions flickered over Sophia's face. Hurt and despair for herself and worry for Annie. The problems with her marriage were evident from her warning. Annie wanted to pull Landers aside and properly dress him down for the pain he was causing Sophia.

"Soph—"

Sophia shook her head. "No, I don't want to hear it. I'm not a fool, Annie. I'm very aware of where my choices have led me."

This was the first time Sophia had voiced that anything was amiss with Landers. Since they'd wed, Sophia had tried so hard to keep things happy and light. The revealing words used as a warning to Annie were not something Sophia shared easily. Her sister never wallowed in sadness. Still, Annie was a self-acknowledged fool because all she wanted was to speak with Miller.

"I know. Thank you for wanting the best for me," Annie said, leaning in and hugging her.

Sophia smiled sadly at her, knowing she wouldn't heed her warning.

"I will be fine. I promise I won't be rash, but I need to speak with him."

Was she headed down a reckless path? No, but she told herself she needed answers before she could consider any proposal.

Sophia nodded. "Go. I think I will walk for a bit."

Annie rushed through the maze pathway, back to the house. As she stepped through the terrace doors, she ran directly into Bromley. He was dressed impeccably, and when he saw her, he smiled in delight.

This man could be her betrothed, more than that, he could be her husband. She took in his broad shoulders, his blond hair, and face that women sighed about. Bromley, even with his rogue reputation, had been the epitome of what a lady should want when being courted.

"Lady Annabelle. I was hoping to see you. I had the best conversation with your brother."

No! She couldn't have this discussion right now. A flash of anger coursed through her that he would approach her brother today. She forced it away knowing he was sincere in his actions. She smiled. "I am feeling unwell. Can we speak more this evening?"

He frowned at her and guilt filled Annie. "Are you sick? Shall I call a maid or have someone fetch a doctor?"

"No, I think I just woke up too early. I need some rest."

He reached for her hand and placed a light kiss on it. "Then I look forward to sharing with you details of my conversation with your brother this evening."

She nodded and forced herself to casually leave the room, walking up the main stairway. She raced towards the hall where the guests were staying, her feet flying across the thick carpet. Annie stopped before Miller's door, realizing she was acting mad. An unchaperoned lady knocking on a man's door was highly unacceptable. What was she doing?

Annie raised her hand to knock but froze when the door opened. A young maid stared at her in surprise.

"My lady, you startled me. I just started to clean up, but Mr. Miller left quite a few of his belongings behind. Shall I send them back to London or will he be returning?"

Miller was gone. He had left so quickly. Why? Annie smiled demurely at her. "I can handle that."

The maid's eyebrows shot up in shock. Perhaps Annie shouldn't have said that. Yes, it was slightly inappropriate that she volunteered to collect his personal items.

"What I meant to say is, if you would give me a moment to look around the room, I can tell you what to send back to London."

The maid frowned at her in puzzlement but nodded. "I will be outside."

Annie stepped through the door and her eyes ran over the elegant room, decorated in masculine colors of deep blue and gold. Small items were left behind but nothing that most would notice if they weren't tasked with preparing a room. She walked towards a small table that held several newspapers and documents.

She sifted through the papers, frowning. What was she even looking for? This was probably pointless, she thought. Her eyes widened as she made it to the bottom. The small leather notepad that Miller took everywhere laid on the surface.

She lifted it up and flipped through the pages. Annie couldn't believe he left it behind. As she reached the last few pages, a piece of paper was placed between two sheets. The front was blank, but she turned it over and gasped. It was the top half of the portrait she had thrown at Miller's feet the night of the Ball of Sin. He kept it.

Why?

"My lady, may I enter?" the maid asked.

Annie snapped the notepad shut, sliding it into a hidden pocket in her skirts. "Of course. Please pack up any documents that are not newspapers and have them sent back to Mr. Miller's residence in London. There is no need to rush. I didn't identify anything he may need urgently."

The maid looked at her curiously as if she wanted to say something. Annie flushed, grateful that the Peyton staff were so discrete and dedicated to her family. If not, she had no doubt her behavior would become *ton* gossip. "Of course, my lady."

Annie breathed a sigh of relief that the maid didn't ask any further questions. She probably had written Annie's behavior off as just another Kincaide quirk. She smirked. At times, it didn't hurt that her family was considered scandalous. Little missteps were easily forgotten thanks to Jack, Sam, and Sophia's previous actions.

She made her way to her room, more confused. Annie shut the door and leaned against it. Miller had kept her portrait. Why and where had he gone in such a hurry? She couldn't accept Bromley's proposal without knowing.

A knock on her door startled her. She sighed, wanting to peer through Miller's notepad. She smoothed her skirts and opened the door. Sam and Clara stood before her, studying her with concern. Annie's brows drew together in puzzlement.

"Bromley said you felt unwell. Jack sent for the town doctor," Clara explained.

Could nothing go her way? She rolled her eyes. "That's a bit drastic. I'm just feeling ill."

Jack's protectiveness bordered on insanity at times. Heaven help any of them if they said they were unwell.

Sam smirked at her, letting on he knew she had lied. "The doctor is already on the way."

Ugh…brothers! "I'm fine."

Clara, not picking up on her false illness, said, "I will stay with you until the doctor arrives."

Her gaze darted to Sam, and he pressed his lips together to prevent himself from laughing. He placed a kiss on his wife's cheek. "I will leave you here, my love."

Clara smiled back at him in adoration. Sam knew she wasn't sick! She would have to look through the notepad at another time.

~

Simon kept his impatience contained as he followed the carriage ahead of him down one of London's main thoroughfares. What he really wanted to do was gallop his horse the remainder of the way to the Den. The shop that he and Miss Markam used to exchange letters was closed. Based on the urgency of her previous letter, he hoped Miss Markam had left further details with someone at the Den. He turned on to the street that led to the gentlemen's club, breathing a sigh of relief before quickening his pace. He urged his horse forward but not too fast to draw attention to himself.

As he approached the Den, a man most would characterize as a drunk stumbled out into the street. He drew his horse to a halt, and the man ambled up to him.

"Sir, do you have anything to spare?" he yelled.

Simon dug in his coat pocket and withdrew some change. The man leaned against his horse, caressing it, before reaching his hand up for the coins. As Simon bent down, the man whispered, "Go around to the entrance used for discretion and wait in the octagon cottage. You are being looked for."

Sam didn't pause but continued to place the coin in the man's hand. "Here you go."

"Thank you, sir," the man said and wandered back to where he was sitting.

Instead of continuing down the street, Simon turned down an alleyway that most would think nothing of. In truth, the back alley was used by the lords and ladies of the *ton* who wanted to use one of the Den's many cottages littered through the grounds for a liaison.

As he approached, the gates were thrown open, and a guard guided him to a decrepit building in the far back of the gardens. The roof of the octagon cottage was partially caved in and clearly hadn't been used for some time.

Simon hopped off his horse, and his eyes darted around. The cottage was not within sight of the other small buildings or the grand house. Still, he guided his horse to the back of the cottage and tied him up, hoping to conceal him from any prying eyes.

He walked to the door of the small building and pushed it open. The small, oddly shaped room was covered in dust. Simon walked in, leaving the door open. He paced back and forth, pulling his long coat around him tightly.

The guard would alert Devons or Derry about his arrival. They were the only ones who would think to send him here. He sighed in impatience. He needed to find Miss Markam as soon as possible. He thought about the two notes she had sent him while at the Peyton estate. The first mentioned the bars and an item. What was the item she referenced?

He should have returned when he received the first note. The second note provided little information, only that they had been discovered. A noise interrupted his thoughts. He turned to see Devons standing in the doorway. His business partner's normal jovial personality was nowhere to be seen. His mouth was set in a grim line. Something was very wrong.
Devons entered the small building, strolling around the room, studying where the roof had caved in.

“What’s going on?” Simon demanded, impatiently.

Devons turned and studied him but finally said, “You’re wanted. The London Peelers, along with an American private investigator and a New York City constable, are searching for you.”

“What are you talking about?” Simon asked, shocked. Why would London or New York City police be searching for him?

“They found the gold bars in your cottage.”

Gold bars? Simon’s mind swirled with confusion. He sat on an old wooden chair and ran his hands over his face.

“What?”

Devons frowned at him and walked over to another dusty chair. He pulled out his handkerchief and swiped it across the seat before sitting. If Simon wasn’t so confused, he would laugh at Devons’ concern with dirtying his clothes.

“Yesterday, an American investigator and constable showed up looking for you. They said your father had stolen money from one of the largest banks in New York City. The constable said that fifty thousand dollars' worth of gold bars were missing. They believed he gave them to you."

Simon shook his head. What Devons was saying was beyond bizarre. "My father is innocent."

Devons leaned back in the chair, folding his arms. "And you?"

Simon rolled his eyes, "Where would I keep that many gold bars?"

"That is what I thought, so when they demanded we call in some London Peelers to search your cottage, I didn't think much of it. I figured you were either innocent or that you wouldn't be stupid enough to keep it hidden where you lived, but to my surprise, they recovered fifty gold bars."

Gold bars in his cottage? That amount was almost the weight of a full-grown man. Simon's eyes connected with Devons. "They aren't mine."

Devons was quiet for a moment. "Who would want to put them in your cottage? They would have to get through our guards to pull something off like that."

"Tobias Walker," Simon bit out.

Devons lifted a brow in surprise. "This gets more and more interesting. I had some of our men investigate who the London Peelers got the tip from to search your cottage. It was Walker."

Simon said nothing.

"Tobias Walker is a dangerous man with many friends in the *ton*. What is this really about?"

"He is setting me up."

"I don't doubt that. He has bankrupted more than one man for speaking ill of him, but you acted like you didn't know him at first."

"I didn't," Simon affirmed.

"Explain it to me."

"Prior to meeting him, I had never spoken with him and only seen him from afar. But I have been studying him for years. I believe it was Walker, not my father, who committed the theft at the bank."

Devons whistled. "He could hang or spend the rest of his life in prison."

"My father died in prison because of Walker," Simon bit out.

"What can I do to help?" he asked, again.

"A maid in his employ, Miss Markam, has been helping me look for evidence against him. She sent me a letter saying that I needed to return, and it was urgent. There was something about an item as well. Can you locate her for me?"

Devons nodded. "You need to get out of London for a bit."

Simon shook his head and Devons said, "Peelers are fanned out around London looking for you. Leave for a few days and I will find the maid."

He wanted to stay in London, but he knew Devons was right. If he stayed he would be caught. Where could he go? Perhaps the town of Blackpool from Miss Markam's letter? He could travel there and figure out what was so important about Allen Lemming. Instinctively, he patted for the leather notepad he carried everywhere. It was gone. He'd left it in the room at the Peyton estate. "Damn it!"

"What is it?"

"I left my notepad at Jack's."

"Does it have any information that could be used against you?"

Just where he was headed, Simon thought angrily. He didn't want Devons to try to talk him out of traveling to Blackpool. He shook his head. "No, it should be fine."

Devons frowned at him. "Are you sure? I could travel to the Peyton estate?"

Simon couldn't let him do that. He didn't want Annie to know he was wanted. Hopefully, he could find evidence in Blackpool to clear him of the charges. If the Kincaides found the notepad, they would never hand it over to the Peelers. He would have to have faith in that.

Simon shook his head. "It isn't necessary. I will leave tomorrow. Tonight, I will find an inn on the outskirts of London, hopefully to avoid the Peelers."

"Don't take the train."

Simon nodded, knowing Devons was right. The Peelers would be all over the train stations. By horse wouldn't be much better. He would stand out too much. He would have to take a coach, less conspicuous. Simon rose. He couldn't stay any longer. He needed to make travel plans.

"There is an inn and tavern known as the Dirty Bell. Stay there, and I will meet you this evening. I can see what I find out about Miss Markam before you leave," Devons suggested.

Simon nodded and made his way to the door.

"You didn't ask if I believed you were innocent," Devons said, stopping him.

Simon looked back. "You know me."

Devons nodded, satisfied with his answer.

Chapter 8

The Peyton estate dining room reverberated with chatter and laughter from the guests making the most of the last night of the week-long party. Annie forced a smile as Lord Connolly's aunt told a long-winded story about her sister. Goodness, the woman could talk.

She pressed her palm against the small notepad hidden in her gown. All she wanted to do was retreat to her room and pour over the contents of it, but she resisted. Everyone was already watching and fawning over her.

After the debacle with the doctor, she didn't know if she would ever tell such a lie again. He had quickly caught on to her ruse. Luckily for her, he didn't flat out tell Jack she was fibbing. Instead, he prescribed her rest. Clara, the saint she was, insisted she stay with her. The only peace and quiet she got was when she announced she was feeling better and would dress for dinner. That was short-lived as then her maid arrived to prepare her for the evening.

"I am glad you are doing better," Bromley whispered, seated next to her.

She forced herself to smile. "Thank you for being so concerned."

"I would like to speak with you after dinner. Perhaps we could get some air."

The proposal was imminent. Why did she feel like she wanted to flee? She looked up at his handsome face made up of a strong jaw and the bluest eyes. This evening, he wore an outrageous waistcoat in a bright red, giving him the appearance of a rakish angel. One who had been nothing but a proper gentleman during his courtship of her.

“May I ask for a reprieve?” she said quietly so only Bromley could hear her.

He lifted a brow in surprise. “May I ask why?”

What could she say? That another man had kissed her and fled, but she couldn’t stop thinking about him? It was preposterous.

“When we spoke privately, you said you would give me time. The news that you have spoken with my brother is a little startling.”

He was quiet for a moment, and Annie thought he might turn cross, but he smiled. “Take all the time you need. I’m a patient man.”

Immense relief filled her, and Annie knew even if there was no Miller, she couldn’t marry Bromley no matter how wonderful he was. He deserved more than what she had to offer him. She deserved more. Miller still may not be an option but if she couldn’t have love—

Love! What was she thinking? She pushed the disconcerting thoughts away, not wanting to face them. For now, she was happy she had put off an awkward conversation with the gentleman sitting next to her.

She smiled at him. “Thank you.”

He was quiet for a moment but finally said, “If you accept my offer, just know that I want all of you.”

She blushed and shook her head. “I don’t know what you mean.”

“I think you do. Even though he is no longer here, he affects you.”

Her blush deepened, knowing he was talking about Miller. She said nothing in response and turned to Lord Connolly and his aunt.

"What are your plans for the season?"

Connolly's aunt launched into a lengthy explanation of their agenda. Apparently, Lord Connolly would be completely embroiled in the marriage-mart this season. The man's coloring turned green at his aunt's ambitious schemes.

Annie's mind wandered back to Miller. Why did he leave? Was it because of their kiss? Every practical thought she had told her to forget Miller, but then the smallest part of her told her that it was impossible.

After the estate party, they would be back in London to immerse themselves in the season as well. Miller was in London, so perhaps they would have an opportunity to speak when Annie and her family returned. She needed answers from him. Once she got something in her mind, she couldn't let it go until she figured it out.

A bell chimed, signaling dinner was over. Everyone rose, and Bromley held his arm out to Annie. They headed towards the ballroom as music drifted down the corridor. The event was a much smaller affair tonight with only the guests Jack had invited to stay at the estate. Annie and Bromley walked silently as the other party attendees threw speculative glances their way.

She couldn't let Bromley propose in front of everyone or let the speculation continue. She may not want to wed him, but she respected him far too much to cause him such embarrassment. She stopped, and Bromley looked at her quizzically.

"I changed my mind. May we speak in a way that won't alert everyone that we are meeting?" Annie said.

A flicker of disbelief and sadness passed over his face. He knew.

Bromley nodded. “After we enter the ballroom, wait a few moments, and then meet me in the library.”

Annie nodded. They entered the expansive room, and Bromley bowed, excusing himself.

She sighed.

“Annie!” Sophia said, looping her arm through Annie’s.

“Did he propose?” she added.

Annie frowned at her sister. “No. Of course not.”

Sophia smiled mischievously “He is expected to. What will you say?”

“Stop. This isn’t a game. Not everyone lives like they are in some type of novelette,” Annie snapped.

Sophia stiffened. She pinched her lips together and her eyes became watery. Annie’s words had been too harsh.

“Sophia—”

“No. Don’t. You’re right. I am being silly. Had I been as practical as you, perhaps I wouldn’t be where I’m at now.”

The wind went out of Annie at her sister’s honest words. “Sophia—”

“I think I will go speak with Mercy,” Sophia said, walking away, not giving Annie time to stop her.

Annie watched her sister flee, feeling awful that she had so callously hurt her. Her blasted tongue was too sharp. None of her anger should have been directed at her. She walked towards the door and discreetly stepped out before heading to the library.

As she entered the room, Bromley turned. He was drinking brandy.

"I suppose since you wanted to do this privately your answer is no," he said, not bothering with niceties.

She frowned. "I don't know what I want right now."

"I can wait."

The problem was if he waited, it wouldn't change her mind. Her decision wasn't about Miller. As much as she should want to spend the rest of her life with the extraordinary, titled lord in front of her, she didn't. "I don't want to marry you. That won't change, and you deserve more."

He took a sip of his brandy. "It's Miller, isn't it?"

She shook her head.

His mouth twisted into a smirk. "Really?"

"Even if there was no Miller, I wouldn't say yes. You said earlier you wanted all of me, but I don't feel that way about you. Trust me, life would be much easier if I did."

He took another sip and was quiet for a moment. Annie wasn't sure he would say anything else. Finally, he said, "He is a bloody fool if he doesn't want you."

Annie smiled at him. "Thank you for being so understanding."

"I'm here for you if you need anything. I will take my leave now, so people don't wonder where we both are."

He lifted her hand to his lips and placed a lingering kiss on it before departing. She threw herself on the sofa. Was she a fool?

She sighed and rose to make her way back to the ballroom. A sudden pounding on the front door halted her steps. Who could that be so late?

~

Simon sat in the Dirty Bell, eating a roast while impatiently waiting for Devons. He wasn't planning to leave until tomorrow, but he needed to know what he found out about Miss Markam. Yes, he wanted to know what she was retrieving, but Simon was struggling with an immense amount of guilt that she may be harmed or worse.

His eyes roamed around the packed tavern. It wasn't much of a place, but the food was good, and unlike some taverns he had been in the last few months, it appeared clean. He was grateful to Devons for the recommendation. He nursed his ale, doing his best to stay alert, knowing he was sought after.

He was fairly confident the Peelers and the Americans would be searching for him closer to the railways. It was becoming the more common form of travel. If they weren't looking for him there, they would likely be looking for him at the docks, assuming that he would flee. Tomorrow he would board a coach for Daventry, then on to Liverpool before making his way to Blackpool.

He wasn't fleeing; innocent men didn't flee. He pondered when Walker had caught on to him. Was it the first night he had met him at the Den or was it over time? He clenched his glass. Fury simmered within him.

He needed to stop Walker. For a brief insane moment at the Peyton estate with Annie in his arms, he had considered giving up his quest to prove his father's innocence. Then he had received Miss Markam's letter.

Allen Lemming. He mulled over the name in his mind. He still didn't know who he was or how he was connected to Walker. The town of Blackpool had come up before, but now he understood why.

"Hello, luv. Would you like some company?" a young shapely server asked.

Simon glanced at her and wished he did want company. But if

he wasn't wanted, then it would be Annie that prevented him from flirting with the server. He couldn't get their moment in the maze out of his mind. Her response to him was what haunted his dreams. A temptation he couldn't claim. He shook his head but smiled, not wanting to insult her. She shrugged and sauntered off.

Where was Devons? On cue, he stepped through the door, and Simon's eyes widened in surprise because the Marquess of Derry entered behind him. He hadn't expected both of his partners from the Den to show up.

The corner of Simon's mouth ticked up in a smile as he studied the two men. Devons seemed completely at ease in the rough tavern, but Derry glared around the room in contempt. They spotted him and made their way over.

Almost simultaneously, both brushed off their seats before sitting. Simon was struck how similar they were not in looks but in mannerisms. Over time, Simon had learned they were actually half-brothers and fiercely devoted to each other. Why they didn't share their connection more broadly, Simon had no idea.

Gratitude coursed through him that they were both here. Their loyalty and friendship had never been more evident.

"So, I hear you are behind one of the greatest robberies of the decade," Derry said dryly.

"I told you he is innocent," Devons reminded him.

Derry raised two fingers, and a server placed two glasses of ale on the table. She winked at him before she left, and Derry smiled back at her. The girl giggled, and Devons rolled his eyes.

"I'm innocent," Simon said, not wanting his friend to think the worst of him.

The marquess lifted a brow. "Do you think I would believe you are capable of this? Now Devons here, I wouldn't think twice."

Devons chuckled.

The marquess continued, "Regardless, we would help you."

Still, Simon didn't want him to think he was the culprit. "My father was convicted of the theft but on little evidence. I knew he was innocent but couldn't prove it."

"How did you suspect Walker?" Derry asked.

Simon took a sip of his ale. "My father had mentioned Walker once long ago. He didn't believe he had anything to do with the crime, but I quickly determined he was somehow connected. Still, I didn't have any evidence beyond that he had left the country."

"How are the Kincaides involved in all of this?"

"They knew none of this. I kept it to myself. Part of why I took the job with them was that their passenger vessel company had stops in England. Over time, I never came across Walker, likely because most of my time was spent in Liverpool. Prior to the Kincaides permanent relocation to England, I was in London preparing for their move, and I saw him at the tavern you both own. As I watched him, I knew I needed answers."

"But you still don't have any proof he is guilty?"

Simon shook his head. He didn't, but now that Walker had played his hand, Simon had no doubt he was the real culprit behind the theft.

"Not until the gold was discovered in my cottage. That is the act of a man who doesn't want his past to catch up with him. Still, it is his word against mine."

"We think we know when Walker had the gold placed in your cottage," Derry explained. "Walker requested the use of a cottage not far from yours a few nights ago. If he wanted to set you up, it was likely that night."

Simon had miscalculated Walker. He had assumed he had long moved on from thinking about the theft or getting caught.

"Is there any other evidence that would prove his guilt?" Devons asked.

"The discovery of those bars at your residence is pretty damning," Derry added.

"Potentially. I don't want to involve either of you in this mess," Simon said.

Devons and Derry looked at each other before Devons said, "You can trust that anything you confide in us will not be shared with anyone. If you need anything, we are here for you."

Simon nodded, grateful. "Did you find any information on Miss Markam?"

Devons shook his head. "Not yet, but I have my men out searching."

Not what Simon wanted to hear, but he was happy that he could trust Devons and Derry to do everything in their power to find her. "Thank you. I appreciate your help."

"Where will you go? Tell us so we know where to find you if something happens," Devons insisted.

Simon frowned. He really didn't want to further embroil his friends in his predicament. Still, he needed someone to know where he went if he disappeared. "Blackpool. I think there is evidence there."

"Do you want us to let the Kincaides know what is happening?" Derry suggested.

Simon's gaze jerked back to him. "I don't want them involved in this."

"They would help," Derry said.

Simon shook his head and Devons frowned at him. "It's the sister. You're worried about her getting wrapped up in this."

Only Devons knew Annie came to him during the Ball of Sin. He scowled at him but didn't deny it. "I don't want her involved in this at all."

Annie likely despised him now. He practically deserted her after the passionate kiss they'd shared. The only goodness in his awful actions was hopefully she would decide to forget him. A little sliver of doubt clouded his thoughts.

Chapter 9

Annie stood outside of Jack's study, trying to hear what was being said. The men at the front door turned out to be Americans and London Peelers investigating Miller. Shock didn't even begin to describe Annie's reaction. Her brothers had seemed just as startled before ushering the men into Jack's study.

She cursed the solid wood door that prevented her from hearing what was being said. Sophia came up next to her. "What's going on?"

"Jack and Sam are speaking with some men searching for Miller."

Her sister's eyes widened in alarm. "Well, you won't hear anything standing there like that."

Sophia nudged her out of the way, not caring if she appeared to be prying and pressed her ear to the door.

She looked utterly ridiculous with her ear smashed up against the oak and for some odd reason, Annie felt emotional. After she was so harsh with her, her sister was still helping her.

"Soph—"

"Don't. I'm still cross with you."

Annie smiled at the back of her sister's head. She couldn't see anything, but her red hair tied up in curls cascading down her back.

"Still, I'm sorry I hurt you."

"Shh…I can't hear."

Sophia yanked her head away from the door, bumping into Annie. “Someone is coming,” she whispered.

The door was thrown open and Annie and Sophia froze. Jack's eyes widened in surprise. His gaze jumped back and forth between the two of them. They both stared back at him, feigning innocence. He rolled his eyes and said, “Annie, can you come in for a moment?”

“I will join her,” Sophia insisted.

Jack sighed but nodded. Her practical brother probably suspected it was easier to include her now. Sophia always figured out what was going on. Not that Annie’s family kept many secrets from each other.

They entered Jack’s study to find it filled with men. Annie’s gaze shifted around and saw multiple men dressed in Peeler uniforms, but two men, in everyday attire, stood closer to the windows.

The older man caught her studying him and bowed slightly. “Hello, Lady Annabelle. I’m Bill Collins. I am an investigator hired by the New York City Common Trust Bank, and this is Constable Tom Shell. We have some questions about Simon Miller. We have been told you may have been the last to see him.”

Annie’s eyes narrowed. “What is this about?”

“That isn’t your concern,” Constable Shell asserted.

Her eyes connected with Shell’s. Annie knew instantly she didn’t like the man. He wasn’t much older than her brothers, but he had a weasley and domineering appearance. He frowned at her with contempt. She sensed he was trying to make her uncomfortable or nervous. She tilted her chin up in defiance, unimpressed.

She turned to Jack and stubbornly said, “I am not answering any questions until I know what is going on.”

“My lady—” Shell started.

Collins raised his hand to silence him. “That is only fair, my lady.”

He took one of the chairs and indicated for her to sit on the sofa. Annie looked at Jack and Sam, who both nodded for her to sit. Her stomach dropped as a sense of foreboding fell over her. She sat, and Sophia joined her, lacing their fingers together.

Jack and Sam both took a seat on the arms of the sofa. Annie’s family surrounding her did nothing to ease her concern. The Kincaides rallied together in the worst of times. What was this man about to tell her? Unlike Shell, he didn’t have the appearance of an ass.

Collins glanced at the Peelers. “Can we have some privacy?”

The majority of the men filed out except for her brothers and Shell. The obnoxious man leaned against a wall, scowling at her.

Collins rolled his eyes and turned back to Annie. “Mr. Miller is being charged with theft. His father worked at the New York City Common Trust Bank, and right after his shift, the contents of a vault went missing. Part of what was taken was a large amount of gold bars. I was hired by the bank to try to retrieve the items in the vault. Constable Shell is here to bring any culprits back.”

“Are you insinuating Miller is involved?” Annie questioned, horrified.

“We know he is. We found the gold bars in his cottage,” Shell said tauntingly.

Sam scowled at the man. Annie could tell he was growing tired of the man's tone. She turned to Jack. "You can't believe this."

Jack squeezed her shoulder. "I don't, but we can't impede their investigation. The butler said you were the last to see Miller before he left. They want to ask you questions about your encounter."

"I was with her," Sophia added.

Both Jack and Sam nodded.

"Before Mr. Miller left, did he share anything out of the ordinary with you?" Collins asked.

She flushed. Nothing besides kissing her until her body burned with desire for him, she thought. Her eyes connected with Sam's, and for some reason Annie felt like he could see everything she was hiding. She looked away and willed the pink hue covering her body to disappear.

"Not really. Sophia was with me. He received a note and said he had to return to London. That is all we know."

Shell sighed, indicating to Annie he didn't believe her. Collins glared at him before turning back to her. "I have met Mr. Miller. He seems like a decent sort, but regardless of if he is guilty or not, it is imperative we meet with him. Are there any details you can give us that may indicate where he is at or what was in the note?"

"He was headed to London is all I know," Annie said.

Sophia nodded. "He left right away."

"There is nothing else?" Shell asked, skeptical.

Perhaps it was hard for some people to lie, but Annie's upbringing had taught her that a lie sometimes was the only thing that led to survival. Ignoring the notepad pressed against her leg, she stared him straight in the eyes and said, "There is nothing."

The man frowned in disbelief.

“Why did New York City send a constable to England to investigate this? What is so special about this case?” Annie demanded, annoyed with the man.

The man didn’t say anything. His beady eyes glared at her.

Mr. Collins interrupted the staring contest and asked, “Can we inspect the room he was staying in?”

Jack nodded. “I will show you to the room, but I believe my staff has already cleaned it.”

They all rose and made their way up to the guest wing. Annie knew she should excuse herself, but she didn’t. Nerves filled her that perhaps she or the maid missed something. She stood in the doorway of the guest room that Miller had used, watching the Peelers and the Americans look around. The room was immaculate.

Collins turned and asked Jack, “Was anything left behind?”

Jack shrugged. “If so, my staff would have sent it back to London.”

Shell sighed, annoyed that they were no help. Mr. Collins handed Jack a paper and said, “This is the hotel we are staying at in London. Please let Mr. Miller know that Ben Collins would like to speak with him.”

Jack nodded. “I will escort you out.”

The guests were still down in the ballroom, oblivious to the Peelers and Americans. Annie didn’t have the energy or desire to join them. She made her way to her room, confused by what she had learned. She didn’t believe Miller was a thief.

Once in her room, still dressed for dinner, she sank into a chair, overjoyed to be alone. She pulled Miller’s notepad from her pocket and ran her fingers along the spine. A tiny nibble of guilt ran through her. She was about to go through Miller's personal item. She shouldn't open it, but she did anyway, flipping to the back where her portrait was tucked in between a few pages. Nothing was written on those, so she flipped back to the front and started looking at Miller's neat and methodical handwriting.

Most of it was information about the Den, but on one page the name Tobias Walker was scribbled along with the name Miss Markam and the word Blackpool. Who was Miss Markam? Was it a lady friend? She frowned, wondering if Miller had a lover. She pushed the thought away and mulled over the word Blackpool. What was it?

A knock distracted her from her thoughts. Her maid entered.

"My lady, I didn't expect you to be here. Would you like to prepare for bed?"

"Yes. Thank you, Nancy."

Nancy nodded and started readying her for bed. Annie sighed as her maid released her hair from the many pins holding her curls up. Nancy chuckled.

"Aye, my lady. I bet that feels nice."

They stood, and Nancy helped her out of her dress before helping her into her nightgown.

Nancy smiled. "Anything else, Lady Annabelle?"

Annie hesitated, and Nancy's smile turned into a frown. "What is it, my lady?"

She was acting odd. Nancy probably thought she was overwhelmed with the events of the night. Truth be told, she was.

"Just a question. Have you ever heard of Blackpool?"

Nancy seemed relieved at her simple question. "Yes, that's a town north of Liverpool."

It was a location. Why would Miller write it down? The town had to be connected with what was going on. She groaned inwardly, realizing that if questioned, Nancy would share their conversation.

Annie said, "I think I must have misheard what Lord Sutton said earlier. I'm looking for the name of a black tart?"

Nancy paused to consider her question. "Hmm. Perhaps a chocolate treacle tart?"

"Yes! That's it," Annie said, faking her excitement. "I hope to have the chef make one for Jack's birthday."

Nancy nodded vigorously. "They are awfully tasty, but I would also recommend a traditional treacle tart if you haven't eaten one."

Annie smiled, relieved that the Blackpool question seemed to be forgotten. "I think both would be good."

"I will be sure to have the chef add them to the menu," Nancy said.

"Thank you, Nancy. You are the best. I don't know what I would do without you."

The woman did a quick bob and departed. Annie shook her head and sank back into her chair. She pondered what she would do next.

She was startled by another knock on her door. She sighed. Why couldn't she be left alone?

"Enter."

Jack and Mercy entered her room, still dressed in evening attire. Jack asked, "Are you okay?"

Was she okay? She didn't know. "I don't believe it."

"I don't know what I believe." He then added, "But is there anything you haven't told us about your encounter with Miller?"

More than she would ever share, she thought. Still, he hadn't told her much beyond he was going to London. The notepad wasn't really part of the discussion. A lie is a lie, her conscience whispered to her.

Both Jack and Mercy frowned at her with concern. A sliver of guilt weaved its way through her. She considered telling them about Miller's notepad but couldn't bring herself to. She shook her head. "There's nothing."

"This will all get sorted out," Mercy reassured her.

Annie nodded. "I think I would like to rest."

They left her room. Annie rose and flopped down on her bed. What was she doing? She knew exactly what she was doing. She was considering doing something drastic. The town of Blackpool ran through her mind. Was that where Miller was headed? How would he get there?

~

Simon sat in the coach heading to Liverpool. His assumption had been right that they would assume he was traveling on the rail lines. Coach routes were being used less as trains became increasingly popular. He looked around the coach that was designed to carry six to eight but only contained two other travelers. One was a man close to his own twenty-nine years and an older woman. Beyond greetings, they had ridden in silence.

It would take them two days to reach Liverpool with a stop in Daventry for a few hours and then likely another day for him to reach Blackpool. The time didn't bother him. He needed it to regroup and think about what his next steps would be. He mulled over the name Allan Lemming in his mind. He wished he knew who he was or what significance he had to the theft, but the name was completely unfamiliar.

He wondered if one of the Americans was the investigator Bill Collins he had spoken with after his father's incarceration. The bank had hired him to track down items taken from the vault. It had been so long, would the same man still be on the case? Collins had been the only person associated with the New York City Common Trust Bank willing to hear Simon out.

Simon respected him. The bank and the New York City police had avoided him after his father's trial, unwilling to investigate anything further. He and Collins met multiple times, but without evidence, there was not much he could do.

Simon's mind drifted back to their last conversation on the day his father was buried.

Simon stood in the small cemetery of the neighborhood church that he'd attended his whole life. He glared at the blank headstone that should read John Miller, dedicated father, or something along those lines. Instead, the stone was blank with no indication who was put to rest beneath it. He felt rage simmer in him that the grave contained no name. The priest had insisted the stone would have to remain unmarked as his father was a criminal. Simon wanted to bury him elsewhere, but being buried in this cemetery had been his father's last wish.

If Father Abbott was still alive, he would have allowed Simon to properly bury his father, criminal or not. The priest who now ran the church couldn't care less that his father had been a dedicated follower. His only concern instead focused on keeping notoriety away from the church.

A few friends had paid their respects regardless that his father was considered a criminal. Simon would always be grateful to them. But now, it was just him standing in front of the mark-free headstone. His jaw clenched, and he swore he would prove his father's innocence. Then his father's name would be placed on the stone.

"Mr. Miller, I'm sorry to intrude."

Simon turned to see Collins, the investigator the bank hired to find the gold bars that were still missing. He was an older gentleman. Simon had spoken with him more than once about his father's innocence.

"It's fine, Mr. Collins."

"I wanted you to know I investigated Tobias Walker but found nothing."

Simon scowled. "He fled the country."

"He moved to England," Mr. Collins said gently.

He could get no one to believe him that Walker was likely the thief. He didn't understand why. "I don't care if you believe me. I will keep looking."

The investigator nodded. Simon studied him. "Why do I think this visit isn't about Walker?"

Mr. Collins tugged on his jacket, seemingly nervous. "There are those who think you have the gold bars."

Simon scoffed and laughed bitterly. "Do you believe that?"

"No, I don't, but I wanted to let you know. I briefed the bank and told them I think it's highly unlikely."

The anger in Simon surged. Unlikely? Mr. Collins held his hand up sensing his fury. "Mr. Miller, I spoke with your father several times. There is a good chance he was innocent, but he didn't dwell on that. What he talked about most was that he worried you would not go on with your life."

"It is not your place to tell me what my father wanted," Simon bit out.

"Still, don't ignore your father's dying wishes."

Simon said nothing, and the investigator left, leaving Simon staring after him.

Simon was jolted back to the present by heavy rain hitting the top of the carriage. The man across from him grinned. "You can never guess what the weather will be like in February around these parts."

Simon grunted in response. The man whistled a song, and Simon glared at him. "Can you please stop?"

"Most like my whistling. I'm a musician," he said, kicking the music case under his feet.

"Well, save it for a show. I'm trying to get some rest."

The man nodded, still grinning. For some reason Simon thought he was being intentionally obnoxious. Concern ricocheted through him. Was this man a Peeler? The man pulled a flask from his pocket and took a swig. Simon frowned at him. No, he was overreacting.

"Would you like a drink? Where are you headed to?"

Simon shook his head at the flask offering. He realized he was taking out his anger on this man who was most likely just chatting as he traveled to his next job.

"Liverpool. I apologize for my tone earlier."

The man chuckled. "No problem. Everyone is entitled to having a bad day. Right, miss?"

The woman who had been silent for the entirety of the

transport glared at him with disdain before closing her eyes.

The man shrugged. “Can’t win today.”

Simon laughed but quickly sobered as the carriage came to a stop. The rain was still coming down in large quantities. The door was thrown open. The driver yelled, over the rain, “I would recommend getting a room if possible. The weather will likely keep us here for a day or two.”

Damn it! The man and woman stepped out, and Simon followed. He sighed in annoyance, hoping they wouldn’t be stuck for more than a night. He glanced up at the sky as rain poured down around them. Simon looked at the driver. “Are you sure?”

The driver smirked at him as if he was an imbecile. “I have been using this route for years. This is the beginning of a bad storm coming that will flood the area. I would recommend obtaining a room before the other coaches arrive.”

Simon scowled but made his way into the closest inn. The musician from the coach stood waiting for a room as well, whistling again. Simon's bad mood returned, and he glowered at him. Damn it.

Chapter 10

Annie sat at the dainty desk in her room, frowning. Her brothers were going to be livid, she thought. She picked up the note she had just written and read the contents.

Jack and Sam,

I have decided to follow up on a possible location where Miller might be. Please don't be alarmed, I will send word as soon as I can. I'm writing this note, so you don't think I've been kidnapped.

Annie

The note was awful and would enrage both her brothers, but at least they wouldn't think she had been harmed by someone. Too much had taken place in the last two years to ever let Jack or Sam think that.

Determined to continue with her plan, she folded the note in half. Her eyes moved around the room, trying to determine the best place to leave it. She rose and made her way over to the made-up bed and placed it on her pillow. Nancy had already tidied up her room, so she had a few hours before it would be found.

Annie grabbed a bag that she used for shopping excursions and made her way to the door. "Here I come Blackpool," she muttered to herself.

She silently made her way to the stairs leading to the foyer and descended. A smile crossed her face when she spied the carriage the staff had readied for her. Nancy, the godsend she was, had said she would see to it earlier this morning. She made her way to the front door but stopped when the butler asked, "My lady, may I be of assistance?"

Caught! She told herself to remain calm. She went to town all the time.

"Good day. I'm taking the carriage to Luton," she said, politely.

The butler's eyes narrowed. "Who will be traveling with you?"

Was he on to her? She was likely overreacting. Annie instinctively placed her already full bag behind her. It contained another dress, a nightgown, and a few other items that she needed while she was away.

She wanted to laugh and say of course she was going alone but her nerves had her concerned he suspected her of subterfuge.

Instead, she smiled brightly. He frowned at her. Perhaps too much. Drat!

"Lady Landers will be joining me. It's likely she just overslept. I will go fetch her."

"My lady, I can have a maid do that."

She shook her head. "Nonsense, I can do it."

She slung her bag over her shoulder and ignored the butler's request to take it to the carriage, charging back up the stairs. She quickly made her way to Sophia's room and knocked softly. There was no movement from the other side of the door, so she knocked again. Annie leaned into the door and heard a faint rustling. She drew back horrified. What if she woke up Landers? What if they were in bed together?

The door opened and her sister poked her head out. "What is it?" she asked with concern.

Annie sighed with relief. Her sister was dressed for the day. "I need you to travel to town with me. I wish to go shopping."

Sophia frowned at her. "You hate shopping."

"Just meet me downstairs and hurry. Don't wake Landers."

Sophia flushed. "He is gone. He returned to London."

The damn wastrel, Annie thought. For a brief moment Sophia looked as if she would cry but then a smile formed on her face. "What adventure are you planning?"

"I just have a few items I want to pick up."

Sophia winked at her. "If you say so. I will be down shortly."

Annie made her way back to the foyer and paced, waiting for Sophia. Her eyes flitted to the elegant clock whose incessant ticking seemed designed solely to torture her. At last, she appeared with a small reticule slung over her arm, beaming at Annie. "I'm ready."

They made their way out the front door and into the carriage. The ride to Luton was brief and Annie stayed quiet wondering how she would be able to slip away from her sister. For once Sophia seemed to be lost in her own thoughts as she stared out the window. Why did Landers leave, Annie wondered? The Kincaides would be traveling to London tomorrow.

The carriage stopped, and Annie followed Sophia out before telling the driver they would be there for a few hours. They strolled along a walkway, and Annie eyed the crowded streets. Luton was growing rapidly, and Annie was happy for the once quiet town. Her eyes darted to the small shop that coaches were departing from before looking at her sister.

Annie pondered how she would escape her sister. Even though Sophia loved a bit of fun and trouble, she would likely never agree to let Annie take a coach to Liverpool alone. Still, she couldn't just leave her in the middle of town. She would think she had been kidnapped.

"Why are we here?" Sophia asked.

"I told you to go shopping."

Her sister laughed, her face glowing with humor. "Why are we really here? You are up to some type of mischief?"

Annie flushed. Her sister was right, but she didn't want her to get in the middle of her plans. Jack and Sam would already be cross with her. Sophia didn't need them angry at her as well. "I think I know where Miller is."

Sophia frowned deeply, coming to a halt along the walkway. "Annie, what are you planning?"

She was mucking this up. The frown on Sophia's face only deepened. Annie grabbed her sister's arm and pulled her to the side of the walkway streaming with people.

"I am taking the coach to where I think Miller is."

Her sister's eyes widened in alarm. "Annie, that's ridiculous."

"Women travel alone by coach all the time."

"Not ladies. What if something happens to you?" Sophia insisted.

She had to do this. It was reckless and foolish, but she didn't care. Determination filled her face.

"Sophia, I need to find him. Please. I need to understand why all of this is happening to him." Annie hesitated but then added, "And why he kissed me in the maze."

Her sister smirked. "I knew he kissed you. The two of you were flustered and breathing heavily. If I had to guess, it was more than just a chaste kiss."

Annie nodded. For a moment Sophia's face flickered with amusement, and Annie had no doubt a slew of romantic ideas ran through her mind. Then she shook her head as if shaking away the thoughts that had shaped her entire life. "No. This is reckless. I will not see you make a choice based on a feeling that Miller may not reciprocate. This is dangerous!"

"I'm doing this," Annie said resolutely.

Her sister studied her. "I will tell Jack the moment I return."

"I left a note for him. I didn't want him or any of you to think that something bad happened to me," Annie explained.

"You are attempting to go after a wanted man," Sophia scolded.

Anger built in Annie at her sister's censor. "What would you do, Soph?"

Her sister laughed sardonically. "The me before marriage or after marriage?"

They were silent for a moment. Annie couldn't find the right words to comfort Sophia, and she would never tell her I told you so.

Finally, Sophia said, "Where are you planning to go?"

She was tempted to tell her but stopped herself. Sophia wasn't great with secrets and Annie knew their brothers would easily get it out of her.

"I would prefer not to tell you. Take the carriage back to the estate and take my note to Jack and Sam," Annie said.

Sophia was silent.

"Soph, I need to do this."

She sighed. "The moment you find Miller you will send me a note. Promise me. How far away are you traveling? Tell me that at least."

"Two days."

"You will stay at an inn by yourself!"

Annie smiled, amused at her outrage. Sophia was the most adventurous out of the two of them.

Annie nodded. “I will be fine.”

Sophia frowned, clearly not wanting Annie to go. She took a deep breath. “Promise you will send word in two days whether you find Miller or not.”

Annie nodded. “I promise.”

Sophia smiled at her. A bit of her normal mischievous self coming back. “I can’t believe you are doing this.”

She started digging in her reticule. Annie frowned at her, unsure what she was looking for. Finally, she triumphantly held up a book.

“Here take this for your travels.”

Annie rolled her eyes. “I don’t want to read one of your romance novelettes.”

Sophia shook her finger at her. “You don’t get to look down on my books with disdain. You are practically acting one out at this very moment.”

Annie begrudgingly took the book. “I disagree, but I will take it. Thank you.”

Unexpectedly, Sophia threw her arms around her and hugged her tightly. “Be safe.”

Annie hugged her back. “I will. I promise.”

~

The driver was right. Rain continued to pour down, turning the road in front of the Old Thistle Inn into a soupy, muddy mess. Simon sat in the tavern, frowning at the weather outside. There had been a few moments where it changed to a lighter drizzle but not many. Carriages were still arriving, and people were being directed to inns further down that still had lodging.

Simon doubted they had any more accommodations either. He took a sip of the ale and glanced at the travelers filling the tavern and the entryway of the inn. Exhaustion and disappointment seemed to permeate the crowd, including himself. His eyes darted to the musician in the corner. Well, everyone except his festive co-traveler and the small crowd surrounding him as he played.

His gaze moved back to the open door leading out to the inn, where people continued to congregate even though the innkeeper was doing his best to redirect them to other options. A woman in a pale blue frock pushed her way to the counter, and Simon stiffened. He craned his neck to get a better sight of her.

The innkeeper was shaking his head. He knew those black curls that were trailing down the woman's back. He shook his head. No, he was imagining the similarity.

At least that is what he told himself. Propelled to be certain, he left his items on the table, and inched to the door.

"I have been told all other inns are full. Is there no room at all?" the woman questioned.

His body hummed at the recognition of the feminine voice. He stood next to a man who leered at the woman, licking his lips. Rage filled Simon, and again, he told himself it couldn't be possible.

The lecherous man said, "You can share with me."

The woman spun on her heel and planted her hands on her hips. "Sir, I would ask you leave me alone."

It hadn't been his imagination. Annie Kincaide stood before

him, glaring down the man next to him. She was a rumbled mess but still stunning with her trim waist, piercing blue eyes, and thick black hair.

Her gaze shifted and connected with Miller. A million emotions shot through Miller, but the primary one was fury. What the hell was she doing here?

The man next to him winked at her. "We could keep each other warm."

Simon grabbed the man by his shirt and pushed him up against the door frame. "Leave her alone."

The man sulked like a petulant child. "I found her first."

Simon leaned in close to the man's face. "The woman you are leering at is my wife."

He looked back at Annie, and she rolled her eyes. Did the woman not have any idea how much danger she was in?

The man's eyes darted back and forth between them. "Why didn't you say that to begin with?" he huffed.

Because he was lying, he thought. He glared at her, and she tilted her chin up in defiance. Oh, this woman would be the death of him. Instead, he smiled. "I hadn't realized she'd arrived yet."

The man shrugged Simon off, muttering about wives and husbands. Simon slowly made his way to Annie. He wanted to shake her and send her home, but no one was leaving Daventry anytime soon.

Annie smiled at him. "I was hoping to find you, husband."

The innkeeper frowned at her. "I thought you were looking for a room."

"She was confused about when I was arriving. Please have one of your servers fetch my wife some food," Simon stated.

Simon held his arm out to Annie, and she looped hers through his. His body emanated with anger.

"Calm down. That man has moved on."

As they walked, he leaned in and whispered, "Do you really think that is why I'm angry?"

She harrumphed and took a seat at his table. What was she doing here? Had she lost her damn mind? By now she and the Kincaides had to know he was a wanted man.

They sat down and both were quiet. A server placed a plate of food and ale in front of Annie. Simon bit out, "Eat."

She grimaced at his tone but daintily ate while he studied her. She said nothing. She drank some of the ale, and Simon was drawn to her mouth and throat. He felt himself harden thinking of those lips. What was he doing? He jerked his eyes back to hers. She smiled and said, "I'm so glad I ran into you. I had thought I wouldn't see you until Liverpool."

"Why would you think I would go to Liverpool?" he asked.

Her gaze flew to his, startled at her own words. She guiltily looked away. What was going on?

"How did you find me?"

She looked back at him and shrugged. Annie Kincaide was too smart for her own good. Her lips formed into a small smile. The predicament she had placed herself in was unacceptable. She didn't seem the least bit upset about it. As a matter of fact, she appeared downright victorious.

"Eat, then we are going upstairs. I don't know what you think you are doing but whatever choice that led you here is quite reckless."

She hissed back, “Regardless, it is my choice.”

He scowled back at her. “Yes, an idiotic one.”

Silence fell over the table. She ignored him and continued to eat her meal, acting as if she was all alone at the table. He glanced back at the musician on a break from entertaining the crowd. He frowned at them in concern. Why the hell was he watching them? Simon scowled at him, and the man raised his mug.

His gaze swung back to Annie and their eyes connected.

“I’m not leaving until I have answers,” she insisted.

“Well, the weather has seen to that, but you are returning to your brother’s estate the moment the skies clear.”

“We shall see,” Annie murmured.

She went back to eating. A bit of cream landed on her lower lip, and she swiped her tongue across it. This wasn’t good at all. She was a distraction he couldn’t afford. He needed to get her back to her brothers as soon as possible.

She wiped her mouth and placed her napkin on the table. “You will give me your word that you won't be cross with me.”

“No.”

“Perhaps I will find lodging elsewhere then.”

Definitely not. “Are you done?”

She pursed her lips and her eyes flashed with anger. What did she have to be angry about? She nodded, and he stood abruptly holding his hand out to her while grabbing her bag. Without another word he pulled her down the hallway and up the stairs. This woman had the ability to drive him mad.

Chapter 11

Annie followed Simon as they walked along the second-floor corridor. He moved like a man keeping a tight leash on his temper. His footsteps didn't just proceed along the floorboards but stomped in a way that made Annie wince. She shook her head at his antics. He stopped abruptly, and Annie skidded to a stop behind him.

As he fished the room key from a pocket, she let out an annoyed sigh. He froze and turned his head towards her. His mouth pressed tightly together. His jaw clenched. She raised a brow, and he scowled at her before turning back. He unlocked the door with more force than necessary and strode in. Annie followed him and shut the door.

Miller remained silent and stalked over to a table before pouring two brandies. He turned and presented her one. She swallowed, nervous now that they were alone, not that she would ever admit it to him. Her eyes roamed over him. He didn't look like the charming, proper Simon Miller she had been friends with over the last several years. He had a shadow of a beard that gave him a dangerous air. Her heart raced and not because he was a wanted man. She blushed at her improper thoughts.

"Annie," he bit out, pushing the glass into her hand.

"Thank you."

"What are you doing here?" he asked, bluntly.

She made her way to a maroon-colored wingback chair and settled herself. Simon paced waiting for her response.

"I came to find you. I was worried. There are men looking for you."

He ran his fingers through his hair in a fit of frustration. She would not be bullied by Simon into leaving, she told herself. She didn't care how upset he was. He took a large gulp from his glass before placing it on the fireplace mantel. Her eyes widened as he pivoted and beelined for her in the chair. He braced his hands on both sides of her seat and leaned down, so they were face to face.

Goodness, he looked villainous. Annie's body hummed at his closeness. Was she crazy? He was a wanted man being sought by both the London Peelers and the Americans. No, of course not! Miller wasn't a danger. She had the mad urge to lean up and press her lips to his but kept it clamped down.

"I'm a wanted man. Have you lost your mind?" he hissed.

She glared at him. "I don't believe for a moment that you are guilty of what they are saying."

His eyes moved to her mouth before they flicked back up to her eyes. "You don't think I can be dangerous?"

Annie gulped. The air crackled with an intensity, and Annie wasn't sure they were talking about theft any longer. She felt breathless but declared, "No."

He pushed off the chair and grabbed his drink from the mantel. He took another gulp. "This may be the most foolish choice I have ever witnessed you make."

She shrugged. "Well, it's done."

His eyes connected with hers. "They found the missing gold bars in my cottage. That is a pretty good sign I'm dangerous."

He was right, but she knew him too well. "I don't care what the Americans say. You didn't do it. Tell me why this is happening?"

"You need to return home."

She hated this bossy Miller. She took a sip of her own brandy. "Why did you kiss me in the maze?"

He looked startled by her question. Did he think she would just go on with life? His brown eyes lingered over her. She knew he was reliving the moment he had pulled her against him in the gardens. Good. She had played their garden interlude over in her mind more than a dozen times. She continued, "That wasn't just a chaste kiss. It was more. Deny that you want me."

His jaw tightened, and Annie, regardless of his anger, was confident she'd made the right choice in seeking him out. "I want an answer," she stated.

Miller took another drink from his glass. "Of course, I want you. I have wanted you from the moment I saw you."

She felt a flutter of happiness surge through her. She hadn't been wrong.

"That doesn't mean you and I are right," he said.

And just like that, her happiness plummeted. His handsome face became shuttered. "I'm not right for you."

Oh, how she detested him. For months now she had thought he didn't care for her and all because he decided it was his choice alone. Too damn bad, she thought. She would decide what was right for her.

"You lied and said that it was nothing more than a friendship. You made me think it was all in my mind."

"I did what I thought was best," he said, taking a seat in the other maroon chair across from her.

She tamped down her anger. They would discuss his asinine views later. "Why is this happening? How did the gold bars end up in your cottage?"

"My father was found guilty of stealing from the bank he worked at. He died in prison shortly after. Gold bars were some of the items stolen from the vault that was broken into. Perhaps he gave them to me."

Annie sensed he was trying to scare her. He was attempting to make her think he was guilty, so she would leave. She frowned at him. "I don't think so."

They were both quiet for a moment until Annie asked, "Was your father guilty?"

"Does it matter?"

Her frown turned to a scowl. She was tired of his evasiveness. He sat quietly drinking his brandy. She took another sip of her own and looked out the window. Large drops of water still filled the air. She wondered if it would rain all night. She arrived at the inn much later than she expected because of the weather. It had been a harrowing ride as the driver did his best to avoid areas of flooding.

"You shouldn't have come," he reiterated again.

She smiled slyly. "You know me well enough to know that I will do as I wish."

"How did you know where I was going?"

He still hadn't told her he was innocent, but he didn't have to. Miller may look devilish right now, but thievery was not a part of his traits. She should tell him that she found his notepad and her portrait, but something made her hesitate. She wasn't ready to share, yet. She shrugged. "I figured that you would leave London and guessed Liverpool was where you were headed. I didn't anticipate running into you in Daventry. I suppose I have the weather to thank for that."

"So you traveled all alone on a hunch? What would you have done if I wasn't headed to Liverpool?" he said grumpily.

It was more than a hunch, but she didn't say that. Instead, she rolled her eyes. "I would have stayed at my family's townhouse there. Liverpool isn't some exotic locale that I'm not familiar with."

He glared at her. This Miller was so different from the man she spent the last few years commiserating and laughing with. Gone was the always affable man, ready to help. In his place was a man who she barely recognized, harsh and specifically furious with her.

"I want to help," she said.

"This is not a game, Annie. The people involved are dangerous. You could be hurt. I already have one associate missing. Do you think worrying about you makes this situation any better?"

"Why not ask my family for help? You have done everything for us. Do you really think Jack and Sam wouldn't be there for you? That I wouldn't be there for you?"

He said nothing. Annie wanted to rail or demand he speak, but she doubted the angry man before her would be swayed into talking.

"Miller," she beseeched.

He shook his head. "It's getting late. We need to get some rest, but you are returning as soon as it's safe."

She rolled her eyes. "If you send me back to Jack's, the investigators will know the direction you were headed in."

He stilled at her words. His brown eyes connected with hers. Annie wasn't a saint. She couldn't prevent the victorious curve of her mouth. She had him. Miller was stuck with her whether he liked it or not.

"Bed," he bit out.

She huffed and stood. "Where shall I change?"

"Behind the dressing screen," he said, jerking his head in the direction of it.

~

Simon sighed as Annie stomped to her bag and pulled out a nightgown. Her blue eyes glanced back at him, flashing with anger and frustration before she moved behind the screen.

She grumbled in her semi-private area about idiots and fools. He shook his head. "I can still hear you."

He was met with icy silence. He leaned his head against the back of the chair, closing his eyes. How did she figure out he was heading towards Liverpool? Luck is what she had insinuated, but Simon suspected that was crap. Did she find his notepad? No. She would have told him. Christ! Her portrait was in the back of it. If she found it, his true feelings would be revealed.

"Is it really luck that led us to end up at the same inn?" he asked.

She sighed, annoyed. "It would appear so."

"Did the investigators and Peelers find anything at the Peyton estate?"

Annie shook her head. "By the time they arrived, Jack had sent any items you left back to the Den."

Relief coursed through him. Annie didn't know about her portrait and his notepad was secure. He felt fortunate to have such good friends. Regret filled him that perhaps he should have shared his past with the Kincaides, Devons, and Derry. If not Devons and Derry, at least the Kincaides, but the last few years had been rough for them. Simon didn't want to add to that. He didn't want Annie to endure anymore hardship. That is why he tried so hard to keep her at arm's length.

He scoffed. Yet, here she was, stuck in a room with him anyway. Damn woman! Damn Walker! Simon still couldn't believe how blind he had been. Walker had been playing him this whole time, making his own plans. His hands itched to seek him out on the streets of London and give him the pounding he deserved, but he couldn't. Gone was the lowly bank worker, and in his place was a very rich man who was married to a highly respected lady.

A rustling noise pulled him from his vengeful thoughts. He turned his gaze towards the thin privacy screen, and his throat went dry as he studied the outline of Annie's slender form, accentuated by a candle. She swayed back and forth trying to shimmy out of her dress. At one point she arched her back, and the silhouette presented on the screen made him swallow hard. Her exquisite breasts tilted up, and all he could think was they were the perfect size for his hands.

Temptation coursed through him. A crazed laugh erupted from his mouth, surprising him.

Annie turned towards him, and the captivating shape of her bosom disappeared. Simon breathed a sigh of relief. Though his traitorous body screamed for her to show them again.

"You try getting out of these dresses. The other dress I brought with me is much easier to maneuver myself," she snapped, annoyed.

He rose and made his way to the screen. The closer he got the more his brain tried to warn him it was a bad idea. "Let me help."

She gasped. "Absolutely not!"

"I have seen the female form once or twice," he said dryly.

"I bet you have. Plenty I'm sure," she said snarkily.

He smiled at her tone. It was so Annie. Yes, he'd had his fair share of encounters, but he suspected not as many as she thought.

"Annie, I will avert my gaze."

She was silent for a long time, and Simon wondered what she was thinking. Finally, she said, "I don't want you to see my scars."

His merriment subsided, and he sobered. What a damn ass he was. He hadn't thought about them. "Annie, I have seen them," he pointed out.

"Just the ones on my arm."

Simon rested a hand on the screen, wanting more than anything to pull her into his arms. To tell her that she was the most beautiful woman he had ever known. Nothing good would come of telling her his thoughts, but he couldn't and wouldn't let her think she was undesirable.

"I think after the maze you know how much I want you," he said softly.

"That is because you haven't seen them."

"Do you think your scars would truly change my desire for you? I have been sitting here being tortured by your silhouette for the last few minutes. Put me out of my misery."

She gasped.

"Let me help," he insisted.

Annie nodded, and Simon moved behind the screen. Her back was facing him. Even though her dress was stuck around her waist, she still wore her chemise and corset. The buttons along her lower back were the culprits preventing her from pulling the dress down any further.

Simon unsnapped the remaining buttons and then worked to untie her corset. The corset fell to the floor, and she stood in only her chemise, a thin petticoat, and knickers. He untied her petticoat, and they slid to the floor. The air between them emanated with desire and also Annie's embarrassment.

He hated that she was self-conscious. Trying to lighten the mood, he asked, "How the hell do you undress on your own?"

She remained silent. Simon wondered what was going on in that quick mind of hers. He should step away but his need to make her understand how stunning she was both inside and outside overpowered him. He brushed her hair away from her scarred shoulder.

"Miller, don't," she pleaded.

Discolored and marred skin covered her side. As Simon looked at Annie, he didn't see anything that she should be ashamed of. He saw a beautiful warrior. Without thinking, he pressed a kiss to her shoulder and trailed more down the back of her arm.

"Do you really think anything could take away from your beauty?" he questioned, his voice thick with emotion.

She attempted to turn, but he wrapped one arm around her, holding her in place. The scars forgotten, his hunger for her propelled him to kiss her along her neck and shoulder. He cupped one of her breasts through her chemise.

"So alluring," he murmured.

She trembled at his touch. Hell, he was trembling. He kissed and teased her, nuzzling her ear, and tasting her neck. She moaned, and Simon's hand ran farther down, wanting to touch her, needing to touch her in the most intimate place. His hand grazed her belly, and she pushed into him.

A knock on the door jerked him out of his heightened state of arousal. They both froze, and the knock came again. He cleared his throat. "Finish dressing. I will get that."

He yanked opened the door. "Yes?"

"My wife thought you may want some sweets for you and the missus," the innkeeper said.

Simon forced himself to smile and took the basket. "Thank you."

He shut the door and placed the basket on the table. What was he thinking throwing the door open? It could have been anyone. He wasn't thinking. That was the problem. He was distracted by the woman emerging from behind the screen. His body stirred at the sight of her even though she was covered from head to toe in her nightgown. He glowered at her and started tossing blankets on the ground.

"You can't sleep on the floor," Annie said, bewildered.

He glowered more. "Go to bed."

She folded her hands across herself stubbornly. "No. We still need to talk."

He laid on the ground and closed his eyes. "No."

Her feet stomped across the floor as she made her way to the bed. He forced himself to keep his eyes shut. It was going to be a long night.

Chapter 12

Annie stretched before pushing the blankets away from herself. She spent the better part of the night tossing and turning. She blinked several times, adjusting to being awake. Her gaze flitted around the small cozy room that wasn't much larger than some of the rooms she'd slept in as a child or the Kincaide's first family home. A bed big enough for two took up the majority of the room with a massive fireplace taking up most of one wall. Stuffed in between the bed and fireplace stood the two wingback chairs that she and Miller sat in the previous evening.

The room was quiet, too quiet. She scooted to the edge of the bed and peered over, but Miller was gone. The blanket still laid on the ground, but he was nowhere to be seen. Curse it, she thought. Her gaze shifted to a window and rain powered by heavy wind splattered against the glass. Would he really leave in such weather?

She pulled the practical sage day dress from her bag and started readying herself. She retrieved her chemise, petticoats, and knickers from behind the dressing screen. So many layers she thought to herself, grumpily. Still, the dress was much easier to get on than the one from yesterday. She buttoned up her clothing before wandering over to the small mirror over the table holding a water basin.

Annie frowned at her frightful black hair, and she adeptly removed the pins before plaiting her hair. She smiled at her much simpler reflection. Gone was the sister of a duke, she thought, amused. She smoothed her skirts down and looked around the room again.

Miller's belongings were still there. He couldn't have left, likely only because the rain had prevented him from doing so. Last night ended quite unexpectedly. She could still feel Miller's lips on her and his hand running up and down her body. His caressing hands left her wanting more than she should for an unmarried lady. She pursed her lips. Stubborn man. Too bad, she was more stubborn than he.

She made her way out the door and the floorboards in the hallway creaked as she walked along them. Once she made it to the first floor, she headed to the one place that everyone could congregate, the attached tavern. She peeked in and noticed it was fairly crowded but spotted Miller sitting at a small table, staring out the window.

She strolled over to his table and tried a smile, hoping they could start fresh.

"May I join my husband for breakfast?" she asked, teasingly.

He turned away from the window and frowned at her. She rolled her eyes. "Thanks, husband, for being so loving."

He raised a brow at her exaggerated use of the word husband. She took a seat. "The weather still looks awful."

Miller nodded. "It's flooding in the area and isn't expected to stop until tomorrow."

She drummed her fingers on the table, feeling antsy. He motioned for the server to bring Annie tea. Annie smiled. "You are the most considerate husband."

He snorted. "Thanks, wife."

Her lips tilted up. "See it isn't that hard to play along."

Miller took a sip of his tea. "I would prefer to be wife-free."

"For a moment when I awoke this morning, I thought you left me."

He scowled at that. “I wouldn't abandon you. Still, when the weather clears, you will depart in a private coach back to Luton.”

Annoyance grew in her. “Your behavior has been awful to me since I arrived. Are we not friends? Even if you are upset, I’m here. You would never treat anyone the way you are behaving now.”

He planted his elbows on the table and leaned in so only she could hear him. “Everything I have done regarding you has been to protect you. But even with all my efforts, you still decided to attend a scandalous ball and now you have run away from your family. Your actions are too bold.”

“There was a time you liked me bold. Judging by your choices last night, you still like how bold I am,” she said, tartly.

“You are an innocent lady. You should not be gallivanting across England, especially in a coach.”

She glared at him, placing her own arms on the table, leaning in. “I am twenty-six years old. Almost twenty-seven. Do not treat me like I’m so naive. I have lived more than most.”

Annie hated that Miller was acting like she was some wide-eyed innocent. She bet as a child she saw and endured far more than Miller ever did, but because he happened to be born a man, he was considered worldly.

Miller was silent but then said, “I apologize. I didn’t mean to insinuate you’re not capable. I just would rather not have you involved in this.”

“I want to talk about everything that has taken place,” she insisted.

He stared back at her. His handsome face was drawn with deep lines. “Can I convince you to go back home?”

She tilted her chin up defiantly. "No and if you send me back, I fear they will get your location from me."

It was a lie, but Annie wasn't above using it. Neither the Peelers nor the Americans would get anything out of her she didn't want to share. Or her brothers for that matter.

Miller stretched his broad shoulders and rubbed the back of his neck. Exhaustion covered his body. Annie got very little sleep, and from Miller's state, she assumed he didn't either.

"You need to rest."

He smiled wryly at her concern. "There are several things I need to do, but the weather is preventing all of them."

She wanted to pounce on his words but held back. "Still, rest is something you can get."

He glanced around, frowning at the crowd in the tavern. Annie stopped herself from rolling her eyes. "Go sleep. I will be fine down here. I brought a book with me."

He ran his fingers through his brown hair, conflicted. Annie looked around amused and said, "Go."

"If you leave the tavern, come straight back to the room."

She did roll her eyes then. "Yes, husband."

He rose and trudged out of the room. Thank goodness. He needed sleep more than anything. Yet, she still didn't have any answers. He hadn't confirmed or denied his involvement in the bank theft. Miller had been around a plethora of money since being in her family's employ and had been nothing but careful and deliberate with their holdings. So how did the gold bars end up in his cottage?

She sighed and shook the unanswered questions from her mind. The innkeeper's wife placed a plate of food before her, and her stomach growled in response. She ate quickly and once full, opened the romance novelette that Sophia gave her. Not really her preference, but she was grateful she had it to pass the time.

"Excuse me, may I take this seat?" a man close to her age inquired with a grin.

She glanced up at him. He was handsome in a debonair English way with black hair and hazel eyes, but it was his smile that grabbed her attention. It emanated a playfulness similar to Bromley's. She should refuse but looked around and realized that there were no other seats available.

He smiled. "We have hours of time to pass. If you allow me, I will sing a song for you."

Her eyes wandered down to the music case he was holding in his hand. It would be unfair to deny him a seat, but she would keep her distance. She nodded. "That is fine. No need for entertainment. I'm reading."

She lifted her book up and attempted to ignore him. It was silent on the other side of the table, and Annie peeked over the top of her novelette. He was still studying her.

He beamed at her. "What is your name? I'm Benjamin Clark."

Goodness! What was her name? She hadn't asked Miller what he was calling himself. Had she called him Miller? She smiled stiffly. "Annie is fine."

He sat. "Well, Annie, what song would you like to hear?"

"That's unnecessary."

He chuckled. "It is barely mid-day, and we have hours to waste. Why not have some fun?"

Her eyes pierced his, wondering what exactly he meant. He

held his hands up. “Innocent fun. How about an ale?”

She wanted to ignore him, but honestly she was dreadfully bored. “Yes. That sounds lovely.”

The man smiled at her. “I promise just some songs, ale, and conversation. I saw how your husband handled the other man who made a lewd proposition to you. Rather protective sort.”

Annie laughed. The man signaled for the server to bring them their drinks.

“Now, what songs can I sing for you?”

~

Laughter and loud voices echoed up to where Simon stood on the landing. His brows lifted in confusion. It sounded as if the entire tavern was singing. The walls of the inn shook from the noise. He wiped his eyes, hoping to shake off the sleepiness he still felt. He had planned to only sleep for an hour, but his body had insisted on more than that.

He descended the stairs and stood at the door of the tavern. The dark heavily wooded room was filled with people swaying back and forth with mugs. Even the innkeeper and his wife joined the crowd. A bit of panic shot through him. Where was Annie? His eyes quickly roamed the room, and he couldn’t find her. The crowd shifted slightly, and he spied her at a table with the musician from his coach.

Annie was seated on the table, her feet placed on the seat of a chair while the man sat next to her strumming his guitar. Her face was flushed as she beamed at the man. He winked at her before turning back to the large crowd singing “The Lass that Loves a Sailor.” As the song reached an end, everyone sang louder and lifted their glasses higher, finishing it off with gusto.

But the standing toast, that pleased the most, was the wind that blows, the ship that goes, and the lass that loves a sailor!

She clinked her mug with the musician before tilting her head back and laughing loudly. If Simon wasn't completely infatuated with Annie Kincaide, seeing her right now would have made him so. Gone was the proper lady and in her place was the mischievous, fun woman that she only showed the world in glimpses.

Everyone applauded and whistled before yelling for another song. The musician held his hands up. "A break, then we will get back to it."

The crowd groaned but moved on. Simon made his way through the people just as Annie hopped off the table. She stumbled a little, and he reached out to steady her. Her sapphire eyes twinkled in amusement.

"There you are! You slept forever," she said, slurring slightly.

She beamed at him glassy-eyed, and Simon realized she was drunk. His lips tilted up at her state. He should be annoyed but there was something endearing about this drunken Annie Kincaide.

"Simon, my husband, join us," she declared before taking the seat her feet were previously resting on. He glanced across the table, and the musician watched them. Something about the man irritated Simon.

He shot him a glare before turning to search for a chair. He found one abandoned against a wall and carried it over. Annie giggled as he sat down next to her.

"Simon, you must meet Benjamin or, if you are being formal, Mr. Clark."

The musician nodded a hello. "We are acquainted. We traveled by coach together."

Annie propped her elbows on the table and looked at Benjamin like he was her everything. "That's lovely."

Christ. How much did she drink in the hours he was asleep? Simon didn't like the way she was staring at Clark or, as Annie informally addressed him, Benjamin.

"Yes. Your wife told me all about the two of you. You are married and on your honeymoon. Though if I had such a beautiful bride, I don't think I would be napping while she charmed everyone. Your loss is my gain, friend."

"You are a wise man, Benjamin. I'm sure you have been told that many times," Annie said with a wink.

He grinned back at her.

Yes, Simon didn't like Clark. Annie smiled at him again. "You, Benjamin, are an exquisite musician."

Simon rolled his eyes.

Annie waved her hand. "Another glass, please."

Simon frowned. "Perhaps a nap will do you good?"

Her beautiful mouth turned into a frown. "Why are you no fun?" She turned to Benjamin and said, "Do you know I used to love speaking to my husband but now he has become a complete bore?"

Benjamin Clark choked on the ale he was drinking but said nothing. Still, Simon could see the amusement in his eyes.

"Let's go upstairs, Annie," Simon said.

She sighed. "We are having a great time. We can sing a few more songs. Benjamin said with enough ale, he will sing the naughty ones."

Definitely not. Simon glared at him. The blasted musician just seemed more amused by the situation.

“What is the naughtiest song you can think of?” Annie asked Simon.

He started to speak, but she cut him off and poked him in the chest. “No lectures. Give us a song.”

Simon smiled tightly. “If you will excuse us, I need to speak with my wife privately.”

She shook her head, and Simon thought he may have to carry her upstairs. But Benjamin shook his head. “I suggest you go with your husband. There will be more time for singing.”

Simon glanced out the window and frowned. He wasn’t wrong. It was still pouring. He turned back to Annie prepared to cajole her upstairs, but she nodded at Clark, shocking Simon.

“I suppose you are right. Well, Benjamin, or Mr. Clark I should say, since we are back to being proper, it was lovely to meet you.”

He winked at her. “Aye, it was. If only we had met before your honeymoon.”

She flushed and Simon skewered the musician with a glare that would leave most men heading for the door, but Clark just smiled back at him.

Annie rose and Simon assisted her as she stumbled to the stairs. They quietly made their way back to their room, and she threw herself on the bed.

“What is our name?” she asked.

“What?”

“Our name. When Benjamin asked me who I was I had to tell him just Annie because I didn’t know a name to give him.”

Simon hadn’t thought about that. Again, he was failing at all of this because he was too distracted by her.

"I gave them the name Lennox."

Annie rolled to her side, curling up, not bothering to take her boots off. She snuggled deep into the bed.

"Hmm...I suppose an okay name," she mumbled, already drifting into sleep.

Simon pulled her boots off. He looked out the window, and the rain was still coming down. Instead of heading back downstairs, he took a seat at one of the chairs by a small table and sighed. Annoyance still filled him that she had sought him out but hidden away was a small bit of happiness that she believed in him that much. Her plump lips relaxed as she fell deeper into sleep. He wanted to kiss her, and that was the problem. Simon wasn't a saint. The next few days it would become increasingly difficult to keep her at arm's length.

Yet, he resisted the temptation to touch her or take her in his arms. He couldn't involve her. The hope had always been to see Walker transported to prison, but he wasn't sure if that was an option anymore. Walker had outsmarted him. If the system wouldn't grant him his justice, then Simon would make sure he paid for his crimes. He not only had blood on his hands for his father but now possibly Miss Markam. If he did anything to her, Simon would allow him no mercy.

Whispers abounded at Walker's cruelty, but he could never find anyone who had been the actual victim. Miss Markam had mentioned maids who were sent away after he tired of them, but unfortunately that was not uncommon for the gentleman of the *ton*. Selfish wastrels all of them. A few men had lost their fortunes to him as well and one even killed themselves over it.

Yet, he was unsure if Walker used his own hands for violence or just destroyed people, similar to his actions against Simon's father. He hoped that Miss Markam was simply hiding.

His main priority was discovering what secrets he held in Blackpool, and then he would figure out how to use them against the man.

For now, he closed his eyes and imagined Annie's face as she sang along with everyone in the tavern. That was how happy he wanted her to be every day. His lips tilted up in a smile. Of course, she had been more than a little foxed.

Chapter 13

Annie opened her eyes and groaned from the pounding in her head. She grabbed the covers and pulled them over her head, hoping for the pain to subside. She peaked out from the blankets and discerned that it was evening and had stopped raining. She sat up pushing the bedding down and examined the room. Miller sat in one of the wingback chairs with his feet propped up on the bed, reading a book. His brown hair hung down over his forehead, and Annie had the urge to reach over and brush it from his face.

He looked up and frowned at her. "How are you?"

The headache. She groaned and threw herself back against the bed. "Awful. Too much ale and I need food."

"Definitely too much ale," he said waspishly.

She closed her eyes and willed herself to feel better or at least not to have to tolerate Miller's tone while she felt this way. She sensed his presence and opened her eyes to find him peering over her. He held out his hand, and she took it, allowing him to pull her from the bed. A tingle ran down her fingertips and across her palm as she steadied herself on her feet. He released her hand quickly, and she stumbled a little but managed to stay upright. Hmm…those sensations were not just hers alone.

Across the room on a little table were plates of food. She made her way over to it and plopped into a chair before drinking from one of the glasses. She took bigger gulps as she realized it was water. She didn't think her stomach could take anymore ale. Miller grabbed his wingback chair and dragged it closer to the table. He was still frowning at her.

She pointed a finger at him. "No lectures. You are a wanted

man."

He pursed his lips and Annie giggled.

"You are still bloody drunk."

She rolled her eyes. "Look at you sounding so English. You should have joined us. Benjamin is quite the musician."

He bristled at her compliment but said nothing. She stuck her fork into the meat pie on the plate and ate with a relish.

A chuckle stopped her mid-bite. "If the ladies of the *ton* could see you now."

She rolled her eyes. "I'm hungry. No matter how many lessons I take in etiquette, you can't take the starving girl out of me."

She meant it as a jest, but Miller immediately sobered.

"I'm joking, Miller."

He smiled at her softly and Annie warmed. She was happy to see him without his scowl. "Well don't slow down on my account."

Annie didn't. She continued to eat until every piece of the meat pie was gone. She sat back and stretched. "I needed that."

"The weather is starting to clear," he said.

"Good, then we can continue on to wherever you are headed."

"I hired a private coach to take you back to Luton."

Her lips twisted in annoyance. So, he was going to send her away. "I want to help."

His mouth flattened into a straight line. "You can't help me, Annie."

"I think I can."

"What if I am a thief and simply trying to flee?" he speculated, lifting a brow.

She leaned forward, looking intensely into his brown eyes. "I don't believe it. You are too decent."

He shifted closer to her, so they were only a couple of inches away. "You have this saintly vision of me that just isn't real. I own a gentleman's club, I collect facts on people, and I use them to my advantage when I feel the need."

"That doesn't make you a thief. I want to know how you ended up in this situation."

He paused for a moment and said, "Finish eating."

"I have been done for a while now. Completely clean," she said, pointing at her plate.

She stood and walked over to the window. The rain had stopped and the water on the ground seemed to be quickly disappearing. She needed to convince Miller to take her with him. How did she do that?

Her family was undoubtedly looking for her now. If she returned to the Peyton estate by coach, the investigators and constables would assume that she had been headed to Liverpool. The main hubs of the coach route that went through Daventry were Liverpool and London.

Still, even if Liverpool wasn't Miller's final destination, it made more sense to take her there instead of sending her back.

She turned back to him. "I have been thinking it would be best for you to take me with you as far as Liverpool. If you send me home now, they will quickly pick up on the direction you are headed. I can only assume you took a coach as opposed to using the rail line so you wouldn't be discovered."

His eyes narrowed. "Again, what made you so confident that I would be on this route? Perhaps Liverpool is my final stop."

His notepad sitting in her bag is how she knew, but she wouldn't tell him that until he revealed some of his secrets.

She shrugged. "Chance."

He was lost in thought but finally he stood and walked to her. "I will take you as far as Liverpool, but then we are to go our separate ways. You will go to your family's townhouse there and contact them. Do you understand?"

She couldn't stop herself from smirking. Miller's eyes flicked down to her mouth, and he scowled. Annie forced herself to look solemn and nod.

"Why are you doing this?" he whispered.

"Why do you keep kissing me?"

Again, his eyes flicked down to her lips. He reached out and brushed his thumb against her lower lip. "I have told you multiple times I desire you. What more do you want me to say?"

She flushed at his touch. She wanted more than desire. Annie wanted him to confess that he cared for her, but she couldn't bring herself to say the words. She had revealed her feelings once, expecting him to return them. Pride prevented her from doing it again. Still, she knew he cared for her. Why else did he have her portrait? He would have to say those words of his own free will. She would not beg for them.

"That will do for now," she said in a snooty voice she saved for when dealing with members of the *ton* she wanted to leave her alone.

He nodded and made his way to the door.

"Where are you going?" Annie asked.

He looked back at her. "To make new arrangements for our private coach."

~

Simon walked back from the stables, relieved that the driver of the private coach he hired for Annie had no problem changing direction to Liverpool. He had considered himself fortunate when he was able to secure private passage for her with all the people milling around Daventry. A public coach was an unacceptable option for her even if she didn't agree. Like it or not, she was a lady and the sister of a duke.

He shook his head at his own insane logic. He was letting her travel with him, a wanted man, but traveling in a public coach was too much. The ridiculousness of the situation was not lost on him. He entered the inn and noticed Clark strumming his guitar, sitting at one of the tables in the tavern. The room was much quieter. Simon assumed most people were getting ready to depart the next morning. The musician looked up and said, "Where is your lovely wife?"

Annoyance covered Simon's face. "She isn't your concern."

"Any trouble securing seating on one of the coaches? I'm headed to Liverpool. I can offer you or your wife my seat."

"We are fine."

Clark chuckled. "It's interesting. She kept calling you Miller yesterday, but the innkeeper said your name was Mr. Lennox."

Miller's face turned to stone. The man just smiled back at him amused. Again, Simon had a sense that there was something more to Clark than just being a musician. "Why would you ask the innkeeper about us?"

Clark's eyes widened at the question, realizing he had revealed too much. He recovered and smiled. "I wanted to make sure your wife was well."

The two men stared one another down. Simon would be glad when they could depart tomorrow. Being caged in with so many people was making him paranoid. He pushed his suspicions about Clark aside.

"Safe travels. I'm sure we won't see you prior to departure," Simon said pointedly.

He spun around, ending the conversation. Clark's laughter echoed behind him.

Simon stomped up the stairs and down the corridor before throwing the door to their room open. Annie jumped. She was preparing for the night, already dressed in a nightgown. Her thick black hair swirled over her shoulder as her fingers quickly plaited it into a practical style for bed.

He had the overwhelming desire to shake it free from the plait and watch her hair swirl around her. Perhaps run his fingers through it as he grabbed the back of her head for a kiss. Christ! What was he thinking? Her nightgown covered her from neck to ankle and still he hungered for her.

His eyes followed her as she moved to place a brush on a small table. The fabric of her sleepwear swirling around her, at times tormenting him by clinging to her waist, her shapely legs, and her bosom. He sighed in frustration, and she glanced at him in concern.

"What's wrong?"

He shook his head and started unfolding a blanket on the ground. He was so distracted he didn't realize how close she was until she stilled him by placing her hand on his forearm. He tensed at her touch, glancing at her face. Her full lips were pursed in a frown and her blue eyes filled with concern.

"You can't sleep on the floor. There is plenty of room for both of us in the bed," she said.

His body screamed to touch her. Was he insane? He shook his head. "No."

"Miller, stop it. You are being childish. I promise I can go an evening without throwing myself at you," she bit out, sarcastically.

Annie stomped to the bed and climbed in, turning her back to him. His body came alive with desire, and he knew it was a bad idea for them to share the bed. It would be hours of hell for him. He left his pants on but yanked his shirt over his head and walked over to the bed, filled with trepidation, as if it would be his undoing. Temptation whispered that it wasn't the bed but her.

He pulled the covers back and climbed in. Annie didn't turn around but said, quietly, "See it isn't all that bad."

He snorted. If she thought that, she didn't desire him as much as he craved her. "If we are found, you will be ruined."

"I am likely already ruined," she pointed out before yawning. "Not that I care."

Simon rolled his eyes. Of course, she didn't. This damn woman did as she liked, said what she wanted, and pursued what she wanted. The problem right now was she was pursuing him, and not only did he want her, but he wanted her for every day of his life.

An impossible option. He had done his best to make sure she wasn't hurt, but Annie had seen through his attempts to keep her at arms-length. Not that he had been very good at it. He had kissed her more than once now and touched her intimately. Now that he had crossed that barrier, the urge to do more was almost overwhelming.

He heard her breathing start to even out and soft snores

coming from her. He smiled slightly, amused that Annie snored. She rolled on to her back and Simon studied her. She made a light moan and snuggled deeper into her pillow. His eyes wandered along her heart-shaped face, down her slender neck covered in awful ruffles, and landed on her bosom. He reached out a hand and swiftly jerked it back, shocked by his inability to resist her.

Simon would not yield to temptation. He rolled away and closed his eyes. Time ticked by, and he was tempted to go back to his spot on the floor, telling himself it was best. She shifted towards him, pressing her forehead up against his back, and he knew he wouldn't leave. He ran sums in his head, hoping that eventually the boredom of the numbers in his mind would overpower the lady snuggled up against him.

A few hours later, Simon opened his eyes and realized the sums had done their job. At some point, he'd drifted off to sleep. His eyes blinked rapidly, adjusting to the sunlight drifting through the window and birds chirping. He sighed in relief that the weather was magnificent. He attempted to roll to his side but was held down by Annie's head against his chest. He looked further down and saw one bare leg wrapped around his torso. At some point her nightgown had shimmied up to her thighs.

Simon groaned, and she squeezed him tighter with her shapely leg. He lightly ran his hand along her back, giving in to not the desire he felt for her but the tenderness. What would it have been like if he had given up his pursuit of Walker and pursued her instead? His mind wandered to thoughts of marriage, children, and having this woman in bed with him every day.

Her plait still laid across her shoulder but slid along his stomach as she breathed up and down. He picked it up running his finger over her thick strands. No, it was impossible. His fixation on Walker didn't allow him to give Annie the happiness she deserved. Vengeful men did not make ideal husbands.

There was much to do, including finding out what secrets Allen Lemming held, tracking down Miss Markam, learning about her mysterious item, and most importantly proving Walker's guilt. What if he couldn't? Simon would not think about that now. He was prepared to make him pay no matter the cost but for now he had leads on proving his guilt. He would pursue those.

Again, Miller cursed his naiveness in thinking Walker didn't suspect what he was up to. He hadn't been nearly careful enough and playing cards with the man had been too much. But Simon couldn't resist those games with him at the Den. They allowed him to understand Walker better and collect facts about him. Likely Walker was on to him from the beginning. It would have taken some time to convince the Americans to travel all the way to England.

Simon was surprised that they had made the trip. It seemed rather drastic for a crime more than five years old. Annie's leg flexed around him, and his body hummed in response. Unable to take any more torment, he hopped up.

Annie sat up, blinking at him wide-eyed. Her eyes wandered down his chest, and he had to stop himself from placing a kiss on her mouth.

"Get dressed. We leave as soon as you are ready," he said hoarsely.

He threw on his shirt and cleaned up before stomping out of the room. In the hallway he was startled to run into Clark. He glowered at him. The man held his hands up.

"I am actually looking for you."

"What is it?" Simon bit out.

"There are some constables looking for Simon Miller and

possibly a lady. The innkeeper said that he had no one here by that name."

"What did you tell them?"

Clark studied him. "Is the lady safe with you?"

Simon scowled. "I will protect her with my life."

Clark shrugged. "I didn't say anything. I let them assume perhaps they were on the wrong route, but I suggest you and your lady be on the way."

Skeptical, Simon asked, "Why wouldn't you tell them?"

"I'm a musician, but I am also many other things. Sometimes things are more complex than they seem."

Who was this man? Simon studied him as if he was really seeing him for the first time. Perhaps a swindler? Regardless, Simon nodded. "Thank you."

Chapter 14

Annie sat in the carriage watching the landscape whirl by. She smiled slightly, amazed at how green everything looked after a bit of rain. It was only February, but spring was already starting to show. She turned away from the scenic view and frowned at Miller. He was back to being moody and had practically hauled her out of the inn this morning. Since their departure they both sat quietly, looking out the window.

"We should be in Liverpool in a couple of hours," Miller said, breaking the silence.

She rolled her eyes at the insufferable man. "I wanted to say goodbye to Benjamin."

Miller didn't respond, and she glanced at him. He glared at her. His brown eyes filled with an emotion that seemed to border on jealousy. Well, good, she thought. She tilted her chin up at him defiantly.

"The musician is not who he seems."

She raised a skeptical black brow at him. "How would you know? You barely said a few words to him. He was the most entertaining part of this awful trip so far."

"I didn't realize it was supposed to be all about fun," he bit out.

"You know it isn't," Annie snapped.

Miller grunted. She threw her hands up in the air annoyed. He returned to looking out the window looking like a sullen child.

"Why did we leave in such a rush?"

He heaved a sigh and turned back to her. If she had something to throw at him, she would do it.

"I ran into your friend. He informed me men were looking for a Simon Miller."

She wrinkled her nose in confusion. "Why would he think that was you?"

"Someone who had too much ale kept calling me that," he said dryly.

Annie flushed. Had she revealed that to him? Her antics could have caused Miller to be captured. "I'm so sorry."

"Luckily for me, he didn't reveal I was at the inn. He chose to warn me instead. What did you talk about with the musician?"

"Perhaps we could use his name, Benjamin," she said, tired of the contempt he used addressing him as the musician.

"Clark," he said, disdainfully, choosing to use his last name.

Perhaps not, Annie thought. She rolled her eyes. "We didn't have any in-depth conversations. We mostly sang and drank."

"Did he ask about me?"

She flushed, embarrassed thinking about the tale she made up. "He asked how we met."

"What did you say?"

"I said we met at a ball, and you fell madly in love with me. It took me a little longer to be won over but eventually I was by your kindness and intelligence. Not wanting to wait, we eloped, and our parents were unhappy with us."

The corner of his mouth lifted up in almost a smile. "Quite a tale."

Her cheeks heated thinking about what else she said. Annie drunkenly elaborated on how Miller desperately loved her. There was no need to share all that. It was too embarrassing.

"It was after several ales."

He nodded. "Maybe he was just someone who doesn't like the law."

"Perhaps," Annie said but now she doubted his intentions.

For a random stranger, he had been extremely attentive. Even when the tavern emptied out, he stayed sitting with her. She assumed he was trying to flirt with her but maybe that wasn't the case.

"Will you tell me everything now?"

"Will you tell me how you knew I was traveling in the direction of Liverpool?"

She thought of the notepad residing in her bag that rested on the floor between them. He should know she was the one that found it. She was surprised he hadn't brought it up. Instead, she shrugged.

His eyes narrowed, and she changed the subject. "Thank you for getting a private coach. It's a much smoother ride. In the public coach I was bouncing all over the place."

"That was likely the weather."

The ride to Daventry had been nerve racking but some of her feelings were caused by her memories of Maggie and Joseph's death in a carriage accident. She didn't dwell on it often but something about bouncing along the road in the storm alarmed her and made her fixate on their last moments. She rode the last half of the way to Daventry terrified and tormented.

"Are you thinking of your parents?"

Hey eyes widened in surprise. How did this man know her so well? Miller never met her parents. They died right before he started to work for the family.

"I am sorry you had to endure that."

"If Maggie was here, she would tell me I was being dramatic. We all have to get around and a coach is the main option."

"Still, I know it must be hard to think of them and their last moments."

She felt a pain in her heart. It was unbearably painful to miss two people she loved so much. She smiled softly, thinking about the long bumpy road that led her, Jack, and Sam to becoming Kincaides. At first Annie feared them like a child would fear a monster, but they worked so hard to prove they cared for all of them.

In the beginning, she wanted to hate them. They were the people who left her and Jack at an orphanage because of a madman. The Duke and Duchess of Peyton had brought their children for a tour of America and perished unexpectedly from a disease outbreak. Her biological father's man-of-affairs then paid Maggie and Joseph to kill her and Jack. They took his money but only because Sophia was desperately ill and needed very expensive medicine. Instead of doing his bidding, they left them at an orphanage.

Miller knew the story. He knew all the Kincaides secrets. Before Jack revealed he was alive to the *ton*, Miller was the only one outside of their immediate family who knew she and Jack were the children of the Duke and Duchess of Peyton.

She smirked. Her brother was becoming more duke-like every day. Initially, there had been a fight over the title between Jack and their cousin Phillip but all of that was over. Phillip, or Viscount Muttonbell as he was known in formal settings, was currently overseas scouting out shipping routes for the family's passenger company.

"I wish I had been able to meet them," Miller said.

Annie wished that too. Maggie and Joseph would have adored him. Joseph would have known from the beginning that he would capture Annie's heart. He was the romantic one of the two.

"They would have liked you," she said.

She rubbed the scar along the inside of her wrist. His eyes roamed over her but not in a way that made her think he wanted to kiss her. She fidgeted under his stare until she couldn't take it anymore. "What is it?" she huffed.

"How did it happen?"

Annie felt her stomach drop. He was asking about her scars. In the past, she'd shared with Simon that she received them during her time in the orphanage, and they were the reason she, Jack, and Sam ended up living with the Kincaides but not much more. If any other person dared to ask, she would have snapped at them to leave it alone. But Miller was different. She found herself wanting to share the story.

"One day, when I was eleven, a man came to visit the orphanage and the headmistress Mrs. Seawald lined up all the girls to be inspected by him. I knew instantly the man was there to take one of us away," she said, with a sad smile before continuing. "I acted like a heathen, hoping he would think I was too much to deal with. It had the opposite effect."

She closed her eyes, remembering the moment as an adult, not a child who had no idea what nefarious plans the man had for her. Simon reached across and grabbed her hand. He stroked the inside of her palm with his thumb.

"Sam and Jack were away. They were reaching an age where they couldn't stay at the orphanage much longer, so they spent most of their days looking for a place we could all move to. Anyway, the man selected me, and I was quickly taken to his carriage. I was so confused. The man didn't address me the entire time we rode to his house. I was beyond upset, but my survival instincts kicked in and I knew I would escape as soon as I could. His house was enormous, and I remember being in awe of the place but still scared. He had a servant take me to a room."

Simon brought her hand to his lips and sprinkled kisses across her fingers. She couldn't stop the words from tumbling out.

"Once inside, I heard the servant lock the door. Little did the man or the servant know I could pick locks, and I did right away. I escaped and made my way back to the orphanage. I was so naive; I thought I would be in trouble, but I didn't understand the man had paid an enormous sum for me. The moment Mrs. Seawald caught sight of me, she was furious. We fought in the kitchen and a boiling pot of water was knocked over scalding me. She left me on the floor."

Annie took a deep breath. "You know the rest. Jack and Sam brought me to the Kincaides."

A tick formed in Simon's jaw, and his eyes blazed with anger. "Where is she now?"

"She died shortly afterwards. Killed by one of the children in the orphanage. The Kincaides paid for the boy's defense. His legal team was able to prove Mrs. Seawald's cruel care forced the boy to act. He now lives in the country outside of Philadelphia."

She frowned at him, sadly. "It wasn't until I was much older that I learned the nefarious plans the man had for me." She took a deep breath but added, "Joseph sat me down one evening and explained everything. He also told me the man died shortly after Maggie and Joseph took us in. Drowned. For years there was talk that several of the men in the neighborhood had made sure he could never hurt any girls again. My father included."

They sat there quietly, and Simon finally said, "If you were my daughter, I would make sure the man never took another breath."

Startled, Annie realized tears were streaming down her cheeks. "Revenge and justice are difficult. I think Joseph's part in his death tormented him for a long time."

He cupped her face, looking at her with such tenderness it made the tears fall faster.

"Thank you for sharing your story with me. You are the most remarkable, courageous woman I have ever known," he said, his voice trembling with conviction.

He pulled her to his side and looped his arm around her, holding her tightly.

~

The private coach came to a stop outside of an inn on the outskirts of Liverpool. Simon still had his arm around Annie as she slept soundly against him. He was humbled that she had shared her story with him. The coach jostled as the driver hopped down, and he gently shook Annie. "We are here. Time to wake up."

Startled, she sat up. "Where are we?"

She moved to the other side, stretching. His eyes roamed over her ravenously. Simon needed to send her home immediately.

"At an inn on the edge of Liverpool."

Annie nodded, and Simon knocked on the carriage wall alerting the driver they were ready to depart. The door swung open, and Simon stepped out, first.

They made their way into the small tidy inn and the innkeeper stood. “Good day. How may I help you?”

“I need a room for the evening.”

The older gentleman nodded. “Just sign here and it will be three shillings.”

Simon signed the ledger and pulled the money from his pocket. He slid two more shilling across the desk. “I would like to secure a private coach for my companion to a townhouse in Liverpool for later today. Can you also have some food sent up to my room for both of us?”

The man nodded again. Simon looked back at Annie to see her glaring at him, but she said nothing. They made their way up to the room silently, following the innkeeper. The silence was tense, and Simon had no doubt Annie was going to explode the minute they were alone.

The innkeeper maneuvered around the room, explaining where everything was. Every time Simon glanced Annie’s way she glowered at him. Finally, he departed.

He turned to her, and she stood glaring at him with her hands on her hips. “You didn’t speak with me before you booked my coach.”

“Annie, you need to return to your family. Nothing that I’m involved in will bring you any happiness.”

She stomped over to him and poked him in the chest with her finger. “You don’t make decisions for me, Simon Miller.”

Even emanating with fury, she was lovely. A few strands of her black silken hair fell haphazardly, and she flushed from her anger. He was tempted to tell her how beautiful she was, but Simon sensed she would likely slap him. He wanted to kiss her, but he kept his emotions tamped down.

“Annie, this has gone on long enough. You need to find a proper gentleman. You will eventually forget me."

She did slap him then. His head snapped back, and he stepped away, rubbing his cheek.

"Do not presume to know what I will get over. And what about you? You will simply get over your feelings for me?"

He said nothing. He would never get over her.

"Tell me you will forget me. That this is a passing fancy," she demanded.

"We are on different paths. Eventually you and I will be just a small memory in both our lives."

The lie spilled from his lips, and he hated himself for it. He again was hurting her to protect her. Pain crossed her face, and she bit her lip to prevent it from trembling.

"Annie—"

She spun away from him, her skirts swirling around her. She stomped over to her bag. She threw clothing and other items out of the bag, digging for something. What was she doing?

Finally, she found something that made her look back at him victoriously. She walked back over to him with a smirk on her face.

"You will forget me. Do you really expect me to believe that?"

He said nothing. She pulled a paper from behind her back, and he knew it was Annie who'd discovered his notepad. She dangled her portrait in front of his face. All this time she knew about the picture.

He slowly reached up and grabbed it. He told himself the night of the Ball of Sin to burn it, but he couldn't.

"Tell me you will forget me even though for months you have carried this every day on your person. Then explain to me how

I will so easily forget you," she spat.

He remained silent.

"You think you can protect me, but I don't need your protection. When you care about someone, you are there for them. I want to be there for you, but you keep pushing me away. I want the truth, Miller. Will you really forget me?"

He loved her and would for the rest of his life, but if he told her, she would never let him go. He didn't want Annie to endure any more hardship because of him. What if he was shipped back to America? What if Walker tried to harm her? His concerns kept him silent until Annie spun around and headed for the door.

"Where are you going?" he demanded.

"Home. Your notepad is in my bag. That is how I knew you were going to Blackpool."

She reached the door and Simon closed his eyes, knowing he couldn't let her walk away like this. Even though logically it would be for the best.

He repeated the words seared to his soul. The words from the note that she attempted to give him that night at his cottage.

"I love you, Simon Miller. Be mine as much as I am yours. Grow old with me. Let us be happy and live life as we see fit, just you and I."

She slowly turned back to him, her expression covered in shock that he knew the words by heart.

He continued, "You said 'let us be happy.' I can't give you that."

Her brows drew together in confusion. "Why?"

"Annie, I love you too much to involve you in this. You deserve to live a life filled with so much joy. A husband who comes home to you every night. Children to love on. I will never stop pursuing Walker until he pays for what he has done. The misery that will bring is not something I'm willing to put on you. Damn it! Even if I could, I'm wanted."

Chapter 15

Miller loved her. He had finally said it. For some absurd reason Annie started to laugh. Miller stared at her with concern. She didn't know what to tell him. The situation was ridiculous. He cared for her, but they could never be together. It truly did seem like one of Sophia's romance novelettes.

She took a deep breath and composed herself. Annie walked to him and set a hand on his chest. He placed his hand over hers.

"I can wait until this is over," she said.

He squeezed her hand. "I can't ask that of you."

What Miller didn't understand was he didn't have to. A brisk knock on the door stopped the conversation. He sighed and opened the door. An older woman carried in Miller's requested food.

"Good day," she said happily, not picking up on the tension in the room.

She set about laying out the food on a table while Annie and Miller stared at one another. There was still so much Annie needed to know. However, Miller had revealed his true feelings.

"Will that be all, sir?" the woman asked.

"Yes, thank you."

The door closed behind her. Annie smiled at him, and he looked back at her with a variety of conflicting emotions crossing his face—annoyance, frustration, concern and most importantly love.

She moved to the table and sat in one of the chairs. "Please sit with me."

He sat down across from her. "I will tell you anything you want to know."

"How did the gold bars end up in your cottage?"

"I was set up by a member of the *ton.*"

Annie's brows drew together in confusion.

"How much do you know of the actual theft that took place in America?" Simon asked.

"A little. An investigator and constable from New York City provided that your father was sent to prison for stealing money from a bank vault, and then they found the missing gold bars from that vault in your cottage."

He frowned. "Was the investigator, Mr. Collins?"

"He was. Do you know him?"

Miller nodded. "He was investigating the theft for the bank, but it has been at least six years. I assumed he was no longer looking into it. He isn't a bad sort. He couldn't help me, but honestly, after my father went to prison, he was the only one willing to speak with me."

Annie agreed. Collins seemed very reasonable. Shell was a different story.

"The constable with him was a confrontational lout. He insisted my family was hiding something."

Miller smiled wryly at her. "One of you was."

Annie rolled her eyes. "If you met him, you would agree with me."

Simon barked out a laugh. He ran his hands through his hair and Annie had the strange desire to cup his face and tell him everything would be fine, but she didn't. She waited patiently for him to continue.

"Six years ago, my father was arrested for the theft at the bank and eventually convicted of the crime. Within a year he died in prison. Until he took his last breath, he insisted he was innocent, but no matter who I spoke with, they wouldn't pursue any other leads. I didn't understand why. My father wouldn't accuse anyone else of the crimes, but he did mention one other man who worked with him, Tobias Walker."

"Tobias Walker. Why does that name sound familiar?"

Miller rose and grabbed two glasses, pouring brandy into them. He handed one to her and drank from his before sitting again.

"Because he lives in London now and is married to a lady. He is very well-established and well liked among the *ton*. In America, he was a bank worker without any prestige, and he didn't mingle with the upper echelons of New York City."

Annie nodded. She had attended balls where Tobias Walker and his wife were present. How did a bank worker rise so quickly?

"Prior to moving to Philadelphia, I looked into Walker, but he fled to England shortly after my father's conviction. Mr. Collins and I discussed this, but he pointed out Walker could have simply chosen to leave the country. It wasn't enough to prove guilt."

"The police didn't find it odd that a bank worker fled the country?"

"Left, not fled," Miller emphasized mockingly.

"Rubbish! It is the same," Annie exclaimed.

"I agree but the police didn't. To them, once my father was convicted, there was no interest in pursuing the case any further. Everything was turned over to private investigators to pursue as leads to recover the items from the vault."

Annie took a sip of her brandy, enjoying the warmth of the liquid as it slid down her throat. If the case was over, what caused the Americans to journey to England now?

"Why did they start looking back into it?"

"I believe Tobias Walker reached out to them."

Miller stood and strode over to the fireplace. He seemed lost in thought. "Miller—"

He took a large drink of his brandy and said, "Part of the reason I took the job with your family was the ability to travel to England. I planned to continue my investigation of him. As time went on, my desire to find him started to fade. Maybe not fade but justice wasn't my all-consuming focus."

Annie took a drink and waited for him to continue. Their eyes connected, and he said, "I met you."

She flushed.

"I need you to know when I kissed you in Philadelphia, I believed that was the start of a different path. A happier one. I wanted us to spend our lives together."

An ache bloomed in her chest, and her eyes filled with hurt. "Yet, you didn't choose me."

He threw the last bit of his brandy back and placed his glass on the mantel. "No. I didn't. But to protect you."

Annie tried her best to form a response, anything, but she couldn't. She clutched her skirts with a combination of anger and sadness. She wouldn't cry. She pushed away her wounded feelings. She needed to hear the rest of the story.

"Continue," she whispered.

His eyes roamed over her, and he looked as if he would rush

across the room and gather her up in his arms.

She shook her head. "Tell me more."

He continued, "When I traveled to London to prepare for your family's move, I randomly crossed paths with Walker in Devons' tavern. To see him doing so well made my obsession to prove my father's innocence come roaring back. I started to investigate him. A few months ago, we began to play cards together and I think somehow he caught on to who I was. But I still had no evidence he was guilty."

"How were you so sure he was involved in the theft?"

Miller shrugged. "It was mostly circumstantial until the gold bars ended up in my cottage. The only person who had a reason to set me up was Walker."

All the information swirled through Annie's mind. "How did Walker find out you may be a threat?"

"I'm unsure. A lady's maid in his household has been working with me. The note I received from her while at your family's house party stated that it was urgent I return to London. I suspect she discovered Walker was on to me. She's now missing. But I think he has been aware of my investigation of him for months."

"I don't understand why these Americans would travel all the way to England for this case?"

Miller shrugged. "I don't know. The value of the items in the vault was exceptionally high."

Annie rose, shocked at the information Miller had shared. Fury grew in her that he had decided to handle this alone.

"Why would you not come to my family for help?" she demanded.

"Because I didn't want you involved. Who knows when this

will end? Your family has been through so much over the last few years."

She hated stubborn men, and she was looking at one right now. She stomped over to him. "My family has done nothing but put you in dangerous situations over the last few years. We owe you."

He clenched his jaw, and they glared at one another. Finally, he said, "Because I know you. You would involve yourself even if I asked you not to. Walker is a savvy opponent and will become more dangerous the closer I get to the truth."

She threw her arms out, dramatically. "Yet, even with all of your attempts to keep me away from this, here I am."

He stepped closer to her until they were almost touching, chest to chest.

"Miller, you're a fool," she said softly.

He grabbed her and pulled her against him, slamming his lips down on her mouth.

~

Simon kissed her deeply, savoring her tongue against his. He ran his hands down her waist, kneading her back. He teased her lower lip with his teeth before pulling his mouth away to sprinkle kisses down her neck. She moaned as her fingers curled around his shirt, clinging to him. His hands roamed down to her bottom, needing to have her pressed up against him.

He was losing his head, but he didn't care. Annie pressed up against him was the sweet torment he craved. Hell, he craved to have her naked in bed with him. He wanted so much from her. So much he had denied himself, but now the secret was out. He loved her.

She pulled away, startling him. Her eyes sparked with anger, and he knew that Annie had more to say. He stifled the desire to groan in frustration and instead ran his fingers through his hair, trying to calm his raging emotions.

Annie, the feisty woman he loved, planted her hands on her hips and glared at him. "I'm not leaving."

He growled in response. "Annie—"

"We can do this together.

"I'm wanted! Be reasonable. When I get this sorted out, I will return."

She muttered something Simon couldn't hear, but he was certain it wasn't favorable to him.

"Absolutely not. We do this together."

He shook his head. She paced back and forth and finally spun around to face him again. "Do you think you can really deny me the opportunity to help the person I love? Do you really think you or anyone else has that power over me? No. If you try to send me back to my family's townhouse, I will just take another coach to Blackpool."

She was right. He could no more stop her from helping him than he could stop breathing. She alone would make that choice because he knew if he did, it would destroy the very thing that made her Annie.

He had caused her so much hurt already. No more. He would only deny her help if she was in danger. He owed her and their potential future that.

"I won't stop you," he said quietly.

Her mouth dropped open, and he almost chuckled.

She beamed at him. "So we do this together."

He rolled his eyes and nodded. She smirked victoriously.

"We need to be careful. Walker is dangerous. His lady's maid's disappearance may be related to him."

"Or she may be in hiding," Annie pointed out.

She was right. Miller had often wondered that himself. Still, more than one person in Walker's life had disappeared when they became an inconvenience. He was a snake.

Simon walked back to the table and motioned for her to join him. "Let's eat some of this food and then we can go for a walk. Get some air."

She stood staring at him, perplexed. She flushed and nodded before sitting down across from him. Annie frowned as she poked at her food.

"What is it?"

She bit her lip and Simon had the desire to nibble on it himself. "Annie?"

"I just thought you would kiss me again."

He stilled and smiled at her like any proper rogue would. "Are you asking me to kiss you?"

"Of course not!"

"All in time," he murmured, adding a wink.

She rolled her eyes at him. They silently ate the roast and potatoes laid out before them. Once Annie was full, she leaned back in her chair lost in thought. Simon ate the last portion of his roast and said, "What are you thinking about now? Kissing?"

"Perhaps you are but no," she said, tartly.

Simon held his hand to heart, mockingly, and she giggled.

"Actually I was wondering why you are traveling to Blackpool."

Simon wished they could keep on with their light conversation, but he knew Annie deserved all the answers to her questions. "Miss Markam, the lady's maid that is missing, mentioned in a note that there is a man named Allen Lemming there who may be connected somehow."

"Do you think he could help prove your father's innocence?"

"I hope so. Right now it is pretty damning that the gold bars were found in my cottage. Without additional proof, I'm not sure how I will get out of this."

"We could leave. Go to the continent," she suggested quietly.

Simon would never do that. He would not let Walker win. He would not allow him to continue to live his extravagant life here in London.

"No," he bit out.

Annie drummed her fingers on the table and Simon could tell she wanted to say something else. He raised a brow in her direction.

"Is this about proving your father's innocence or making Walker pay?"

"Aren't they the same?"

She shook her head, frowning. "Having the world know your father is innocent is a great deal different from seeing justice served with Walker."

"Ideally he would be arrested."

"And if he is not?" she questioned.

Simon rose, unwilling to talk anymore about what ifs. Right now he hoped whatever they found in Blackpool would be enough to clear both him and his father of any wrongdoing. If not, perhaps the mysterious item Miss Markam mentioned was another option. Simon assumed Miss Markam's disappearance was connected to Walker but maybe she was in hiding, as Annie suggested. Simon hoped Devons and Derry would be able to find her.

For now, he would choose to believe everything would work out. That hope meant he could have a life with Annie someday. Still, a nibble of doubt filled his mind. The fact Walker set him up meant he was willing to do anything to keep fingers from pointing at him.

"We will find the evidence we need in Blackpool," he said with confidence he didn't really feel.

Annie frowned at him, skeptical. He held his hand out. "Let's get some air. We have been cramped up in inns and carriages for the last few days. A nice stroll will be beneficial."

Chapter 16

Annie and Miller strolled along the walkway by the inn, enjoying the early evening air. Miller had been right. It was refreshing to get out and walk around after spending countless days cooped up. Still, something felt unfinished. Annie flushed. It wasn't unfinished words but unfinished actions.

He patted her hand that held his arm and her body tingled. She looked up at him and realized she wasn't alone in regard to those unfinished actions. His eyes were filled with desire.

"Shall we return?" she suggested breathlessly.

He nodded.

They entered the inn and made their way up the stairs and down the hallway leading to their room for the evening. She stepped in and started to remove her cloak. Miller stood behind her. He brought his mouth to her ear. "Let me help with that."

He unclasped her cloak and pulled it from her shoulders. Annie thought he might step away, but he didn't. Instead, he placed a soft kiss at the back of her ear, causing little shivers to shoot down her spine.

"Do you know that behind the ear is one of the most sensitive spots on the body?"

His tongue ran over the spot where her ear and neck met. She shook her head, slightly.

"You can kiss and suckle enough to drive a person mad."

Her body swayed towards him, and he continued teasing her ear. She sighed. "You are torturing me."

He chuckled, and the sound echoed off her neck. "A good

torture I suspect."

Annie, done with his torment, turned, and faced him. She pulled his head down to her and their lips were barely a breath apart. "I can play this game as well."

"You have been playing this game with me far longer than you realize," he whispered before placing his lips on hers.

He cupped the back of her head, kissing her as if this was his only chance. He teased her mouth open with his tongue, and she allowed him in. Their tongues sparred with one another. Annie sighed as his hands left her head and roamed over her body. She splayed her own fingers across his firm chest enjoying the heat emanating from him. She started to slide her fingers into his shirt but stopped as he stepped back, breathing heavily.

His eyes raked over her. She started to pull her hair free of the pins holding it. "What are you doing?"

Annie had no idea and grinned sheepishly. "I don't know; attempting to seduce you. For some reason letting my hair down seemed like the perfect start."

His eyes glowed with desire as he watched the curls fall around Annie's shoulders. "What should I do next?"

"Annie, we—"

She lifted a finger, shaking it at him. "Ah…ah…none of that. What should I do next?"

He ran his hands through his hair, torn between being the proper Miller who did everything right and the man standing before her now.

"Just for tonight, let's not think," she pleaded.

Their eyes connected and the emotions between them crackled.

"Take your dress off," he said.

She smiled at him before reaching up and pulling at the ties holding the top of her dress together. The dress slid down revealing her chemise, slender arms, and shoulders. He watched her, and she continued with the ties at her waist. The dress fell fully to the floor. Next, she untied her petticoats, and they landed in a heap on the floor with the rest of her clothing. She stepped over all the fabric, standing before him in only her chemise and knickers.

"What next?" she asked.

"It's your turn. What do you want to do next?" he said, leaning against a wall.

Nerves filled her. She tilted her chin up defiantly. She would not let her nerves get the better of her.

"Take your shirt off," she requested.

"Gladly," he said, yanking it over his head.

She walked to the bed with Miller's eyes devouring her. She stood by the bed and pointed at it. "Sit here."

He took his spot on the edge of the bed and Annie stood in front of him. Simon looked up at her; concern caused his brow to pucker. She pressed her forehead against his. "Stop with the worries."

"I won't take your innocence," he murmured.

Annie drew back and frowned. "Miller—"

He pulled her between his splayed legs. "There is so much we can do. Let me show you."

He kissed her bosom and stomach through her chemise. "Let me make you feel good. Don't overthink this as you pleaded with me."

Annie groaned as his tongue flicked across the underside of her breast. She nodded and pressed her fingers against his broad shoulders.

"You have changed since leaving America," Annie murmured.

"I have been boxing with Devons," he said, his voice gruff.

He ran his hand down her side, and her body warmed, knowing only a thin piece of fabric prevented him from touching her. Annie tugged her chemise over her head, tossing it to the floor. His breath hitched a little. For a moment she worried about her scars but when she studied his face all she saw was hunger.

Miller pulled her down flipping her onto her back as he leaned over her.

"You are exquisite," he said.

She smiled at the conviction in his voice. He kissed her shoulder before smattering kisses along her collarbone. Then he moved further down, and Annie closed her eyes torn between desire and embarrassment. His hand cupped one of her breasts as his tongue made contact with the hard pebble jutting out from the other. She gasped at the new sensation. Her body rocked against his thigh that at some point he had maneuvered between her legs.

She murmured in frustration, the ache in her most feminine place intensifying. She needed more, more of him. His kisses moved down her stomach, and she stopped his hands as he started to pull her knickers down. He stared up at her, smiling with tenderness.

"Let me touch you. You don't know how often I have dreamed of touching you like this."

Her body ached for that touch but blushing furiously, she

asked, "Is this common?"

He chuckled against her stomach. "It should be."

Miller kissed her belly. "What do you say, Annie?"

She nodded. He smiled at her wickedly and continued. Her knickers disappeared in a heap. Annie wondered if she should feel embarrassed, but she didn't. She felt like the most beautiful woman laid out naked before him. He kissed her hip before gently opening her legs.

The scruff on his face slid along her inner thigh, making her shiver. She moaned and tentatively ran her fingers through his hair. He placed a kiss on her most intimate spot, and she started to shake her head. He couldn't do that! But the sensation emitting from her body stopped her from saying as much. He teased and suckled her sex. Annie grasped his hair and pushed herself against his mouth. Wanton didn't come close to describing how she was behaving right now.

The ache within her intensified. He cupped her bottom as his sinful mouth continued to taste her. She writhed back and forth, and her legs shook as she rushed towards the release her body demanded. Finally, her body exploded. She fell back, throwing her hand over her eyes as her heart beat rapidly and the sensation of her release slowly evaporated.

Miller inched his way up to where she lay on the bed, smiling. "Happy?"

She smiled. "Happy does not describe what I am feeling."

He kissed her forehead. "Let's get dressed and eat in a tavern tonight."

She groaned. "I don't think I can move yet."

He chuckled. "Come on."

Miller stood and pulled her off the bed. She fell into him and felt his manhood pressed up against her stomach. She kissed him and said, "What of you?"

He shook his head. "We have time."

She frowned at him, knowing he didn't believe they would end up together.

"You and I will find evidence against Walker. You must believe that. I'm far from optimistic and I'm willing to believe it."

~

They had found a quaint little tavern further down the road to have dinner. A group of musicians played lively tunes as everyone ate. Simon and Annie were able to obtain a table far enough away that they could still speak but also enjoy the music. Annie's face was flushed as she clapped along with a song. This singing and dancing Annie was new to Simon. At society balls and events, she was always so composed. The song ended and Annie raised her glass with the rest of the patrons. Simon chuckled, and she smiled at him.

"What's so funny?"

"I don't think I realized how much you enjoyed music. Your enthusiasm for these musicians is so different from your interest in any *ton* event."

"No one here cares what I do. I can yell and waive my mug around. The *ton* is vastly different. They are always waiting for something to gossip about."

"I didn't think you cared about gossip."

She frowned at him. "Of course, I don't, but I have no desire to embarrass my family. I guess during our travels I have felt freer."

Simon reached across the table and held her hand. "I like this freer Annie."

She rolled her eyes. He pulled her hand to his lips and added, "But I like all the Annies you show the world. Even the prickly one."

She laughed loudly. "You can be prickly yourself."

They sat for a moment staring at each other, amusement dancing in both of their eyes. He wanted this forever. But if they found nothing in Blackpool, he couldn't continue to be with Annie. He knew that even if she wasn't willing to accept it.

"Why do you look so serious all of a sudden?"

He shook the thoughts from his mind. "I just hope Allen Lemming and Blackpool have answers that can help me prove my father's innocence. And mine."

"Even if it doesn't, we will figure this out."

"Annie, at some point you will have to return home."

She pursed her lips, clearly not agreeing.

"If the evidence isn't there, I will have to leave or go into hiding. There is no way I will allow you to be with me."

Her eyes flashed. "So, I'm supposed to go home, knowing you love me, knowing I love you?"

He reached for her hand again, squeezing it. "Let's figure it out after Blackpool. Can we agree to that?"

Simon knew she didn't want to agree. Hell, he didn't want to agree but neither of them knew where this was headed. He didn't want to promise her something they couldn't have.

Finally, she nodded. "I want you to prove your father's innocence."

He smiled wryly. "For all these years I have imagined this

ending in a specific way."

She tilted her head waiting for him to continue.

"My father was buried in a grave without a name on the headstone. That is how they bury criminals. He lies in our neighborhood cemetery, but no one knows it is him because his name was not allowed to be placed on the stone. At the end of this when he is proven innocent, I want to return to where he is buried and make sure he is given that respect."

Annie's eyes filled with tears. They didn't fall, but they were still there. "It will happen."

He wanted to believe that, and it was his ultimate goal.

Yet as Walker continued to destroy his life, another desire had started to grow and fester, revenge. He hoped Walker would eventually be arrested but if not, Simon wasn't sure he could just let him go. He wasn't sure what that meant and didn't want to dwell on it.

He looked at Annie who went back to listening to the musicians and clapping. He pushed the thoughts from his mind and started clapping his hands as well. He would enjoy this moment. Enjoy having Annie with him and in his arms.

Chapter 17

Annie sat in the carriage beaming at Simon. She couldn't help it. They were not far from Blackpool and had spent the better part of the evening before and during the carriage ride enjoying each other. Well, as much as Miller would allow. He was adamant that he wouldn't take her innocence unless they were wed. Doubts still lingered in his mind that they could be together.

Still, whether he wanted to acknowledge it or not, she was truly ruined. There was no way word had not gotten out that she had disappeared, and the assumption would be she left with someone. To her it didn't matter if they were wed or not. She was his, and he was hers.

"Sometimes you have the most expressive face."

She laughed, knowing she couldn't deny her happiness. "Then what am I thinking?"

His eyes roamed over her in a slow perusal that made her heart skip. "You want to torment me more with that mouth and delectable body of yours."

"It doesn't have to be torment," she challenged.

He rolled his eyes upward. "You are making my self-control hang by a thread."

"My reputation is destroyed, and you know what? I don't care!" she declared.

And the truth was she didn't. Even if there was no Miller, she hated how society treated young women as virtuous flowers that needed to remain untouched or unplucked until the wedding night.

"Annie—"

"Do you really think I would be with someone whose primary concern was my virtue? What hypocrisy. You aren't innocent. Most men aren't when they go to their marriage bed."

He threw his hands up. "Annie, I don't dictate how the world sees these things."

She glowered at him and then shook her head. "We are getting off topic. This will end with proving your father's innocence and then it won't matter because I will be wed to you."

He smiled, and she smiled back at him. She wouldn't let him ruin her hope. She had enough for both of them.

"I'm glad you are here," he said.

She warmed to his words. Her eyes wandered over him, and she flushed as her body filled with want. Miller could be a roguish highway man in his current state, or what Annie imagined most ladies thought one would look like.

He sat sprawled in the seat across from her. His unkempt brown hair and beard gave him a wicked appearance. Her eyes moved down the front of him, taking in his broad chest, flat stomach, and hard thighs. A body she had been pressed up against more than once in the last day. She flushed and yanked her eyes back to his. They twinkled devilishly.

"Lustful agony," he bemoaned.

"Shall I tell you what I'm thinking right now?"

His lips lifted, and he shook his head in mock pain. "We are about to arrive. I can't take anymore."

Annie smiled cheekily at him but changed the subject. "What is the plan? It is still fairly early. Will we try to visit Lemming's today?"

"You will stay at the inn, and I will go see Lemming."

She started to shake her head, but the carriage came to a stop, disrupting their conversation. The door swung open, and Miller held his hand out to her. She stepped out, looking around. Blackpool was a rather small town. Annie now understood why public coaches traveled to the tiny village so infrequently.

The town was no more than a few streets and the only inn appeared to be the one the private coach driver deposited them at. Miller had paid the man to stay close so they could leave as soon as they met with Allen Lemming.

She frowned remembering Miller's words that she would stay at the inn. Absolutely not. They were going to do this together. Something could happen to him. Lemming could attack him. What then? She was so distracted by her thoughts, she jumped when Miller said, "Let's go in and get our room, then we can discuss what will happen next."

"Yes, our plan to visit Lemming," she said, emphasizing the word our.

He rolled his eyes and left her in the foyer as he obtained a key for a room. The inn was very quiet, and Annie assumed that they didn't have very many visitors. It was likely most of the town knew each other.

Miller walked back to her, dangling the key. She nodded and followed him up the stairs. Annie had been in more inns in the last week than the entirety of her life, she mused. The situation they were in was incredibly serious but in some weird way she was happy that she had this time with Miller. They made their way down the hallway similar to the last few inns they'd stayed at. Miller stopped at a door, and she waited while he dealt with the lock. He opened the door, directing her in first.

She walked to the center of the room and turned, folding her arms, and pursing her lips. She was going with him.

Miller dropped their items on a dresser and turned to her. His eyes took in her stance and face. He sighed. “I know you want to go, but please don’t fight me on this.”

“I don’t understand why I can’t go?”

“Because when you love someone, you don’t put them in harm's way. I couldn’t live with myself if something happened to you.”

A shy smile formed on her face. “It makes me so happy that you are so open about loving me.”

He chuckled. “We are way beyond questioning whether I love you.”

Her shy smile grew wider. He wrapped her in his arms. “I love you more than I can ever vocalize. That is why I need you to stay here.”

She pulled away and shook her head. That wasn’t what Annie wanted. She wanted them to go together. “If you love someone, you are all in.”

“Please wait here. I need you to be safe,” he pleaded softly.

She didn’t want to sit by the window waiting on Miller, but she also didn’t want to fight with him. She acquiesced, reluctantly, and nodded.

“I promise I won’t be long. I asked the innkeeper about him, and he was able to tell me where his cottage was. If I leave now, I will be back well before it’s dark.”

She pulled him towards her, pulling his head down to hers and placing a kiss on his lips. “Be safe.”

He kissed her nose. “I promise.”

He stepped away and headed for the door. Annie realized she had never reciprocated in telling Miller she loved him. “Miller,” she called out.

He glanced back at her and lifted a brow. “I love you,” she said.

A stunning smile crossed his face, and he winked at her before walking into the hallway and closing the door. She made her way to the window and watched him walk out of the inn before turning down a quiet street. She plopped down in a wooden chair next to the window, scowling. She hated waiting.

~

Simon stood out front of the small but tidy cottage nestled between two trees in a grassy field, frowning. He'd assumed Allen Lemming's dwellings would be more extravagant than the small home before him. The assumption was formed from how Tobias Walker lived among the elite in London. Again it begged, who was this man?

He took a deep breath, preparing himself for what he was unsure. He checked the pistol hidden under his jacket but hoped he wouldn't have to use it. It had been difficult enough getting it out of the room without Annie seeing.

He was here for the truth. Today he would get answers on how Lemming, Walker, and his father were connected.

The front door was yanked open, startling him. A much older man with silvery hair peered out at him. His eyes widened as he stared at Simon. A moment of recognition crossed his face. Simon thought he would slam the door but instead he hobbled out dressed in practical pants and a shirt.

“Sorry to startle you. I noticed you standing out here and grew tired of waiting.”

Simon remained silent, unsure what to say.

"You're the Miller child, right?" the man said in a gruff voice.

How did he know? The similarity between him and his father was striking, but it had been many years since his death. Simon nodded.

The man tilted his head and studied him more. "You look just like him, except he was a much better dresser."

Simon's thoughts swirled, shocked this man was openly acknowledging that he was acquainted with his father. The man sighed and beckoned him into the house before hobbling back through the door. For a moment Simon wondered if it was a trap. He patted where the pistol was on his person and cautiously entered the small cottage.

As his eyes adjusted to the light, he took in his surroundings. Lemming's home wasn't much larger than some of the inn rooms he and Annie stayed in. A small bed resided in the corner, two chairs stood by a heavily used fireplace, and the rest was taken up by a table and kitchen area.

The man poured tea into a cup. "I was just getting ready to have my afternoon tea, when I glanced out the window and saw you standing there. Would you like some?"

"No," Simon said, unsure why this man was being amicable.

The man nodded and made his way to the table in the kitchen area containing two chairs. He sat and motioned for Simon to sit across from him.

"You are Allen Lemming?"

The man's eyes connected with his. They were filled with both sadness and relief. He nodded.

"Do you know why I'm here?" Simon asked sharper than he

intended.

Lemming was quiet for a moment while he considered Simon's question. He took a sip of his tea. Simon wanted to pound his fist on the table in frustration. Finally, he said, "I'm assuming to gather information to prove your father was innocent."

"And was he?"

Fear clutched at Simon's heart. For so long he had been adamant that his father was innocent. Yet, a sliver of doubt reared its head. He needed to hear Lemming say his father was not guilty of the crimes he went to prison for.

Lemming glared at him and acting somewhat annoyed that Simon had even asked the question. "Of course, your father was innocent. Your father didn't have a criminal bone in his body."

A sense of relief washed over him, and for a brief moment he thought he may actually cry but he forced himself not to. In all the years since the crime, no one had ever so confidently said those words.

Regaining his composure, he questioned, "What happened? How did you know my father?"

Lemming took another sip of his tea. "I worked in the bank with him, but I was a cleaner. It was my job to clean the vaults. Your father would unlock them for me, so I could go in and do my work. You can't imagine the stuff the elite store in those vaults. Money, gold, jewelry, and more. I have never seen so many fine things."

How did a cleaner break into a vault? Simon didn't understand. Lemming smirked. "I can tell you are underestimating me, boy. Without me, Walker would have never pulled it off."

"How does Walker fit into this?" Simon asked.

Lemming snorted. "He convinced me to give him the combination for the safe." He looked down and took a deep breath before looking back up. "I am the one that damned your father to that godforsaken prison on Blackwell Island."

"How?"

"When I had to clean the vaults, your father and I's first stop was retrieving the keys from the safe. At first, he was diligent about making sure I couldn't see what numbers unlocked the safe but the more familiar we became with each other, the more careless he became."

Simon shook his head. It couldn't be that simple. "Why would you think no one would find out?"

Lemming scowled. "The plan, at first, was never to steal from just one vault. I was so tempted by everything in those vaults and Walker used that to his benefit."

"So, you gave him the combination?"

The old man nodded. "He said he would take a little here and there but that isn't what happened. He took everything from one vault. He said he was afraid he would be discovered if he spent time opening all the vaults."

Lemming took a deep breath and continued. "Afterwards, everyone who had access to the combination was questioned. It was swiftly determined your father worked the last shift before everything was stolen. From there everything happened so quickly, your father was arrested and convicted."

Simon glared at him. "You didn't think to confess."

Lemming slammed his hand on the table. "I tried. I didn't find this out until later, but Walker has close ties with several people in the police department. They told me I was a crazy old man and not to come back. Shortly after that, Walker wooed me over here. He said we would live like kings. The only one who did that was him. Hell, I didn't even know how much he took."

Rage built in Simon, thinking about how easy it was for Walker and Lemming to allow his father to go to prison.

"You have been here since?"

A snort came from Lemming. "No, I tried London for a bit but lost everything and then Walker carted me out here. He said I was not to leave Blackpool. So, I have been here since."

"Why wouldn't you leave?"

Lemming shrugged his slim shoulders. "I am an old man. All I have is what Walker provides me." He shivered and added, "Walker can be a very dangerous man if you cross him."

He stood and made his way to a hutch, digging through the cabinet. Simon almost asked him what he was looking for but stopped when he hobbled back carrying a sack. He handed the sack to Simon. "Open it."

He did and looked back up at the man shocked. In the bag were two bars of gold. He pulled one from the bag.

The man sat back down. "I have spent several years in this boring little village. I don't like it, but it has given me time to think. I think about your father a great deal. His kindness and professionalism. He didn't deserve any of this. I remember I witnessed you one time trying to get into the bank to speak with someone about your father's case. You were so determined but the guards threw you out. That is when I went to the police."

Simon wanted to yell that he didn't do enough but refrained. Why didn't the police look into it? Was it because of Walker's connections?

In the bag along with the gold bars was a folded letter. Simon retrieved it and opened it up. His eyes scrutinized the words.

To whom it may concern,

Tobias Walker and I are guilty of the New York City Common Trust Bank theft. We stole five hundred thousand dollars' worth of items. John Miller was innocent of all crimes. As proof of my guilt within this bag are two stamped gold bars obtained from the vault.

Allen Lemming

Simon looked back at Lemming, and he had tears in his eyes. "If I could go back and change all of this, I would but I can't. Do what you will with me and take the bag. I am ready for my life to end."

The man thought Simon was here to kill him. The pistol pressed against his side, but temptation to use it never came to fruition. He had his proof. Part of him was shocked. He thought he would have been more tempted to end this man's life, but he felt nothing but victory that he had the proof he needed.

"Does Walker know you have this gold?"

Lemming shook his head. "No, he thinks I traded it for drinks and women long ago. But I held onto it because someday I knew I would have to unburden my soul of my crime. I'm ready for any consequences you think I deserve."

"You will have to find another person to put you out of your misery. It won't be me. It's Walker I'm after."

Lemming didn't appear relieved that he would live another day but just nodded. "Be careful with him. He enjoys his high-society life. He won't let anyone take it away from him."

Simon stood and said, "Don't go far. I am sure there will be questions for you."

Lemming said nothing. Simon strode from the house and once outside let out a guttural gasp. He had the evidence that proved his father's innocence. Fury festered in him that Walker had done so much damage all for selfish reasons and the police hadn't even bothered to investigate him.

Chapter 18

Annie paced back and forth in the small room. Miller had only been gone a few hours, but it seemed too long. She studied the movement on the street below, willing him to appear. She hoped that Miller obtained some type of proof from Lemming that would help confirm his innocence and his father's. She drummed her fingers on the wall, impatient.

Her gaze went back to the blasted window and her heart skipped a beat. He was back. She studied him as he made his way down the street. He appeared lost in thought, his brows drawn together in a look of concern. Her stomach dropped.

Had his visit been for nothing?

He glanced up at the windows of the inn and their eyes connected. A wide grin filled his face, and she bolted out of the room. She quickly made her way down the stairs and out the front door of the inn. The smile was still on his face, and she smiled back at him.

Annie, not caring who saw, threw her arms around him, and he squeezed her back tightly with one arm. She stepped back and lifted a brow questioningly at a sack he was holding in the other arm.

"Let's go inside," he said.

They made their way back to their room, and he dropped the sack that was slung over his shoulder. It landed with a hard thud on the wooden floor.

Her eyes widened, and she studied the bag, intrigued.

"Is that some of the missing gold bars?"

He picked her up and swung her around, startling her even more. She laughed at his enthusiasm, and he deposited her on her feet, placing a kiss on her lips. Miller beamed even more. It had been a long time since she had seen him this cheerful.

"Yes. And Lemming wrote a letter admitting his part in the crime."

Her own smile grew wider at the news. "And where is Lemming?"

"He is still at his cottage," Miller said. "He isn't going anywhere. He is an older gentleman that doesn't get around very well. He thought I was there to end his life."

Annie gasped. "Did the thought cross your mind?"

Miller frowned at her. "No. Perhaps it would have at another time in my life but not today."

She nodded. "This evidence will clear your father's name. We can go back to America and have another service for your father. One with his name on his headstone. Justice will be served."

"Walker still needs to pay," Simon said, his voice filled with anger.

She stepped back. "The police will see to it."

Miller clenched his jaw. "I hope so, but the police have done nothing so far. He must pay."

Fear filled Annie that Miller would try to confront Walker on his own. "Promise that you will not try to deal with him yourself?"

He shook his head. "I won't lie to you and promise you that."

His face was filled with determination and Annie frowned back at him with concern. If Walker didn't go to prison, would he attempt to exact justice on his own?

The thought sent shivers through her. A choice like that would change him and would be on his conscience for the rest of his life. She pushed the dark thought away, wanting to enjoy the success of the day.

"But this should exonerate you and your father!"

He grinned at her, some of his previous optimism coming back. "It should."

Relief filled Annie. "What did he tell you?"

"He told me how the crime happened, and what role Walker and he played in it. It was Lemming who provided Walker with the ability to get into the bank vaults. There was a safe that held the keys and Lemming by chance in his work with my father gleaned the combination. The note and the gold should prove my father's innocence," Miller said.

Annie wrapped her arms around him and said, "I am so happy you have the truth."

"Me too," he murmured.

He leaned down and kissed her. His warm lips pressed against hers. Annie moaned as his tongue teased the inside of her mouth. Their bodies molded to each other, and she sighed, enjoying the moment. Miller's hands loosened the ties on the back of her dress, and it fell to the ground, leaving her only in her chemise, knickers, and petticoats.

She stepped back and smiled at him. "What are you doing?"

"I want to see you."

He maneuvered her to the bed, but before they went further Annie stopped him. "I want you, Miller."

He looked at her puzzled. He was against taking her innocence, but she wanted all of him, and she wanted to give all of herself to him.

"I want us to lay together as if married," she said breathlessly.

His eyes darkened with desire, but he shook his head. "I can't. We aren't wed."

"I don't care," she said simply before kissing him.

The kiss deepened, wrapping them in a haze of lust and anticipation.

He said in a serious tone. "Are you sure?"

"Yes, I have never been surer of anything in my life. I want to be with you."

Miller groaned, and Annie giggled at his weakening resolve. He pulled her chemise over her head. Her body hummed in anticipation. Next, he untied her petticoat and knickers, and they fell to the floor. His eyes roamed over her, and he took a ragged breath. "You are exquisite."

She blushed at his compliment. He knelt before her and pushed her legs further apart. Starting at a foot, he trailed bites and kisses up one leg. "Miller," she moaned.

"Simon," he said, pausing.

Her eyes flew down to him, and he grinned up at her wickedly. "I think Simon is more appropriate at this point."

She let out a small chuckle.

He continued on, leaving kisses along her thigh. "I am going to make you explode with pleasure before I take you."

Her body shivered with delight.

"Do you want that?" he asked.

His lips slid along her stomach, inching closer to her sex.

Her stomach contracted at the sensation. She looked back down at him. His eyes watched her face intensely. Her knees shook with desire, and she nodded.

"Yes, I do, Simon."

He smiled again before dipping his head down and tasting her with his tongue. Her body arched at his touch, and she tumbled on to the edge of the bed.

He grinned up at her. "Even better."

He placed her legs over his shoulders. His beard tickled her inner thigh causing Annie to tremble before his tongue found her most feminine spot again. She fell on her elbows back against the bed watching him tease and torment her. Her body rocked against his mouth until her whimpers grew into cries of desire.

She dug her heels into his broad back as her body cried out for release. She arched against him, reaching the peak of exquisite torture. Her body moved on its own until the overwhelming intense ache at her core exploded. Her muscles relaxed, and she fell back against the bed. She threw her hands over her face, taking deep breaths.

She peaked down at him to see him sitting back on his calves, smiling at her and looking quite proud.

Annie scooted further back on the bed, and she beckoned him with a hand. He stood and pulled his shirt over his head before disposing of his trousers. She had seen dozens of statues capturing the male form but none of them prepared her for Simon. He was all muscle. Her eyes wandered down him, stopping at his manhood. Nerves erupted in her stomach, and she bit her lip.

He joined her on the bed before leaning over her and kissing her. "Are you sure?"

She cradled his face in her hands. “Yes.”

He sprinkled kisses across her shoulders and collarbone before capturing her mouth with his. He hovered over her as their tongues sparred with one another. Slowly he slid his body along hers. Her body again instinctively pushed towards his, opening her legs to allow him more room. She felt his member press against her sex.

He gently rocked his way further in her until he reached the barrier of her innocence. She looked up at his face that was filled with desire and love. “Simon, please.”

In one swift thrust, he pushed all the way into her, and she felt a burning sensation. She flinched, and they lay against one another with Simon sprinkling kisses across her mouth and throat. Very slowly, he started to move again. The burning began to subside and the ache at the apex of her thighs came tumbling back.

Annie was not unaware of the pleasure her body could provide, having long ago discovered it on her own, but she was awestruck at the level of pleasure she could obtain from another person. With her Simon, she thought tenderly. She moaned as their bodies moved against each other. She wrapped one leg around him trying to push him in deeper, and he groaned, “Annie.”

He pumped into her deeper and faster. She bucked her hips upwards meeting him stroke for stroke until they were both panting and rushing towards a release. He continued his onslaught as he pressed his lips to her hungrily before withdrawing from her body. He pumped his member as his release covered her stomach. Her body yearned for him to still be in her, but she knew he was protecting her from any unplanned choices.

Annie’s body still trembled with her own heightened need.

He kissed her again before sliding his fingers in her. The touch intensified the ache within her and her hips, finding momentum, moved against his hand. Her body shook, and she panted as she raced to her own release, wanting it. No, demanding it. With a loud whimper, the ache dissolved, and she fell against the bed.

For some reason Annie laughed. She laughed at how absolutely perfect and exquisite the moment was. Using a cloth, he cleaned them both up before lying down next to her. He ran his hands up and down her as she caught her breath.

She rolled towards him, and they pressed their heads to each other. He smiled and said, "I'm glad you stayed."

Her lips curved upwards. "I'm always right."

His chest shook and Annie realized he was laughing. Finally, he said, "I cede to you, my lady."

~

A few hours later, Simon and Annie sat on the floor of the tiny room, enjoying a tray of wine, cheese, meat, and bread brought up by one of the inn workers. Annie sat cocooned in Simon's shirt, and he in only his trousers. How she loved this man. He pulled her to him for a slow lingering kiss. She sighed contently.

The moment was perfect. She smiled wryly. Well besides that they were hiding out in an inn and had been traveling for days. Still, she didn't want to be anywhere else in the world. Though she did have to admit she was starting to miss London, shockingly. And her family, not so shockingly. Soon this would all be over, she thought to herself. This would just be a silly story they talked about as they grew old.

Simon sighed and ran his hand along his jaw. "I need to shave."

Annie pursed her lips, studying him. "I don't know, I like you this way."

He lifted a brow. "Why is that?"

"I'm not sure."

He grabbed her hand and placed kisses on her fingers. "I assure you whether I look like a proper man, or a scoundrel is irrelevant to how I can make you feel."

A red hue started at the top of her head and ran all the way down her. She laughed at his confidence but didn't disagree.

His face turned serious. "Once I'm cleared of all this, I want us to marry right away."

Her tempting mouth turned into a smirk. "Still so proper deep down," she said, dryly.

He ate a slice of bread, ignoring her lighthearted jab.

Annie said, "Tell me something about you I don't know. You know so much about me and I know so little about you."

"What would you like to know?"

"Did you know your mother?" she asked.

Simon sat back and thought about her question. Finally, he said, "My mother, when I was two, left. She wrote my father a note and said she was headed west."

Annie's face filled with concern. "That must have been devastating for your father."

Simon shook his head, smiling slightly. "My father was perhaps the most compassionate man I knew. One time I said some unkind words about my mother. I was about fourteen. My father sat me down and said that my mother was a wanderer and to have forced her to stay would have been good for no one. He then said he would always think of her fondly because she gave him me."

A lump formed in Simon's throat as he remembered the moment and how defiant he had been at the time. Annie reached across the table, squeezing his hand and said, "Still, to leave your child."

Perhaps, he had more of his father in him than he thought because he felt no rage towards her. He shrugged. "She left me with the best father a child could ask for."

"What about your parents? Do you have any memories of the late duke and duchess?"

She shook her head sadly. "Not one. Sometimes I wish I did and sometimes I'm grateful I don't. Maggie and Joseph are the only parents I have ever known, and I still grieve that we lost them far too soon."

"From everything I heard they were rather remarkable."

She smiled softly. "They were. They had so much guilt over what happened to Jack and I in the orphanage. After we moved in with them and I recovered from my injuries, I was horrid to them. I was so angry."

"Yet, you forgave them. The always stubborn Annie Kincaide."

She nodded. "I did. Completely. Sam, Jack, and I came to them as practically savages. We could steal, cuss, and fight like any other kid in the orphanage. Well, except we could all read thanks to Jack's education. That is how we became close with Sam. Sam agreed to protect us and help get us food if Jack taught him to read."

"Your family is remarkable," Simon said and meant it.

She snorted. "Irrational, insane, but perhaps remarkable."

"I won't disagree," Simon said with a wink.

She laughed and teasingly slapped his hand. Simon rose. "I'm going to head to the shop across the street and see if I can send a letter to the Americans and your family."

Annie frowned at him. "Are you sure we should do that now?"

"I want everyone to know as soon as possible that I'm innocent, so I can marry you."

She laughed and stood.

"First you need to give me that shirt."

Annie yanked it over her head, tossing it at him. He sucked in his breath at how beautiful she was. He made a move towards her, and she wagged a finger at him. "No. They are bringing up water for a bath momentarily. You go to the shop, and I will bathe."

He growled, and she pulled her nightgown over her body.

"I will be back shortly."

She blew him a kiss and Simon left the room. He made his way out of the inn and headed towards the shop, still smiling. Distracted by his thoughts, he didn't notice the carriage outside of the shop until the door swung open and a man grabbed him.

Simon attempted to swing at the man but was easily pushed into the carriage. He sprung up on his knees ready to fight. Leveled at his face was a pistol being held by Tobias Walker. Even brandishing a weapon, the man looked like the perfect dandy. His blondish silver hair was coiffed to perfection and his waistcoat was styled in the latest fashion.

Walker smirked at him. "Sit," he said.

Simon scowled but sat on the bench across from him. Walker leaned back on his own side, still holding the pistol. "I knew you were somehow connected to John Miller. It took me time to confirm you were his son. Even after that, I had hoped you would give up this chase."

"Never. You will pay for your crime whether it is by my hands or the law."

Walker laughed loudly. "That's rich, especially since I am the one with the pistol."

Simon's eyes moved around the carriage, trying to figure out a way to grab the pistol from him. Walker put it away. "My man is standing outside of this carriage ready to shoot you, if I ask."

The tension in the carriage was almost smothering. They had played cards with each other for months, always cordial, but now all that insincere politeness was gone. "Nothing will stop me from making sure you pay for your actions."

"Are you sure about that?" Walker asked. He pulled the curtain aside and Simon looked out the window. From where they sat, they had a direct view to a window located in the room Simon and Annie were staying in.

Fear clutched at Simon. He glared at Walker. "Touch her and I will kill you."

The man chuckled again. "So brave but what you don't understand is I am the one that will decide what happens next. I visited my dear friend Allen Lemming after you left. Unfortunately, he has departed this world."

Cold fury raced through Simon as Walker continued, "He told me about the gold bars and the letter. You are going to give those to me."

Simon shook his head and Walker pointed back out the window. In one of the windows on the second floor of the inn stood a man. He tilted his hat to Simon and Walker.

"If you don't, not only will I kill you, but I will kill your lady. Quite beautiful. I wonder if her brothers know what she has been up to. Sleeping with a wanted man."

Simon reached across the carriage, grabbing Walker by his cravat. He smirked at him in return. "I suggest you release me, Miller. All I need to do is knock on the carriage wall and my men are ready to act."

Fueled with anger, Simon released him, throwing Walker against the bench. "I will let that go as you are agitated."

Just then the curtains to his room at the inn were pulled back and Annie peered out into the darkness, frowning. She was likely wondering where he was.

"What do you want?" Simon bit out.

Walker had him. "Tomorrow you will send your lady to Liverpool. The investigators have already been tipped off that you are in Blackpool. You will then be apprehended and confess that you were really the owner of the gold bars and that you traveled up here to retrieve what remained of them. That it was you and your father who worked with Lemming."

Simon shook his head, but Walker pointed out the window. "You will do this because if you don't, I will kill that lady waiting on you. What matters more to you? This wasted obsession of proving my guilt or your lady?"

Annie mattered. Simon would not allow her to be harmed even if that meant confessing to something that he was innocent of. He would protect her at all costs. He doubted that Walker was planning to let him live after she was gone but at least she would be safe. Simon would find a way out of this after she was gone.

He nodded. "I will need to send a letter to alert her family to where she is."

Walker shrugged and smiled as if they were friends. "I am glad you could be reasonable about this."

Simon ignored him and threw the door of the carriage open. He stalked into the shop and the man behind the counter said, "You lucked out, sir. We were just about to close."

He forced a smile. "Sorry but I would like to get a letter back to London."

The man provided him with paper and something to write with. "It won't depart until tomorrow."

Simon nodded. He considered writing to the Kincaides about Walker but hesitated knowing that the man was ready to do Annie harm if anything went wrong. He scribbled down a quick note.

Annie is at the Liverpool townhouse. Come as quickly as you can.

Miller

He handed the man the letter and walked out. Walker's carriage was still out front. He looked out the carriage window and nodded to him, grinning as if he was an old friend. Simon didn't acknowledge him and continued back to the inn. He took the stairs two at a time and hurried down the hallway. Before he reached his room, the door next to his opened and the man he saw in the window glared at him. He scowled at him but said nothing before entering his room.

Was there a way he could alert Annie to the danger they were in? He doubted Blackpool had any constables. If he caused a scene, he would likely be apprehended by Walker's henchmen and Annie would be hurt. He cursed, frustrated by the situation he was in.

"Well, that wasn't the greeting I was expecting."

He looked in the direction of Annie's voice and saw her sitting in a tub, studying him.

Chapter 19

Annie's smile turned to a frown as she took in Simon's stony face. "Is everything okay?"

His eyes ran over her and he smiled softly. "Yes, getting the letters sent took longer than I expected. The shop owner was closing when I arrived."

She grinned mischievously up at him. "I thought you could help me bathe."

For a moment, he hesitated but then pulled his shirt over his head and made his way towards her, grabbing a chair on his way. He appeared different, but Annie couldn't explain why. Perhaps he was just exhausted.

"I can get out, and we can get some rest."

He sat behind her and placed a small bite on her neck causing warm sensations to rush down her.

"And pass up this opportunity. Never."

He held his hand out for the bathing cloth and Annie handed it to him.

"Lean back," he said hoarsely.

She closed her eyes, enjoying the pleasure of him running the cloth over her body. He kissed her shoulder and then started exploring her body again. Annie realized he had abandoned the cloth and his fingers were slowly moving down her stomach. She wiggled in anticipation for where they would go next.

As his fingers moved through the curls at her sex, she sucked in her breath. He placed another bite on her neck causing her mind to swirl trying to rationalize the sensations coming from different places in her body. His fingers teased her, and she moaned. His breathing was ragged behind her.

"I have fantasized about you like this in my dreams."

She leaned her head against his chest and the back of the bathing tub as her body moved with his teasing. "In a tub?" she asked.

He kissed her cheek, and she could feel the smile on his lips. "Yes. Naked, wet, and moaning."

Annie wanted all of him and now. She sat up and then stood, startling him. His eyes ran over her body, ravenously. Without another word between them, he scooped her into his arms, carrying her to the bed. He quickly discarded his clothes and kissed her with a hunger that made Annie tremble. He nudged her legs open and entered her with a deep lunge. She gasped at the overwhelming primal need emanating from him. Her body responded the same, needing him just as much and still begging for release from what they started while she was in the tub.

He held her head looking at her intensely as their bodies moved with each other, the tempo increasing. She closed her eyes. "Open your eyes. I want to see you come apart," he demanded.

Her eyes fluttered open, and a nibble of concern flitted through her mind at the desperation she saw in his face. She ignored it and met him thrust for thrust until her body arched as she came apart. She let out a sob, and he kissed her deeply as he drove towards his own satisfaction. Consuming her with his mouth. In the last moment he withdrew from her before embracing his own release. He kissed her lightly before finding a cloth to clean them both up with. They lay in bed, sated but Annie studied him as he laid on his back. He was withdrawn.

"Are you sure everything is okay?"

He rolled to his side, planting a kiss on her nose. "Yes."

Annie ran a hand gently down his cheek, studying him. "You seemed so much happier before your visit to the shop."

He placed a kiss on her hand. "Simply overwhelmed with everything that has taken place."

They laid quietly for a moment and then Simon said, "But I wanted to speak with you about tomorrow. I want you to go to Liverpool without me. I would like to speak with Lemming one more time."

Something was off. Foreboding filled her. She would not desert him. "We leave together, Simon."

"Please, do this."

She started to shake her head, and he cut her off. "I won't discuss this further, Annie," he bit out.

Her eyes widened in shock at his cross tone. She scowled at him, infuriated, and jumped from the bed, before pulling on his shirt. Simon also rose and pulled on his trousers, prior to pouring himself a brandy.

They were both quiet until Simon said, "I don't mean to be harsh. I promise I will only be a few hours behind your arrival in Liverpool. I'm tired of you being cooped up in these inns. Go to your family's townhouse and wait for the arrival of your brothers."

"What has changed that you want to do this?"

"I have a few more things to tie up with Lemming, then I will be on my way."

Annie's heart thumped wildly. Did he mean to harm him?

"Simon, any decision you make, you will have to live with for the rest of your life. You're a good man. It will weigh heavily on your conscience. Revenge is not—"

"I don't mean to harm the man," he snapped, seemingly offended that she had jumped to that conclusion.

She flushed embarrassed that she had assumed wrong. "I just don't want you to do anything you will regret."

He took a sip of his drink. "I promise I won't. I just think it would be better for you to be in Liverpool when your family arrives. They will be worried."

He had a point. She couldn't imagine how upset her family was with her. She missed them and truthfully was tired of sitting in inns. Perhaps she was making too big of a deal out of his request. She studied his face and eyes. He turned away, appearing uncomfortable with her perusal. She couldn't shake the feeling something was wrong.

"Please, Annie," he said.

She closed her eyes, hating her next words. "Fine."

Simon smiled with relief. Annie felt an impending sense of doom. She pushed the concern away telling herself they had the evidence, and everything would be fine.

~

Simon watched the carriage carrying Annie to Liverpool rumble away. She was safe. That was what mattered. He turned to see the man Walker hired loitering in the entryway of the inn. He glared at Simon, but Simon didn't even acknowledge him as he walked through the door. He made his way up the stairs knowing he was right behind him. Simon opened the door to his room, and the man pushed his way in behind him.

"Where is Walker?" Simon asked, trying to determine what his options were.

"He returned to London. I'm to wait here until the Americans and Peelers show up to arrest you. Remember your part. You are to confess, and nothing happens to your lady love."

Surprise is what Simon felt. He was confident that he would never make it back to London, but he guessed it made sense that they would need him to actually confess his part to remove any suspicion from Walker. He thought about fleeing, and as if the man could read his mind, he said, "Don't even think about escaping. Walker doesn't make false threats. He has men following your lady."

Simon scowled at him. Ignoring Simon's response, the man rummaged through the sack and withdrew the note Lemming had written. He balled the paper up and threw it into the fireplace. Simon clenched his jaw as the paper turned to ash. As much as Simon wanted justice, he couldn't chance Annie being hurt.

There was a knock on the door and the man rose to answer it. On the other side of the door stood the investigator Mr. Collins and some other men. They entered the room and Collins studied him.

"So, it was you all along?"

Simon nodded without any hesitation. As much as he wanted Walker to pay, he valued Annie's life more.

Collins said nothing else to him but turned to the man. "Where is the sack you mentioned?"

The man smirked and handed it to him. Collins looked in the bag and frowned. "Is this all there is, two gold bars?"

Walker's henchman nodded. Collins' eyes narrowed. "Why is Walker so involved in this?"

The man shifted nervously but said, “He is just doing his part to make sure justice is served.”

Simon wanted to throw his head back and laugh hysterically. Collins handed the sack to a man. “Shell, take that with you in your carriage. I will ride with Mr. Miller.”

Shell shook his head. “I think you need someone with you.”

Collins smiled at him. “The Peelers will be riding on top, and you will be in the carriage behind us. I’m not sure Mr. Miller here is at risk of escaping as he confessed to his crime.”

“You are an investigator, not an officer of the law,” Shell said, smugly.

Collins' eyes narrowed at his remark. “I might remind you that my clients provide a great deal of support to the high constable in New York City. Let’s not argue who has the authority to do what.”

Shell looked as if he wanted to do just that, and Collins waited patiently for what he would do next. Simon wondered what was going on between the two men. Finally, Shell nodded and left.

“So, all along, even though you have been adamant your father was innocent, you have been guilty?” Collins questioned him again.

Simon’s eyes shifted around to all the men standing in the room, including Walker’s henchman. Collins seemed skeptical of his confession, but Simon would not risk Annie’s safety, so he nodded.

“Completely guilty,” he bit out.

Collins sighed and motioned for him to rise. They made their way out of the inn and to the carriages that would take them all back to Liverpool. From there they would likely travel by train back to London. Collins had Simon enter first before joining him. Walker's henchman attempted to enter the carriage and Collins stopped him.

The man scowled at him. "I am riding with you, so I can get my reward."

Collins shook his head. "You will get your reward, no need to ride with us."

The man glared at him. "Walker wanted me to make sure I saw him delivered to Newgate."

"Well, you can tell Walker we have it from here," Collins said before shutting the door in his face.

They rode in the carriage in silence for at least an hour before Collins said, "What's going on?"

Simon looked at him, stone faced. "I don't know what you mean. I confessed. Isn't that why you are in London. To bring me back?"

Collins leaned back on the bench. "You know with everything that was taken from that vault, the family only wanted one thing back and in all this time, not once have you ever brought that item up. I have waited and waited for you to do so or for it to appear somewhere but nothing."

He must be talking about the item Miss Markam mentioned hinted at in her letter. What was it? "But to my shock Mr. Walker mentioned it in his letter he sent to the bank as well as insisted Mr. Shell work with me on this case. Mr. Shell has very strong connections with High Constable Monroe. My first thought was something was amiss with the accusation Walker was directing at you and Shell was sent to make sure I followed the right clues."

"What is it?" Simon asked.

Collins smiled. "The one piece that will reveal who the real culprit of the theft is. I won't share it with you, but I do believe you are innocent, and I think Walker is setting you up. Why are you going along with his plan? Is it because of Lady Annabelle Kincaide?"

Did Simon trust this man? Did it really matter? He knew the moment he arrived in Newgate that he would be marked for death. It was only a matter of time. What did he have to lose? Annie was what he had to lose. Still, if he was going to survive this, he needed to rely on someone.

"Do I have your word that what I share will go no further than us? It will not be shared with Mr. Shell, especially if you believe he may be working with Walker?" Simon said.

Collins nodded. "I have another associate that Mr. Shell doesn't know about, but he can be trusted. I give you my word for both of us."

"Walker is setting me up and he threatened to harm Lady Annabelle if I did not confess. I was able to meet with Allen Lemming, and he confessed his part in the theft. Unfortunately, I left him there. Yesterday, Walker informed me he is no longer living."

"Did he kill him?"

"I assume so. I didn't see him commit the act."

Collins sighed. "Some of the Peelers are out inspecting Lemming's place now."

Simon nodded. "In the end, he did the right thing or was trying to. He gave me the gold and a letter admitting his and Walker's guilt. Unfortunately Walker's man burned the letter."

"I need you to help me obtain the item from Walker. It should prove his guilt and your father's innocence."

"I will not risk Lady Annabelle's life. She means too much to me."

"If you stay in prison, you will be killed. They are waiting on your written confession, and that is all. You must know this."

Simon scowled at him. Of course, he knew that. He wasn't an imbecile but what choice did he have? "I need Walker to believe that I am going along with him. At least until Annabelle is protected by her family. Beyond that, if there is a way for me to get out of this, I'm game."

Collins nodded. "This is what we will do."

Chapter 20

Annie stood in the sitting room of the Kincaide townhouse. A full day and night had passed since she departed from Blackpool, and she had heard nothing from Simon. She twisted at the folds of her pale blue dress. A lump formed in her throat, and she pushed it away. She worried something had happened to him. It was impossible that he wouldn't come for her. A kernel of doubt filled her before she shook it away. No, she wouldn't doubt him.

She glanced around the luxurious settings of her family's townhouse and felt out of place after spending so much time with Simon at various inns. Once she arrived yesterday, she was quickly ushered to a bath and dressed in a much more complex dress than the one she had been wearing for the last few days. Now, here she sat, perfectly coiffed and dressed as all ladies were expected to be. Irritation shot through her.

The front door opened, jerking her away from her thoughts. Thunderous footsteps made their way down the hallway. She closed her eyes in absolute pain, wishing the footsteps were Simon's, but she knew they belonged to her brothers.

She took a deep breath and turned to the door, ready to be yelled at. Sam stepped in first, followed by Jack. Relief covered both her brothers' faces. Sam swept her up into a hug. "Damn it, Annie. We were so concerned."

She pulled back from his arms with tears in her eyes. "He said he would come for me, but he hasn't. I'm so worried."

Jack and Sam looked at each other. Something was amiss. "What is it?" she asked.

"Miller's been arrested. He was escorted to Newgate prison

yesterday. He is expected to be returned to America in the next couple of days. The Peelers alerted us that you were in Liverpool."

Annie shook her head, shocked. It was impossible. "He sent you a letter by coach."

Both her brothers frowned at her. "We didn't receive a letter from Miller," Jack said, skeptical.

"He sent it!"

"We likely were already headed to Liverpool," Sam said gently.

Perhaps, Annie thought. She clutched her stomach in horror. The squalor conditions at Newgate were infamous. She closed her eyes, repulsed that Simon was there, sitting in some damp, repugnant cell.

"We must leave. He will need our help."

Sam guided her to the sofa, and she stared at him perplexed. She didn't want to sit down for a chat. It was time for action. They needed to help Simon.

"No. We need to leave. Simon shouldn't—"

Jack's face filled with fury. "When did you become close enough to call him Simon?"

A deep flush covered Annie's body. She would not be ashamed of the choices she and Simon made. "I plan to marry him."

Her brother's fury only increased, and Sam placed a hand on his shoulder. "Have some care, brother."

Jack shrugged him off and wandered to a table that held a decanter of brandy. Annie frowned at his back, appalled at his anger.

"Please sit, Annie," Sam said with a smile.

The peacemaker sat in a chair across from her, and Jack joined them, providing them each with a glass. She looked between her two brothers, one so angry and the other frowning at her with concern.

She took a sip of the brandy, pausing to embrace the burning sensation that traveled down her torso. "What is it then? Obviously something terrible happened."

"He was fleeing when he was apprehended. He was planning to leave the country," Jack explained.

Jack could have told her anything, and she would have been less shocked. Impossible, she thought. Simon would not abandon her. "I don't believe it," she declared.

"I think you need some time—"

"Take me to Newgate," she demanded, cutting Jack off.

Jack's face turned hard. "I will not allow you to step foot in that prison."

She had to visit him. If she saw his face, she could learn the truth. Did something cause him to make a false confession, or had he always planned on fleeing? She looked down, betrayal washing over her. She held the pain inside of her, refusing to let it erupt. The discussions over the last week flashed in her mind. There was no hint of deception. She would not believe that of him.

She regained her composure and glared at Jack. "Even if he is guilty of what you said, I must see him."

"No! I will not let you see someone who compromised you."

Annie didn't deny it. She bit back, "How dare you judge me or him. You are not the picture of honor." Annie's gaze flicked to Sam. "Neither of you are."

Both her brothers scowled at her condemnation. She didn't care. She would not let them hold her to a different standard than themselves.

Neither responded. She continued, "Back to the issue of me visiting Miller. I must. He told me he was innocent. If he is guilty, I deserve to confront him."

"Annie—" Sam started.

Annie couldn't prevent the tears from filling her eyes. "Please, Sam."

Sam looked away from her, uncomfortable to see her in so much emotional agony. Neither of her brothers wanted to see her distressed, but of the two, Sam had always been the most understanding. She needed at least him on her side. He proved her right and said, "We can try."

Annie nodded her thanks to Sam, and he smiled softly at her.

"Do you think we can just show up at Newgate and demand to see him?" Jack asked, disgruntled.

"You are a duke. You can make anything happen," Annie stated.

Jack started to shake his head and Sam said, "We will escort her. If seeing him will help her gain closure, then we must try our best."

Annie wasn't interested in closure, but she kept silent. Instead, she smiled at Sam, grateful.

"If we leave by train, we can attempt to see him today," he added.

"You won't be alone with him," Jack insisted.

"Of course not," Annie said.

Hours later, Annie sat in a carriage with Sam and Jack. The

train ride back to London had been a quiet one. Jack was against Annie confronting Simon and the visit to Newgate. Annie was grateful for Sam's insistence that they go.

"You can't believe he is guilty of this," she implored to Jack.

"I don't know what to think. But I know that he spent several days with you alone. Not how a respectable man would behave."

Annie snorted. "You compromised your own wife in order for her to wed you."

"It isn't the same," he barked.

"I sought him out, Jack. It wasn't the other way around. I went after him. He wanted me to leave. He insisted I leave several times."

The carriage came to a stop before they could continue their conversation. "Well, we shall see."

They stepped out and Annie studied the imposing Newgate prison. Simon was in there somewhere. She calmed her stormy emotions. Jack approached a guard at the main entrance. "I'm the Duke of Peyton. I demand to see the warden about a prisoner named Simon Miller being held here."

The guard stared at him, speechless. "Now," Jack snapped.

The man shuffled off leaving them waiting. After a few minutes later, they were ushered into the large stone building. Annie's nose wrinkled at the smell of filth. The walls were covered with decades of grime that seemed to permeate the air. They arrived at a room that was shockingly cleaner than the rest of the massive compound.

"This is Warden Hemley's office. He will be here shortly," the guard said before bowing and departing.

Moments later, Warden Hemley entered the room. He bowed to

Jack. "Your Grace, how may I help you?"

"I would like to see Simon Miller."

The warden frowned at him, and his eyes darted to Annie. "I am not sure this place is appropriate for a lady."

"Can we see him, or do I need to make my request with your superiors?"

Annie sucked in a deep breath. Jack never threw his title around. She felt grateful even if he was furious with her.

The warden blanched at the threat. "No, that won't be necessary. You are lucky he is meeting with the Americans who will be escorting him back to New York City. They must give approval. I have already asked, and they agreed but will attend the visit."

Jack glared at the man, who appeared to shrivel before their eyes. "Lead us to him," Jack bit out.

Annie smoothed the front of her dress, nervous.

The warden led them down another stone hallway, and Annie forced herself to not gag from the stench. The hallway was lined with cells and men peeked through bars on the massive wooden doors that contained them. More than a few hollered out to them. She kept her gaze forward, not wanting to engage. Jack growled at one man's lecherous promise but kept moving.

The warden opened the door to a small cell, and they stepped in. Simon sat in a chair at a table with Mr. Collins and Mr. Shell seated across from him. When Simon saw them, his eyes widened in shock.

"What are you doing here?" Simon bit out, his eyes blazing with fury.

~

The damn woman he was trying to protect was standing in Newgate prison. In his damn cell! Did she have no sense? Fury threatened to erupt from him. He glared at Jack and Sam. How could they allow her to be in such a place?

"You shouldn't have brought her here!" he snapped at the Kincaide brothers.

Jack lunged at him, and Sam grabbed him before he could reach Simon. He had known the Kincaide brothers for years and never thought a time would come when he wanted to do physical harm to either of them but his rage that they brought Annie to the hell he was sitting in threatened that.

"I had to see you," Annie said.

She stared at him defiantly, and he was torn between shaking her and wanting to sweep her up in his arms. She was with her family, safe. He glanced at Collins who remained emotionless. Simon doubted he had time to alert the Kincaides to their plan. Shell studied everyone in the room. The weasel, Simon thought. He had no doubt he would immediately go to Walker after this visit was over.

Simon could not let on that Collins suspected that Shell was working with Walker. "You shouldn't have come," he said harshly.

"You're innocent. I know you are. Allen Lemming told you what really happened," Annie said to him.

"I am sorry, my lady, but Mr. Miller was lying to you. He only met with Lemming to obtain the remaining gold. He always planned to leave," Shell said, gloating.

Annie's eyes flashed. "No, visit Lemming. He will tell you the truth."

Shell shook his head. "Unfortunately, he passed away, and it doesn't matter as Mr. Miller just provided his statement that he is the guilty party, resolving the case."

"Tobias Walker is the one guilty of this crime," Annie said, looking at him confused.

Shell laughed. "My lady, Mr. Walker, is highly respected. His only participation in this, is he alerted us that he thought Mr. Miller may have the gold. We are taking Mr. Miller back to America, and he will be tried for his crimes. The bank wants to get this finalized as soon as possible."

Simon silently pleaded that Annie would say no more, but the stubborn woman he loved shook her head. "Walker worked at that bank as well."

"My lady, I must demand you stop making accusations. Mr. Miller here has confirmed he has always had the gold, and he was fleeing when taken into custody."

She looked at Simon questioningly. "Is this true?"

He needed Shell to think that he was playing the part Walker demanded of him. If not, his plans with Collins would be lost. Out of the corner of his eyes, he saw Collins watching the exchange with cool detachment. They both knew what was at stake. Simon hated himself for his next words.

"I hadn't expected you to find me, Annie. I had to come up with something. You insisted that you wouldn't leave. I told you what you wanted to hear."

Hurt covered her face before fury filled it. She slammed her hand on the table. "You are lying."

He smiled condescendingly at her. His heart breaking. "No, I'm not. Besides, it was convenient to be traveling with a wife. No one looking for me was expecting that."

"Liar! I don't know why but I know you are. The moments we

shared were real."

Her conviction almost destroyed him. He said the next words hoping they would end any further conversations. "It was just a bit of fun."

All the color drained from her face. Jack did punch him then. Simon's head snapped back, and he said nothing. He embraced the pain. He deserved it, even if what he was doing was for Annie's own good and would bring Walker to justice.

Sam pulled Jack away, but Jack shook him off. He grabbed Simon by the front of his shirt. "You are lucky you are leaving, or I would rip you apart. Apologize to her now!"

"I'm sorry," Simon mumbled, not wanting to look at her face, afraid it would undo him.

Jack shook him. "Look at her!"

He turned his gaze towards her, and his legs almost buckled at the agony on her face.

"I'm sorry, my lady."

Her mouth trembled as she stared at him. She appeared to want to say something but instead turned to Jack and Sam and said, "I want to leave."

Simon's mind screamed for her to come back, to not give up on him. She walked out the door without another look back. Pain and grief filled Simon. He had not only lied to her but hurt her possibly beyond repair. There was no way to tell her he was playing a part. How much could you hurt one person before they gave up on you? He allowed himself to embrace the pain of her absence and hurt, still hoping someday he would have the chance to make it up to her.

He turned back to Collins and Shell. "Is there anything else?"

Shell smirked, delighted with the conversation. Simon had the urge to pummel the man but refrained from doing so.

The warden entered. “Was the duke satisfied with his visit?”

“I believe so,” Collins said.

The warden sighed with relief. It wasn’t every day a duke demanded a visit with a prisoner.

Collins rose. “We are leaving. I don’t want anyone entering Mr. Miller’s cell until we return.”

The warden nodded. Simon listened to Collins and Shell’s footsteps as they made their way down the hallway. Later tonight Collins would retrieve him without Shell. He just needed to survive until then. It shouldn't be a problem as long as the warden kept his word to not allow anyone entry. He was putting a great deal of trust in Collins, but he had no choice. It was his only chance.

Chapter 21

Annie sat with Jack, Sam, and their wives in the dining room at the Peyton townhouse in London. The entire carriage ride home had been filled with awkward silence. More than once, Jack had looked as if he wanted to say something, but Sam had shaken his head. She was grateful to him. He understood all his siblings so well, particularly when to push and not to push. The same couldn't be said for His Grace, she thought.

To avoid further questioning, she had rushed up to her room and planned on staying there for the rest of the evening. Unfortunately, it was not long after that a maid arrived to prepare her for dinner at Jack's insistence.

She glanced at Jack where he sat at the head of the table and their eyes connected. His normally impassive face was filled with worry. Sadness settled within her that they were so upset with each other. Pragmatically, she understood his reaction. He had always been her protector during their time at the orphanage, after her accident, and most recently while navigating the *ton*.

Still, she was hurt by his harsh words and overbearingness. She needed his support, not his censor. She tore her gaze away, refusing to dwell on their fractured relationship. It hurt too much, and she already had enough pain to deal with.

The silence around the room was deafening. Clara had attempted small talk earlier, but it had fallen flat. Annie was likely at fault as she couldn't muster enthusiasm for any of the topics. She adored Clara and gave her a small smile. She would never want to hurt her. Clara smiled back at her, reassuringly.

Just when Annie thought she couldn't take anymore silence, the dining-room door was thrown open and her beautiful sister rushed in. Her red wavy hair fell down her back, and she was dressed in an extravagant red gown, likely coming from some grand ball. Her eyes darted around the room until they landed on Annie. The emotion Annie had kept at bay bubbled to the surface and a strangled sob escaped her.

Sophia rushed to her side. She pulled Annie from her chair and wrapped her in her arms. Annie's tears fell freely, and she was unable to stop crying. In her periphery, she noticed Jack sending all the servants out of the room.

Sophia stepped back and grasped Annie's shoulders. "He isn't guilty. I refuse to believe it."

"He compromised your sister," Jack bit out.

Sophia rolled her eyes. "I didn't say anything about that."

Annie glared at him, wanting to toss her glass at his head.

Sophia didn't take her eyes off her. She squeezed her shoulders, reassuringly. "He loves her. He always has. Everyone in this room has made rash decisions in the name of love."

Annie pulled away, taking deep breaths to compose herself. "He confessed."

Sophia's eyes widened in shock and her gaze slid to Sam who nodded. She shook her head. "No, it must be a misunderstanding."

How Annie wanted to believe that but all she could think of was Simon's words about their time together being a bit of fun. Pain and humiliation filled her.

"Sophia, why don't you sit?" Sam suggested.

Sophia gave Annie another squeeze. Annie was grateful to have her there. She sat down in a chair. "What happens next?"

Sam sighed. "He did confess and will be handed over to the

investigators to be taken back to America."

"That's it?" Sophia questioned.

"He is guilty of his crimes," Jack snapped.

Annie was tired of Jack's brooding anger. Simon had done so much for their family. Jack was letting his fury about her and Simon overrule any other thought.

"Would you stop acting like he is the worst sort of man? I already told you, I went to him, Jack. Miller would never take advantage. I pursued him."

"Enough!" he bellowed.

Mercy placed her hand on his and frowned at him. He took a deep breath. "All of your chances are ruined."

"I. Don't. Care. You wanted this world not me," Annie declared, defiantly.

He stood and stalked out of the room. Sam followed him out, leaving Annie with Clara, Mercy, and Sophia.

Mercy grimaced, concerned by Jack's outburst. "He wants to protect you."

Annie knew that but Jack also knew her dreams of finding the perfect husband were never a priority for her. She pursued Simon, not because she needed a husband but because she wanted him. She still wanted him. That is why it hurt so much to find out he didn't care for her. Honestly, part of her still couldn't believe it.

Still, talk would get out that she had been found with Simon. Then she would be ruined. She would go away, she thought. Perhaps back to Philadelphia. No, she couldn't imagine going back.

"What happened?" Sophia asked.

She blushed, unsure of what to share.

“We are here for you. Nothing you say will leave this room,” Mercy reassured.

Annie smiled at her. Her brother was lucky to have her as a wife. Before Mercy came into Jack’s life, he had been so hard, and some might even say harsh. Over the years, she had softened him in ways that he didn’t even realize.

Annie took a deep breath. “I found a notepad of his and discovered he was headed to a town north of Liverpool called Blackpool. I left in a public coach but became stuck in Daventry due to the weather. I was shocked to find him at the inn I was seeking lodging at.”

“Did you stay with him?” Sophia said, not scandalized in the least.

Annie rolled her eyes at her sister's dramatics. “I did.”

She glanced around the table and realized Mercy, Clara, and Sophia were waiting for her to continue.

“He confessed that he loved me. For so long I thought it was one-sided, but he said he had always cared for me. That is why I don’t understand what is happening. He wasn’t fleeing. He was looking for proof.”

“Proof of what?” Clara asked.

Annie smiled at her wryly. “I’m sure you’ve been told most of the story as no one in this family can keep a secret.”

“I haven’t,” Sophia piped up.

“Years ago, his father went to prison for stealing from a bank and a man who is now part of London society is actually the culprit. The man set Simon, I mean Miller, up. Well, that is what he told me but then Miller confessed to being the culprit.”

Sophia gasped. “I don’t believe it.”

Mercy agreed. “I don’t either. Something must have made him confess. Miller cares for you. I have always known that since I first saw the two of you together.”

Clara nodded in support.

“I just don’t know why he would take the blame,” Annie said as much to herself as to everyone at the table.

“You can’t lose hope. People make difficult choices for the people they love,” Clara said.

Annie smiled, grateful to have these women in her life. These were the words she needed to hear. She had missed all of them.

“Thank you,” she said to them.

~

Simon sat in the dark musty cell, watching the lone candle slowly dwindle down. Every time footsteps echoed down the hallway, he hoped it was Collins. The plan was he would be escorted from the prison tonight. Simon was unsure how an investigator would be able to have him released. Only Shell, in his official capacity as a constable, had the power to take him from the prison, but Collins said to leave it all to him.

During their talk on the way to London, Collins had informed Simon that he suspected Shell was working with both Walker and corrupt police officials in New York City. He believed Shell’s sole purpose in being in London was to make sure that Simon and his father were held responsible for the bank crimes.

Simon still didn’t understand what role Collins played in the situation. Collins explained to him that significant changes were in the works to curb the corruption in New York City’s police system but were still months away from being implemented.

The heavy wooden door to his cell opened, and Simon stood expecting it to be Collins but instead two massive men stepped into the room. The door shut behind them. One smiled at him, and trepidation filled Simon. The men were there to inflict pain. There was nothing a pocket of coins couldn't buy, he thought disgusted. This was Walker's doing. He had no doubt.

The smiling man stepped closer and said, "We can make this as pain free as you like. It is up to you."

Simon said nothing, waiting for the men to pounce. He said a silent prayer that he would survive this beating until Collins showed up. The smiling man lunged at him, and Simon dodged him, causing him to collapse onto the rickety wooden bed in the cell. The other man laughed, and the smiling man glowered at him.

The man pushed himself up from the bed and scowled at him. "So, you want it the hard way. I'm fine with that."

Both men advanced towards him, and Simon surveyed them to determine what his best hope was. One man lunged at him, and he easily dodged him, using his leg to trip him and drop him to the ground. Simon turned to the other man and the man's fist hit his chin. His head snapped back. For a moment, he thought blackness would engulf him, but he shook it off and steadied himself, preparing for the next jab.

The one man still laid on the floor as the other advanced on him again. Simon jabbed him in the throat, leaving him winded. He staggered backwards and Simon took the moment to right himself. His hand stung from the impact. The other man rose and charged him, hitting Simon in the chest. He fell against the stone wall, flinching. The man didn't give Simon time to react or move.

He attacked him with multiple punches. Simon pushed him and stumbled away. The man chuckled. Simon, infuriated, pivoted back to him and punched him multiple times. The man fled across the room, catching his breath. He was livid. He looked at the other man. “Grab him and hold him.”

Simon waited patiently until he was within arm’s reach. He jabbed at him multiple times but eventually the man got him in a bear hug from behind, holding his arms. The smiling man cracked his knuckles with glee and made his way to them. Simon struggled against the man holding him, but he didn’t budge. The blows came one after the other until Simon couldn't stay upright. He fell to his knees, and both men cackled with delight.

Smiley held him in place on his knees. “Don’t worry. It’s almost over.”

Was this the end? He closed his eyes and a vision of Annie appeared. The other man took fabric and wrapped it around both his hands, preparing to strangle him. No! Simon would die fighting. The man advanced on him, and Simon, with his last amount of strength jabbed him in the stomach multiple times. He staggered to his feet, propelling the man holding his shoulders backwards until he toppled over. He pivoted and waited for their next attack. Just then the cell door was pulled open. Collins stepped in with one of the guards.

Everyone froze, and Collins bellowed, “What in the hell is going on here?”

The guard looked around confused. “Sir, I am not sure how they got in the cell. I will have a guard escort them away.”

“Now!” Collins demanded.

The man yelled down the hall and two guards entered the room before taking the men away. Simon collapsed on the bed, breathing heavily.

“Are you okay?” Collins asked.

Simon had an uncontrollable urge to laugh but suppressed it. "Barely."

"We need to leave now," Collins said quietly.

Simon staggered to his feet. They made their way down the hallway and out of the godforsaken prison. Simon wanted to fall to his knees in gratitude, but Collins hustled him into a carriage. He collapsed against one of the benches and a man across from him with an American accent chuckled. "I guess just in time."

Simon looked his way and his eyes widened in shock. "The musician."

Clark smirked. "I'm several things. One of those things is a musician."

"What happened to your accent?" Simon questioned.

The man smiled. "Just one of many."

Collins knocked on the carriage, and they started to move. Simon glanced between the two men.

"Clark is a constable as well. He is the one who signed you out."

"Are you working with Shell?" Simon asked, confused.

Clark scowled. "Certainly not. I'm part of a police element established to identify corruption in the police system. Recently, I learned that the highest official of the police in New York City, High Constable Monroe, is connected to Tobias Walker and may have been instrumental in him not being prosecuted."

"How do you know this?"

Clark smiled. "Collins and I are old friends. A few years back he informed me that he didn't think your father's case was handled correctly, but we had no evidence. That was until Walker sent good old Collins here a letter outlining his concerns about you."

"Why do you care?" Simon asked, mistrustful of the man, who until a few moments ago he knew only as a musician.

Clark and Collins' eyes connected. Clark turned back to him. "I will be honest with you. A case like yours wouldn't normally matter to me but because of the connection to the high constable, it does. If we prove he is linked to this, we can unseat him and his corrupt associates."

Simon shook his head. Unbelievable. The only reason these men were assisting him was because of their own agenda.

"I know it is frustrating that no one helped your father but if we can unseat Monroe, the attorney general plans to implement a new police system. One modeled after London's but first we need to prove he is corrupt. This new system will prevent things like what happened to your father."

Simon grunted, skeptical.

"Regardless of Clark's motives, if you help him, your father will be exonerated. That is what you have wanted all along," Collins said.

"What do you have to do with this?" Simon asked him.

"My clients are some of the wealthiest in New York City and so are their friends. Even if we prove Monroe was connected, he can't be unseated without the city's upper echelon supporting it. My clients will support this system change if they know Monroe assisted Walker in covering up his crimes."

Something was still not right about all of this. The item, both Collins and Miss Markam had mentioned, came to mind.

"What was in the vault besides money and gold bars?"

"Do we have your word you will help us?" Clark questioned.

Simon scowled at him. “Regardless of what your intent is, you had my agreement the moment you said my father would be exonerated.”

Clark nodded and slapped him on his shoulder, causing Simon to wince.

“There was one item in the vault that hasn’t been revealed to the public,” Collins began.

Chapter 22

Annie tossed and turned in her bed, unable to sleep. Simon's harsh words ran through her mind. She kept trying to will herself to not think about their encounter in the prison. She closed her eyes again, hoping that this attempt at sleep would work. The silence of the night was interrupted by faint noises coming from the first floor. She frowned and sat up in her bed, listening intently. Drawn by them, she pulled her wrap over her nightgown and made her way from her room to the foyer stairs.

As she peeked over the railing, she gasped. Simon stood below with the investigator, Mr. Collins, and her brother Jack. She hurried down the steps but froze at the foot of the stairs. Standing with them was the musician from the inn. Her brows drew together in confusion. Her gaze darted back to Simon who looked as if he had been beaten unmercifully.

"You're hurt?" she asked him, drawing everyone's attention to her arrival.

He grimaced. "A little roughed up, but I will survive thanks to Collins and Clark here."

She wanted to rush into his arms but stayed rooted to where she was. Her eyes flashed, and she accused, "You lied at the prison!"

He went to her, but she held her hand up. "No. How could you?"

"He did it to save you, my lady," Clark explained.

Annie's eyes snapped back to the musician. "Why are you here?"

"It's a long story. We were just getting ready to explain to your brother."

Annie made her way to the study, not bothering to wait on any of the men. She would not be left out. The fury she felt wouldn't subside. She had almost lost him, but she kept her raging emotions in. She sat in one of the wingback chairs in the sitting area. The men joined her. She glanced at Simon as he grimaced while taking a seat. What had he endured?

Jack outright glared at him, appearing to have no sympathy for him. Annie wished Sam and Clara had stayed at the Peyton townhouse. Her other brother was by far the more understanding one. Annie imagined Mercy was still fast asleep.

"What in the hell is going on?" Jack demanded.

"As I stated before, I'm the investigator that was hired by the bank to look into the theft Miller's father was sent to prison for. What I have not shared is that the bank now believes Miller's father was not the culprit in the crime."

Annie's gaze darted to Simon. That was wonderful news.

Collins continued, "There was an item the family kept in the vault that hasn't turned up yet. When Walker reached out to me about his suspicions about Miller, he mentioned the item. This led me to believe perhaps it was Walker who was involved. Miller already believed this for years, but I was unsure. We didn't have any proof."

The investigator turned to Simon. "At the time I concluded the police had found the right man, and I am sorry for that. I was unaware of the connection between Walker and the High Constable of New York City."

Annie frowned at Clark. "What does this have to do with you?"

"There are changes going on with the New York City

police system. Rampant corruption exists within the system, including high-level officials. The attorney general asked me to ferret out those corrupt men, no matter the level. Collins informed me of this case and Walker's strong ties to High Constable Monroe as well as some of the watchmen. It is my job to identify if actions were taken to protect Walker and if so, make sure those officials are identified and replaced, paving the way for a different police force in New York City."

Annie frowned, perplexed. "Are you saying the bank theft could bring down the entire police system?"

Clark nodded. "I certainly hope so."

She would have never guessed him to be a member of the police. She had never assumed he was anything but a musician. "So you are a constable?"

He winked at her. "Something like that. I'm someone who stays in the background."

"Clark knew who we were when he took the coach with me to Daventry," Simon pointed out.

"I planned on revealing myself to Miller in Liverpool, but I didn't realize that wasn't his final destination, but Blackpool was."

"Why didn't you confront Miller in Daventry or tell him your concerns?" Annie asked.

"We are being very careful because the high constable specifically requested Mr. Shell work this with me, but Clark and I have reason to believe he is here to make sure we only identify Miller as the guilty party," Collins said.

Annie closed her eyes in horror at the blatant disregard Walker had for Simon and his father's life. Not only Walker but the police. It was a shameful tragedy that disgusted her, but she wasn't the least surprised.

“Why would you confess?” Annie said, looking at Simon.

“Walker and his henchman found us while we were in Blackpool. Lemming is dead, likely by Walker’s hands. He insinuated if I didn’t confess, harm would come to you. He planned to have me done away with while I was in Newgate, but Collins stepped in.”

She glared at him. “You could have lost your life. My family would make sure I was safe. They always do.”

A flash of tenderness crossed Jack’s face, but Annie's gaze flicked back to Simon. “You are an imbecile.”

Clark snorted with laughter and Simon scowled at him before turning back to Annie. “It was the only way I could keep you safe.”

“By sacrificing yourself!” she snapped.

“It was the only way,” Simon reiterated quietly.

“My lady, Walker was in Blackpool and had a man watching you, even when you traveled back to Liverpool. You were unprotected. There were no other options. Collins and I didn’t know you were both in Blackpool until Shell was alerted by Walker’s henchman. I failed you there,” Clark said.

Annie pursed her lips in disbelief. Clark didn’t fail her. The man she loved did.

“I believe the plan was to do away with Miller in Blackpool, but they didn’t expect you to be there. They had to change plans and bring him back to London. In some ways you saved his life with your actions,” Clark added.

Jack growled. “Pure recklessness.”

She glared at her brother defiantly, not regretting anything. Still, anger swirled in her that Simon would have given his life to save her. If he was not so badly beaten, she might consider taking a swing at him.

"So what is to be done about this now?" Jack asked.

"We need to prove Walker's guilt. Once we do that, Collins and I will bring him back to New York City to be tried and the men who protected him will also be removed from their positions. But right now, we only have Miller's word. Unfortunately, he is wanted, and it won't hold up."

"Why all the secrets?" Annie asked.

Collins looked to Clark, who said, "The high constable is the highest-level police official in New York City. He will do everything possible to stay in power, and he has supporters. The attorney general can't remove him unless we have solid proof. Until we have proof, we can't let anyone know that we or the attorney general suspect Walker of the theft or that the high constable helped cover it up."

Annie couldn't believe the tale she was being told. From what Simon said, Walker was a lowly worker at the bank. "How is Walker connected to this high constable?"

"Walker is the high constable's second cousin, not a close connection. Still, once he discovered who was behind the theft, he quickly worked to have Walker's part covered up to prevent any sullying of the family name. He wrote the letters that introduced him into London society," Collins said.

"Walker will be taken back to America and tried," Simon bit out.

Annie's gaze swung to Simon, wishing she could make this all disappear for him. She turned back to Clark and Collins. "How do you prove his guilt?"

Collins and Clark looked between each other silently trying to determine what they wanted to share. Finally, Collins said,

“There is a tremendously valuable necklace known as the Lovely Lotus that was in the vault. The Lotus was made in the Orient over a century ago and contains some of the largest gemstones in the world. Some even speculate it is the most expensive necklace ever created. The piece contains sizable diamonds that drop down into an enormous pendant shaped as a lotus made of diamonds, rubies, spinels, and jade. The family doesn’t care about anything but retrieving it.”

“You think Walker has it?” Jack asked, skeptically.

Collins and Clark, both nodded. Collins added, “It would be difficult to sell. We believe instead Walker hid it away. When he wrote to me he said he believed Miller had gold from the theft and perhaps a necklace. We now believe that Walker was holding both and set Miller up. Only a select few knew about the necklace and no one from the police as the family didn’t trust them.”

“So, if we find the necklace, we will not only prove my father’s innocence but also bring down those who had a part in his wrongful conviction.”

“Why didn’t you come to me with this before?” Jack demanded of Simon.

Annie studied her brother and saw the hurt he was trying to hide. Simon was like family to them. Her brother was angry about her and Simon, but he may be even more upset that Simon hadn’t trusted him.

Simon grimaced as he sat a little straighter. “I didn’t want to jeopardize or involve you in something potentially dangerous.”

“We have done nothing but do that to you. And with regard to Annie, what are your intentions?”

“Jack!” Annie snapped, blushing furiously.

Clark cleared his throat, and everyone turned back to him.

"Before you discuss such a personal matter, I wanted to point out we still need to find the necklace."

"I think it is with Miss Markam. She is missing, and I asked Devons to find her, but I haven't been able to follow-up," Simon explained.

Collins and Clark nodded. Simon turned back to Jack and said, "I need your help. Clark is going to reveal to Shell that he is in London and that he and Collins escorted me from Newgate. The plan is to say I escaped the carriage. I need a place to stay, and a duke's residence is likely not the first place they will search, even if they suspect I'm here."

"Of course," Jack said without any hesitation.

Annie smiled at him. He may be angry at Simon, but he was still loyal. She turned to Collins and Clark and asked, "Won't Shell or Walker suspect something?"

Clark smirked. "Collins offered to let me knock him around to make it look real."

Collins rolled his eyes. "We agreed that we would both take a couple hits."

Clark and Collins rose. Clark said, "We will return tomorrow to discuss next steps. Can Devons be trusted if we reach out to him?"

"I plan to have him pay us a visit tomorrow afternoon. He likely will not tell you anything unless he knows Miller is safe," Jack explained.

"We'll return tomorrow," Clark said, before grinning at Collins. "Let's go give you a thrashing."

Collins snorted. "We'll see who thrashes who."

They made their way out of the house. Jack, Annie, and Simon sat in silence. Jack rose and said, "Leave us, Annie."

Annie stood and said, “Don’t order me about.”

Jack glanced at her incredulously.

She was over brothers and lovers. “I am leaving but not because you demanded me to. I’m leaving you both here because I’m exhausted. Exhausted by all the men in my life.”

Both Simon and Jack frowned at her. She walked out of the room, her head held high and slammed the door.

~

Simon stared at the wooden door, still shaking from the force Annie used to close it. His eyes shifted back to Jack, who appeared at a loss for words. He frowned at the door before turning back to Simon. He scowled and stomped his way over to a table, pouring them both a glass of brandy. He pushed it into Simon’s hand. “Drink. You look awful.”

Jack paced, not saying anything. Finally, he stopped. “Why wouldn’t you share this with us? We have asked you to do so much to help our family. We would’ve gone after Walker with you.”

Anger and frustration emanated from him.

“I only meant to protect all of you. You and your family have been through so much already. I didn’t know how this would end. I still don’t.”

“Walker will go to prison,” Jack said with certainty.

“And if he doesn’t?”

Jack’s eyes widened. “You mean to exact your revenge yourself if he doesn’t pay for his crimes by the courts?”

Simon remained silent. He didn’t know what he would do and hoped it didn’t come to that. Walker had done away with Lemming and there was still the question of what happened to

Miss Markam. Beyond that, he had made Simon a wanted man. Simon refused to let him walk away, and he was skeptical any police system in New York City would see Walker tried. "He will pay for what he has done but my hope is that the courts will handle it."

"And if not?"

Simon shrugged.

"Why not take your revenge now if it means so much to you?" Jack asked.

He knew Jack knew why. It was because of Annie, not because he was a good man. The temptation of a life with her even now still overruled his desire for revenge.

"You aren't a killer. Taking a life, no matter how awful the person is, stays with you," Jack said bluntly.

Simon raised a brow at him, wondering why he was so certain.

Jack sat across from him. "The woman who ran the orphanage Annie, Sam, and I were at was killed by a boy who lived there."

Simon nodded. "Annie told me."

"My family helped him get acquitted in his case. Even years later, he always said his actions still haunted him. My father said the same thing after he participated in ridding Philadelphia of the monster that attempted to buy Annie from the orphanage. There is a lifetime price you pay when you take someone's life."

Simon scowled, not wanting to hear Jack's words. He remained silent, knowing nothing he said would be right.

"So, if Clark and Collins are able to take Walker into custody, you will be fine with that."

Simon nodded. Jack's eyes pierced his. "If not, I will not allow my sister to have to bear the aftermath of your choices. She has been through too much already."

Simon snapped, "I only want the best for your sister."

"A man who spends the rest of his life haunted by the decisions based on his thirst for revenge is not what is best for her."

Simon looked away. He couldn't deny what Jack was saying. He would not lie to him. Jack slammed his glass down on a table. "What is it to be, friend?"

"I want justice, I can't deny that. Clark and Collins seem to think he will go to prison," Simon bit out.

Jack stood, pacing back and forth. He turned back to Simon. "She loves you. I wasn't sure that was something Annie would ever find. Not because she isn't capable of love but because I wasn't sure she would allow herself to be that open with anyone. But then she met you. She would give all of herself to you. I won't see her devotion squandered by a man who can't let go of his past or his anger."

"You have no idea what I have been through."

Jack glared at him. "You're right, I don't, but I know what my sister has endured. If you can't give her a life without misery, then leave now."

Simon could let go of his anger if Walker paid. He would do it for Annie. Walker would go to prison, and Simon would never think of him again. "I'm not leaving. I choose your sister above all else."

Jack studied him. "I hope so. Revenge has a way of lodging itself deep inside you, but I can promise you from first-hand knowledge it is a lonely way to live. I almost lost Mercy because of my own desire for revenge. Every day I am thankful I pulled myself back from it. Hell, I am glad she pulled me. Without her I would not have found the ability to forgive."

He and Jack were more similar than Simon had ever considered. He shouldn't be surprised. Jack, himself, at an early age, had lost everything and revenge had driven him to almost destroy not only his family but his chance at love with his wife. In the end, Jack's better side had prevailed.

"Promise me, you will move on once you and your father are proven innocent of these crimes, regardless of what happens to Walker."

Something held Simon back from promising him that he, too, could be a better man. He was so far away from forgiveness. Walker had not only destroyed his father's life but was on the verge of destroying his.

"I want to help Clark and Collins prove Walker's guilt. If it all works out, this conversation will be pointless. Your sister is the woman I want now and forever."

Jack nodded. "Don't forget that. Focus on that. If you don't, you will lose everything. Put her and your happiness above revenge."

Simon nodded.

"I expect a proposal from you when this is done," Jack stated.

Simon glanced at him, somewhat shocked Jack would consider it.

"You are the man my sister wants and one of the few men I trust in this world. Even if I want to plant my fist in your face right now."

Simon's eyes filled with respect, and he said, "I hope the day comes when I can ask for her hand."

Jack rose and Simon stayed seated. "I think I will stay here a little longer."

His friend passed him and squeezed his shoulder. "Don't lose sight of what you have."

Simon nodded, overwhelmed with too many emotions to say anything. Jack made it to the door and glanced back at him with narrowed eyes. "I expect you to not leave the visitor's wing once upstairs."

Simon had the grace to blush, and Jack sighed, leaving him. Jack had given him much to think about. What did he want more, happiness or revenge? His mind flashed back to a conversation he had with his father during one of his visits to Blackwell Island.

"Promise me you will move on. Find happiness," his father pleaded.

Simon scowled. "How can you ask that of me?"

His father's rough bony fingers grasped his hand. "Because I need you to be happy. I need to know you will not spend your life bitter and angry."

Simon shook his head. "You ask too much of me."

"It is all I ask of you."

Simon came back to the present. Melancholy thoughts lingered in his mind. His father long ago wanted him to give up his quest to see him proven innocent. Yet, Simon had refused, even after his death. He took a sip of brandy. He would once Walker was taken back to America to be tried for his father's crimes. And if it didn't happen? No, he wouldn't think about that. It would happen.

Chapter 23

Annie, dressed in her nightclothes, quietly tiptoed down the hall of the visitor's wing of the Peyton townhouse. She did her best to be as quiet as possible. It would do her no good to wake the house. Still, she needed to see Simon. When she left the study, she had been too angry to deal with him or her brother.

She was only a few doors away from Simon's sleeping quarters when she felt a tap on the back of her forearm causing her to jump. She spun around and came face to face with her brother. Shockingly, his expression was neither fury nor disappointment but concern.

He grabbed her and pulled her into an empty bedroom. She yanked her arm away from him, furious to be manhandled.

"Leave it be until tomorrow," he said quietly.

"I'm tired of your boorishness. You treat me as if I will fall apart. Go lord over someone else."

He looked away, hurt. They stood there silently in the dark room. She and Jack had been through so much. A sliver of guilt coursed through her.

He turned back. "I am your brother, and I will interfere when I feel necessary."

"Yes, because you are the duke."

"No! Because I'm worried for you. It isn't any different from when you, Annie, and Sam have tried to involve yourselves in my life; being a duke is irrelevant. I hate when you say things like that."

Annie took a deep breath, knowing she was taking her anger

out on Jack. Anger that was meant for Simon.

"I need to speak with him."

"You can see him tomorrow. Take tonight to think about what you want to say."

Jack's words weren't unwise. Still, she desperately wanted to confront Simon. Annie swallowed the lump in her throat. "He almost died."

"He loves you. There isn't anything I wouldn't do for Mercy, including giving my life."

She scowled.

He ran his fingers through his hair. "Join me for a drink."

Annie hesitated, still wanting to find a way to see Simon. Her brother walked to the door and held the door for her. She rolled her eyes. The request clearly was more of a demand. Oh, how she wished she could blame his arrogant tendencies on being a duke, but this had always been Jack.

She followed him to the second floor sitting room, still aglow from the fire crackling in the fireplace. She sat on the sofa and Jack poured them both some brandy. Annie was grateful that while ladies didn't often drink brandy, the Kincaide family had made a custom of it as an end of evening drink.

He handed her a glass before settling into a wingback chair and stretching out his legs.

They sat there in silence until Jack said, "My only hope is that you are happy. That your days are filled with laughter."

She raised a skeptical brow at him. "What makes you think I won't be with Miller?"

Jack took a sip of his brandy. "I think if Walker is arrested and Miller's father's name is cleared, you could be. If not, then I worry his life will be consumed by making sure Walker pays for his acts."

"You and I are the last people who can judge him. We came to London for revenge."

"Yes, but in the end, we didn't choose revenge over our loved ones."

She frowned at him. "Partially because our own cousin killed the man who caused us so much grief."

Annie took a sip of her brandy, not understanding how Jack could draw a parallel between the two.

"My point is that even after that incident, we chose to move on and not dwell on it."

"That is what will happen once Walker is arrested."

"And if he is not? If he stays a wanted man?" Jack asked.

Annie didn't want to think about that. She would still love him. If they had to flee, they would. She would stay by his side. She wouldn't desert him. Still, she remained silent knowing that somehow sharing that would prove Jack's point.

"I won't let you go down a path that leads to misery no matter how much you love him. Your love for each other will turn to resentment."

Annie's eyes flashed. "You have no idea if that is true."

Jack stood; exhaustion emanated from his body. "I need sleep. Please do as I ask and speak with him in the morning."

He wasn't the only one that sleep was starting to beckon to. Annie still wanted to speak with Simon but perhaps Jack was right. She could wait until tomorrow. Not wanting to argue anymore, she nodded.

Relief passed over his face. He leaned down and kissed her

cheek. "I love you, Annie, and I hope for your sake that Collins and Clark can sort this all out. But promise me you will think about your own happiness if that doesn't happen."

Her brother never shared his feelings or made loving declarations, so Annie had to force herself to not become emotional. She knew he was worried. She nodded, and he made his way to the door. As he reached the door, she called out, "Jack."

He turned back, frowning.

"I love you too."

Her brother smiled back at her before disappearing down the hallway. Annie stayed on the sofa, sipping the rest of her brandy. She frowned as she gazed at the fire.

The next morning Annie made her way to the breakfast room, hoping Simon would be there. Her hopes were quickly proven real. Simon and Mercy sat at the table eating their breakfast. Simon's eyes roamed over her as she took a seat causing her stomach to flutter with nerves. She pushed them away. She had nothing to be nervous about. She smiled at one of the servers already placing her normal meal in front of her.

"Annie, I didn't think you would be up until much later," Mercy said.

Annie smiled at Mercy. Her sister-in-law was an early riser. She always had been. Her and Jack had many, some would say scandalous, early morning encounters at Hyde Park when he was wooing her. Annie on the other hand was not a morning person. She often stayed up late which caused her to sleep in. But she knew Simon was likely to be up. He was an early morning person as well. She grimaced, thinking about the early risers in her life.

"Where is Jack?" she asked, knowing even though they were

both up late, he wouldn't sleep in.

"He went to visit Devons and possibly Derry. He was hesitant to send a note, thinking it could be intercepted."

"When is the meeting here with them supposed to happen?"

Mercy and Simon glanced at each other. Frustration grew in Annie. "I won't be left out of this."

Simon rolled his eyes. How dare he? After everything she had done for him. She pursed her lips and glared at him. His mouth twitched up as if he wanted to smile. He was still badly bruised from his fight the night before, but he seemed to be feeling better.

Mercy rose. "I think I will go for a walk in the gardens."

"It's February," Simon pointed out.

She smiled cheekily at him. "It is never too early to plan the beds."

As she left, she motioned for the servers to follow her, leaving Annie and Simon alone. They sat across from each other, separated by the massive table. Silence filled the room, only interrupted by the faint ticking of a clock.

"I know you are furious with me," Simon said.

"You lied to me. And said I was a bit of fun."

He winced at her words before covering his bruised but still handsome face with his hands.

"Do you love me or is that a lie?"

The fact she had to ask made her blush with embarrassment. He removed his hands away from his face, frowning in disbelief.

He rose from his chair and pulled her up by her forearms. "I love you. I will always love you."

His eyes blazed with devotion and Annie felt foolish for asking but his words at the prison were so drastically different.

"I'm so sorry I said those things to you, but we couldn't tip Shell off. It killed me to watch you walk away from that cell, thinking I didn't care about you. I wanted to scream out to you."

Annie pulled out of his arms, pacing. Eventually, she turned back to him. "Do you know what I would have gone through if something happened to you?"

He looked away.

She continued, "Do you know the devastation I would have felt if you died?"

"I'm sorry. You are the last person I would ever want to hurt," he insisted.

They both stared at one another, silent. Finally, she said, with a shaky voice. "Promise you will not put yourself in danger again. You will allow Collins and Clark to take the lead on this."

Annie worried that as Jack said Simon wouldn't be able to let any of this go.

"Of course."

She frowned at him. Unsure she believed him. As if sensing her concern, he took her in his arms and said, "Annie, I want a life with you. That is what matters."

Annie wanted to believe him. She pulled him closer and ignored her concerns.

~

Simon Miller stood in Jack's study with Annie, Jack, Sam, and Clark waiting on Devons to arrive. Jack didn't provide Devons with many details in their earlier meeting, just to meet at the townhouse.

"How did your discussion with Shell go?" Simon asked Clark who sat lounging by the fire.

A laugh erupted from Clark. "That man attempted to take a swing at me. He said I didn't have the authority to have you released. I can't stand him."

Simon smiled at Clark's tone. "Was he right? Do you have the authority?"

"Of course, I do. I am here at the behest of the attorney general. Last I checked, that outranked High Constable Monroe."

Jack and Sam laughed at his condescending tone. Simon shook his head at all of them. Annie stood, staring pensively out a window. Simon made his way over to her.

"How are you?"

She shrugged. "Fine. Hoping that Devons arrives with good news."

"Me too. I'm also worried that Shell may come here looking for you."

Jack, eavesdropping on their conversation, said, "I have the same concerns. I would hate for you to be found before Clark and Collins are able to prove your innocence."

Simon's gaze flitted to him, wondering for a brief moment if Jack was being sarcastic. But apparently not; he just stared at him with a concerned frown. "After we speak with Devons, I will leave."

"I am going with you," Annie stated.

He shook his head but didn't need to say anything further because Jack bit out, "Absolutely not."

"That may not be necessary. I believe Shell, Collins, and the Peelers are looking for you in the dock area. Rumors are swirling that you secured passage to the Continent."

"Rumors from whom?" Annie asked.

Clark winked at her. "Some loud drunk at one of the taverns."

Simon suspected the drunk was the man winking at Annie. Annie smiled at Clark, impressed with his cleverness. Simon clenched his fists at his side, annoyed at their friendliness. He forced himself to get over it. Clark was doing everything in his power to help him.

"You are welcome here for as long as is necessary," Jack said.

"And my home is open to you," Sam added.

Simon was grateful to his friends. They were risking so much by offering to house him.

"You should have come to us sooner," Jack muttered.

Simon cringed at the statement. Jack was right. He should have trusted his friends, instead of trying to do everything on his own. He stared at Jack and knew their bond was a lifelong one, but his secrets had tarnished it and only time would repair it.

"I should have," he agreed.

Jack glanced at him, startled, but the butler entering the room stopped any further discussion. He looked at Jack and said, "Your Grace, Mr. Devons is here along with Lord Derry. Would you like me to show both of them in?"

"Who is this Derry fellow?" Clark asked, suspiciously.

"He is someone who can be trusted," Sam said to Clark.

Everyone in the room nodded in agreement but turned to him for his concurrence. No more secrets, Simon thought. These men, their wives, and Annie were his friends. He would not keep them in the dark any longer. He nodded.

"Show them in," Jack requested.

The butler left and a moment later opened the door for Devons and Derry. At the sight of Simon, both Derry and Devons smiled.

"You are here. I suspected that to be the case from Jack's vague request. The Peelers are all over the dock areas looking for you," Devons said to Simon.

"I know. Things are not quite as they seem," Simon explained.

Derry raised an eyebrow. "What does that mean?"

"Clark," Simon said, nodding towards the man, before continuing, "is working to dismantle corruption within the New York City police system. He believes my father's imprisonment was to cover up the involvement of Walker, who is the family member of a high-ranking police official.

Clark took over and filled them in on the rest of the details. Devons and Derry appeared shocked.

"So, you are a New York City constable?" Devons asked.

Clark grinned. "Something like that but I do more undercover work directly for the attorney general."

"And you believe this necklace still exists?" Derry asked him.

"I do. It's very valuable. The family who owns it has been looking for it for years. Even if it were sold in England, word would eventually get back to them."

Simon changed the topic, unable to wait another minute to hear about what Devons had found out about Miss Markam. "Have you discovered the location of Mrs. Walker's maid?"

"I haven't been able to find Miss Markam but something

interesting happened since you left. I had someone watching Walker's house to see if she returned, and she hasn't, but Mrs. Walker has disappeared."

Everyone in the room was quiet for a moment. Simon wondered what it meant. Would Walker dare to harm a lady well known within the *ton* and more importantly his own wife?

"How do you know she is missing? Your man didn't spot her leaving?" Clark asked.

Devons shrugged. "No. The reason I know she isn't there is because Walker is also looking for her."

"Where could she be?" Annie wondered. "Did she have any visitors?"

Devons nodded. "A few. One that struck me as odd. Lord Bromley visited her multiple times before her disappearance. I assumed it was a lover's tryst type of thing."

Was Bromley connected to Mrs. Walker's disappearance?

"Perhaps he was visiting Tobias Walker?" Sam pointed out.

Bromley hated Walker. There was no way. Simon was skeptical that it was some type of lovers' tryst as Bromley had recently been wooing Annie. He looked at Annie, and she flushed from head to toe. Did she still think of him or consider him? Annoyance filled Simon, but he pushed the feelings away. Annie loved him and he loved her.

"No, he was out of town," Devons responded.

"Yes, he was in Blackpool," Simon said, darkly.

"Bromley was close with Mrs. Walker when they were children but once she married that ended," Derry explained.

Sam winked at him. "It is always good to have someone who is caught up on society gossip."

Derry didn't even respond, just glowered at him for insinuating he enjoyed such drivel.

Simon nodded. "I spoke with Bromley briefly at the estate party that Jack and Mercy hosted. Bromley doesn't have a friendship with Tobias Walker. He may despise him as much as I do."

"We need to call on him," Annie said, energized.

Everyone nodded. "I should speak with him," she added.

"No," Simon snipped, knowing he was being a prickly jealous arse.

She frowned at him. "Bromley and I are close. If he knows something, he will more likely share it with me than anyone else. It isn't as if you can go call on him yourself."

"You're close because you almost married him," Simon bit out. "I will figure out a way to visit him."

She rolled her eyes and turned to her brothers. "Tell him, I should be the one to speak with him."

"What my sister wants me to say is you are being unnecessarily irrational. Even though Bromley wanted to marry her, she turned him down prior to leaving on her little adventure with you. He would have been a solid match, might I add."

"Jack!" Annie hissed.

He shrugged. "You are right. It should be you. Sam or I will escort you."

"Can this Bromley be trusted?" Clark asked.

"I would say yes. Bromley never approved of Walker," Derry added.

Jack snorted. “You are really up on the gossip.”

Everyone laughed, including Simon. It was nice to have a moment of levity with his friends. Simon supposed it made sense. Bromley did care for Annie and if anyone would be able to get information from him, it would be her.

“Be careful,” he said to her.

She smiled at him. “I’ll be fine.”

“What he really is saying is don't take one look at the respectable lord and realize you made a mistake,” Jack said dryly.

Everyone laughed.

Chapter 24

Annie stood in Lord Bromley's drawing room with Jack and Sam. The butler had been startled at the unannounced visit and said Bromley likely wouldn't see them. Jack glowered at him, and he escorted them to the sitting room before he sought out Bromley.

Sam shook his head. "It's strange that Lord Bromley has a part in this."

Annie shrugged. "The *ton* isn't so large."

"No it isn't," Jack muttered.

She smiled at her brother. Grateful to have him there, actually grateful both her brothers were there. She was on the verge of ruin, and they were still by her side. So far gossip hadn't gotten out she had been missing and with Simon, but it would eventually. Scandals always did. Yet, neither Jack nor Sam abandoned her or wrote her off. Jack was furious, but that was his nature. She adored her family even when she didn't like them all that much.

She glanced at them. They were handsome, entitled men with the world at their feet. If she closed her eyes, she could picture the three of them at the orphanage curled up in one bed, trying to stay warm. Her brothers not only survived but excelled since those awful days.

"Why are you looking at us like that?" Sam asked bemused.

She laughed and wrapped her arm in his. "I'm just lucky to have both of you. Whether it is in an orphanage in Philadelphia, or here in London. Thank you."

Sam flushed but Jack snorted. "You should be grateful we

are still here, especially with your scandal hanging over our heads."

She rolled her eyes at her brother, knowing he was all bluster. "Funny how easy it is for you to toss the word scandal at me when you both ruined your wives prior to being wed to them."

Sam chuckled. Jack sighed. "It's different for us."

"I know because you are men. Lucky for you," she said dryly.

Jack's expression softened. "I just want what is best for you."

She smiled. "I know and I want Miller. If there was no Miller, I would likely be off somewhere creating a scandal you would hate anyway. Perhaps I would have opened my own tavern or become an explorer. You think men are so special but really ladies can live full colorful lives as well. I was never going to be the proper London lady, but I tried for you."

He smiled softly at that. "I love you, that is why I worry."

Goodness, two declarations of affection from her brother in such a short time was absolutely shocking. She released Sam's arm and looped her arm through Jack's. "I know."

They all smiled at one another, and the moment ended when the door was thrown open by Lord Bromley.

"I was shocked to hear I had a visitor but delighted that my guests were the Kincaides," he said, entering the room before bowing to Jack.

Jack waved him off, and Bromley indicated for everyone to sit. Bromley stared at Annie inquisitively, and Annie realized he likely thought she'd changed her mind. She flushed and not wanting him to get the wrong idea, quickly said, "My lord, we wanted to speak with you about Mrs. Walker."

Both her brothers glanced at her, surprised by her blunt tone, and she ignored their stares. He stared at her in puzzlement and was quiet but eventually said, “I know Mrs. Walker. Our family estates as children were not far from each other. We spent our childhoods together, but we haven’t been close since she married.”

“You haven’t seen her since she was married?” Sam asked.

Bromley forced a smile. “Not often, why all the questions?”

Annie took a deep breath. Hoping she could trust Bromley with what she was about to tell him. “Simon Miller has been charged with a crime he didn’t commit. He believes Walker was guilty of the actual crime. It was a bank theft in New York City.”

Bromley didn’t look shocked. If anything, he seemed as if he was doing his best to not reveal any emotion. “What does this have to do with me?”

Annie continued, “Miller was working with a maid in Walker’s employ. He believed he could find evidence that incriminated Walker but both she and Mrs. Walker have disappeared. Miller has been accused of being an accomplice because they found some of the stolen items in his living quarters.”

Bromley stood and poured himself a glass of brandy. He took a sip. “This is all shocking, but I still don’t see why you would seek me out. I haven’t seen Mrs. Walker since we were young.”

“We know you visited her multiple times before she disappeared. We need to speak with her. There is an item that will implicate Walker and clear Miller’s name,” Sam explained.

Bromley's face turned hard, and his eyes narrowed. “How do you know this?”

Sam and Jack shrugged. Annie rose and made her way to him. She took his one free hand in both of hers. “There is one item that could fix this, and Miller believes Mrs. Walker and Miss Markam have it. Do you have any idea where they might be?”

"I knew you were smitten with him," Bromley whispered.

She released his hand, sensing even if he had information, he wouldn't share any details. He knew something. He didn't seem surprised by anything they shared.

He took another sip. "I will look into it but honestly I don't think I can help."

She nodded, feeling like she'd failed Simon. If Bromley didn't have answers, they had nowhere else to look. She took a deep breath. "I am sorry I hurt you but please don't hold that against Miller. If you have evidence—"

"I would never do that," he stated flatly.

Annie believed him but still she got the sense he knew more than he said. Jack and Sam rose.

"Come on, Annie. I don't think we will find any answers here," Jack said.

She nodded and took his arm. As they made their way to the door, she turned back to Bromley one last time. "If you do know where they are, please tell them if they come forward, they will be protected."

He pressed his lips together in a flat line and gave one nod.

~

Simon sat with Annie, Jack, and Mercy in the drawing room. They just finished dinner and were having an after-dinner drink. Disappointment and tiredness filled the room. He took a sip of his brandy, enjoying how the liquid numbed some of his emotions. They had been optimistic that Bromley would know where Mrs. Walker and Miss Markam were. Perhaps it was ludicrous that it would be so simple.

With that lead dead, everyone was unsure about what was

next. Simon himself was uncertain. Should he leave? Turn himself in? When he suggested giving himself up, Clark had been alarmed and told him if it came to that, to flee.

Still, Clark tried to be optimistic before leaving to inform Collins of the false lead. He believed they would still find a way. Simon wanted to be confident but wasn't. He wanted this finished. His eyes flitted over to Annie. She was stunning in a deep blue dress with her dark hair swept up on the top of her head. He longed to be free to touch her.

Without the necklace, his only option was to leave if he didn't want to go to prison. Or he could go after Walker, he thought to himself. His fury toward the man grew every day. Could he really kill the man? Then what would he do?

His gaze darted to Annie. He thought about Jack's concern that Annie being with him would lead her into a life of misery. He was right. Simon would never let that happen. He loved her too much. He would leave her behind, even if he broke her heart.

A knock on the front door startled all of them. Annie's lovely blue eyes connected with his. They all heard the butler quickly make his way to the door.

"Good evening, I request to see His Grace," a familiar voice requested. Jack stood before making his way out the door. Simon stood to join him, but Annie shook her head, recognizing it as Lord Bromley's.

"We don't know if we can trust him," she pointed out.

She was right. Still, he hated being cooped up while they all did so much for him. He stood and leaned against a windowsill. There was murmuring in the hall. Simon did his best to hear what was being said but then heard a familiar female voice. He placed his glass down and strode from the room.

"Miller," Annie called out, trailing behind him along with

Mercy.

He stood in the center of the foyer and looked towards the door. Bromley, dressed in a shockingly bright orange waistcoat stood with both Mrs. Walker and Miss Markam. Relief coursed through him. Miss Markam was fine. He had been so worried Walker had done something to her on his account. Everyone stood in the foyer staring at each other.

Jack cleared his throat, "Why don't we go back into the drawing room?"

Simon headed into the room and stood by the door. As Miss Markam entered, she stopped, and her eyes filled with relief at the sight of him. "I am so sorry, Mr. Miller. I wanted to reach out but knew Mr. Walker was looking for me."

He nodded, unexpectedly overcome with emotion. He truly worried that he had cost this woman her life. "I'm glad you're fine."

She smiled at him tentatively before continuing into the drawing room. Simon sat down in somewhat of a daze, still shocked by the turn of events. The Bromley lead had seemed hopeless a mere few moments ago. He glanced at Bromley who was studying Annie and a sliver of jealousy unwound itself in his belly, but he tamped it down. Bromley was here to help. It didn't matter why.

After they were all seated, Bromley said, "I apologize for not being forthright earlier, but I didn't want to reveal any information I had about Mrs. Walker or Miss Markam until I spoke with them. They both realize how dangerous Walker is."

"They were at your house when we visited?" Annie questioned.

Bromley looked at Mrs. Walker and she nodded. He turned back to Annie. "Yes. Mrs. Walker and Miss Markam came to me a few days ago. Miss Markam found a keepsake of Walker's hidden away in his study but shortly afterwards, Walker discovered the item was missing. Miss Markam panicked and fled."

Miss Markam turned to Simon. "There was a safe in Walker's study that was never opened. I kept checking it to see if he would leave it open by accident, but he never did. Then one night, he and a few of the men he hires for protection loaded almost a dozen bags with something. I couldn't get close enough to see. After they left, I went in and pulled on the door, and to my surprise it opened."

"It had to have been the gold bars," Jack said.

Miss Markam's eyes filled with tears. "I'm sorry I was unable to warn you what they were planning, Mr. Miller, but I just had no idea."

"You have done so much for me. You couldn't have known."

She sniffed. "Still, to see you as a wanted man in the papers was dreadful. You are a good man."

Simon reached across and squeezed her hand. She smiled back at him and composed herself. "I sent you a letter and then fled to my sister's house. I was too scared to leave her house but when days passed and I saw the information about you in the paper, I knew I needed to do something else. I was able to get word to Mrs. Walker where I was, and that I thought her husband meant to harm me."

"I would never let that happen," Mrs. Walker said to her, reassuringly before turning back to everyone. "Once Miss Markam told me what was going on, I asked Lord Bromley to assist us. My husband has been in a rage since Miss Markam left, looking everywhere for her and for the item she found."

"You have the necklace," Annie asked, hopeful.

Mrs. Walker nodded and pulled out a velvet pouch. She retrieved the necklace and placed it on the table. Simon had never seen anything so exquisite. The jeweled flower was the size of his hand. It was something a king or queen would have. The necklace itself was made of connected diamonds that shimmered.

“It is absolutely magnificent. No wonder the owner wants it back so desperately,” Mercy whispered.

Everyone nodded in agreement. Mrs. Walker looked at Simon. “I always suspected my husband's money came from some type of ill-gotten means, but when you approached Miss Markam, it confirmed what I already knew. This is the only item Tobias was ever protective of. He showed it to me only a handful of times, but he kept it locked up in our safe that only he had the key to.”

“Would you be willing to testify that Walker has had this item since you met?” Simon said.

“Yes, of course. My husband is not a good man, and I hope to use this necklace to obtain a divorce.”

“We will help you in any way we can,” Jack said.

She smiled stiffly at him and continued, “A few days ago, Bromley was able to retrieve Miss Markam from her sister's house. Bromley and I have been meeting to discuss what we should do. My husband has built many connections since arriving in London, so I was leery of going to the police.”

Mrs. Walker took a deep breath. “Unfortunately, a few days ago, my husband discovered Bromley was visiting me and flew into a rage. I knew I had to leave.”

“Leonora—” Bromley said, frowning.

She held her hand up. “After he was done with me, he left for his clubs, and I fled. I have been resting at Bromley’s residence since.”

"I'm so sorry," Simon said.

He studied the petite woman in front of him. She was so different from Annie. She had blonde curly hair and brown eyes with a smattering of freckles across her face. He glanced at Bromley who sat next to her, protectively. Who was she to him? Not that it mattered. Simon was grateful she'd decided to come to the Peyton townhouse.

"No need to apologize. I entered the marriage of my own free will. My father would say it is my punishment for making such fanciful choices."

"If your father was alive, he would rip him to shreds," Bromley growled.

Bromley cared for Mrs. Walker, Simon realized. Pain covered his face, and he seemed to be refraining pulling her into his arms.

She looked down and took a deep breath before looking back up. "My husband is a dangerous man. He will not hesitate to hurt anyone if he needs to protect himself. But if there is a way you can have him arrested for his crimes, I will do anything to help."

"I can't believe he left the safe open," Simon said, stunned.

"It was a mistake. He was yelling and rushing the men loading the bags. I'm assuming that the bags contained the gold bars found at your residence," Miss Markam said.

Simon nodded in agreement.

"So, Miller, can you guarantee Walker will be arrested for his crimes if we provide you with this necklace?" Bromley asked.

"I can," Simon said, feeling hopeful.

He explained to Bromley, Mrs. Walker, and Miss Markam

everything Collins and Clark had told him. Afterwards Mrs. Walker turned to Bromley and said, "This will allow me to truly be free of him."

"You will be, regardless. I will send you anywhere you like but that man will never lay another finger on you again," Bromley said.

She smiled at him, grateful. Bromley placed a reassuring hand on hers. Simon glanced at Annie to see if her suitor's affection for another bothered her, but she was fixated on the necklace. She picked it up and cradled it in her hand in awe.

"It is certainly a lovely piece," Jack said dryly.

She stared at him with so much hope in her eyes. "I couldn't care less what it looks like. It is Simon's proof that he and his father are innocent."

Her eyes moved back to Simon, and he was overcome with emotion but nodded.

Miss Markam smiled and looked at her employer affectionately. "Mr. Miller's innocence and my lady's freedom."

Simon nodded and looked at Jack. "Can you send for Clark and Collins?"

Chapter 25

Annie shut the door to her room and sighed. She had hoped to see Simon before retiring for the evening, but from the moment Clark arrived until the last person left, the house was abuzz with activity. An arrest warrant had been issued for Walker and Simon was no longer wanted.

She smiled that Simon was free.

"Did I ever tell you how much I love your smile?"

Annie spun in the direction of the voice and saw Simon standing by one of her bedroom windows. Her heart thumped wildly as she took in the sight of him. He still had his beard, but it was now neatly trimmed. Her eyes roamed down him in a way that would be inappropriate outside of the private setting they were in. She flushed, envisioning his strong arms holding her and his muscular form beneath his clothes.

Her eyes connected with his and she smiled. His face was filled with happiness, and he appeared more at ease than she had seen him in a long time.

"Proper Simon Miller in my room. I wasn't expecting that," she whispered.

He walked to her, and her desire for him intensified. He smiled at her cockily, and she knew it was evident to him as everything between them always was. Simon pulled her to him and hungrily kissed her. It had been only a few days since their last touch, but it seemed like an eternity. She clung to him, wanting to feel his soft lips against hers forever. He stepped away. "I shouldn't be here, but I need to see you. I love you, Annie. Marry me."

Annie laughed quietly, hoping to not wake anyone. She gently cradled Simon's face in her hands. "Of course. A million yeses."

He took her hands and kissed them, looking at her intently. "Thank you for being you. For believing in me."

She raised a brow. "For even following you?"

He frowned briefly before smiling. "For being stubbornly you. For fighting for me and for us."

She loved this man. He understood her and accepted her like no other person did. She was so happy she wouldn't lose him.

"I'm just glad it's over."

Simon nodded. "I would like to go back to New York City and make sure my father's name is placed on his headstone."

Annie knew how much his father's exoneration meant to him. "Of course."

"When would you like to be married? Tomorrow?"

She smiled at him impishly. "You must be joking."

He chuckled quietly. "I don't want to waste any more time."

"As soon as possible. That way I don't have to endure another season as an unwed lady."

He sighed dramatically. "Is that the only reason?"

Annie kissed him lightly. "Definitely not. Perhaps you could stay for a bit."

His eyes roamed over her, and she knew that he wanted her just as badly. "I shouldn't stay."

"Simon, we are to be wed."

He groaned. "Stop tempting me."

She smiled and turned her back to him. She was wearing one of her simpler dresses and told her maid that she would prepare for bed by herself tonight. They shouldn't be disturbed. Simon quickly undid the ties that prevented the dress from falling to the floor. It fell in a swoosh to the ground. His fingers easily discarded her corset and petticoats. She turned to him only in her chemise and knickers. He sucked in his breath as his finger gently ran over the tip of one of her breasts.

"We can wait until our wedding. Are you sure?" he said, thickly.

She yanked his shirt free from his trousers with a chuckle. "We have already done this. Do I look like the type of person who likes to unnecessarily torture herself?"

"Your brother—"

"We are to be married. What could he possibly say?" Annie said, cutting him off.

She pulled the chemise over her head and then kicked off her knickers before sauntering to the foot of the bed. She turned to him, waiting. She almost laughed at his conflicted expression. Simon, so noble, hesitated but Annie knew what she wanted. Him. Now.

Annie sat on the edge of the bed and crossed one leg over the other. His eyes ran down the length of her legs, and he swallowed. She lifted a brow at him. He pulled his shirt over his head and made his way to her.

"You should tell me to leave."

She let out a hushed laugh. "Why would I do that? Again, we have done this."

"Because you are a lady."

"I am still the same woman you gave in to at the inn."

He stood over her as his gaze lingered down her, warming her skin. "That you are," he said, thickly.

Simon ran one hand down her leg, grasping her heel. She fell back against the bed on her elbows. She gasped and flushed as he straightened her leg. Her stomach clenched as he placed a kiss on the inside of her ankle.

"These legs are so delectable."

He placed another kiss on the inside of her calf before falling to his knees in front of her. He continued with his kisses.

"Simon," she murmured.

He gently spread her legs apart. "You wanted me here, my lady. But to keep me here you must be very quiet. Do you think you can do that?"

Annie nodded. His lips grazed her thigh, and she moaned. He pulled back and smiled at her wickedly. "Too loud."

"You are intentionally causing me to be loud."

His chest shook and Annie knew he was laughing at her. She glared at him. "You won't hear another sound from me."

He lifted a brow at her challenge. Annie hoped she could stay quiet, or they would end up married tomorrow.

"Just a taste."

His tongue touched her most sensitive spot, and she pressed her lips together as he suckled and tasted her. Her body moved of its own accord and a whimper escaped. He lifted his head and looked up at her. "Quiet, Lady Annabelle."

She clutched his hair and guided him back to where she wanted him. He continued to taste and tease her as her body bucked against his mouth. She wanted to moan but held back, frustrated. Her release was imminent, and she chased it. The ache grew so strong that when she finally exploded, she flung her hand across her mouth to keep from screaming.

Simon stood with a satisfied smile. She sat up flushed. He pushed his trousers down and moved to join her in bed, but Annie stayed him with her hand. He looked down at her confused. She trailed her hand across his stomach and his member twitched.

"Let's see how good you are at staying quiet."

He shook his head. "No."

She ran his finger down his shaft and he groaned. She shook her head. "Too loud, Simon."

"I can't stay quiet."

Triumph surged through her. "You can if you really want to."

Her hand circled him, and she stroked her hand up and down his shaft. He grabbed one of the bed posts and closed his eyes. His legs shook. She leaned forward and wrapped her mouth around him. He released the bedpost and bit his knuckles to stay quiet. If not caught up in what she was doing, she would have smiled up at him victoriously. Her tongue slid along against the taut skin of his shaft as she took him in and out of her mouth. He quietly cursed and jerked away from her before pushing her down on the bed.

He entered her in an intense stroke that left her breathless. He kissed her deeply as he pushed into her, and she clung to him, needing him. Simon lifted his head from their kiss and continued his deep strokes. Their eyes connected, and Annie was momentarily speechless by the love and desire she saw in them. A love and desire that she never knew she wanted but now couldn't imagine living without.

A slow ache built in her, and she moaned before he claimed her mouth again. He pushed into her, claiming her, causing the ache to explode. His strokes became frenzied, and Annie pressed her mouth against his to quiet his moans. After one more stroke, he withdrew from her, and with a low groan, found his own release. His chest heaved up and down as the look of ecstasy slowly faded from his face. He grabbed a cloth and cleaned them up before falling against the bed next to her.

She leaned up on an elbow and placed a kiss on his mouth before whispering, “I think I am the victor when it comes to being quiet.”

He smiled. “We need to get married soon. I don’t think I can survive another night of being this quiet.”

She fell back and smiled. Yes, they would have to marry sooner than later.

~

Simon stood in the Den listening to Collins and Clark explain everything they had done to find Walker since he became a wanted man. It had been ten days, and no one had seen or heard from him. He clenched his glass of brandy, frustrated. Not at Clark and Collins but how easily Walker was able to avoid being caught.

Walker was going to get away with it, and it made Simon want to hurl his brandy glass into the fireplace. No, it made him want to pummel someone. How could one man be so lucky? He wouldn’t say it was skill or intelligence because Walker wasn’t that clever. Simon took a large drink. Perhaps he was. He almost had Simon carted off to prison.

“So, what’s next?” he asked.

Collins and Clark looked at each other. Devons, who had joined him for the meeting said, “Why don’t we sit down and have this discussion?”

Simon stalked over to the sitting area of the expansive room that was mostly used in the evenings as a theater room.

He sat and waited for everyone to join him. Finally, Collins said, "We need to return soon."

A sardonic smirk appeared on Simon's face. "So, Walker will go free."

"We'll provide you with all of the information we have to continue the search for him," Clark said.

Simon knew he should be happy. His father was exonerated, but Walker had left a wake of destruction in his path, and he would get away with it.

"I know this isn't how you wanted it to end but we have to act now. Shell has agreed to provide testimony on his part and how his orders came directly from the high constable. This case will likely dismantle the entire police system in New York City, allowing a better system to take its place."

Simon snorted. "Do you really think it will be any better?"

Clark flushed with anger. "That's the whole point."

"Funny, I thought policing was to make sure people paid for their crimes."

The room fell into silence. Clark said, "I won't lie to you. My priority is to make sure we hold those in New York City accountable for their part. Walker has never been the priority. It doesn't mean I don't want him to pay, but we must return."

Simon turned his gaze to Collins. "You agree with this."

Collins rubbed the back of his neck, uncomfortable. Simon waited him out.

He sighed. "I would stay if I could, but my priorities are my clients. The necklace is all they wanted. I would like it back in their hands as soon as possible. Honestly, having control of it makes me damn nervous."

Simon respected both Clark and Collins and always knew their focus was different from his. He would find Walker on his own, and he needed to do it quickly. He and Annie were planning to wed. If he couldn't find him soon, he would have to walk away from his quest for justice. A little nibble of doubt sprang up in his mind whether he could truly walk away without Walker being punished for his crimes, but he ignored it. He would. He had to for Annie.

"When will you leave?" he asked.

"In three days," Collins said.

"We will find him," Devons insisted.

"And if we do find him after you leave?" Simon asked Clark.

"He will be tried and sent to prison for what he did. We will be waiting for him."

Simon nodded, knowing that once Walker was on American soil that Clark would do everything in his power to make sure he paid for his crimes. He didn't doubt that, but someone had to get him there.

"You are confident this case will help the attorney general make the needed changes."

Clark nodded. "I have already sent word. By the time I reach New York City, a great deal should be settled."

Simon supposed he should be happy that corrupt officials would be forced to step down, but he didn't hold Clark's same devout belief that a new policing system and new leadership would make a lasting impact. He was likely jaded from his own experience.

Clark and Collins rose.

"We need to go, but we will continue to search for Walker until we leave," Clark stated.

Simon nodded, watching them make their way out. He didn't blame them that their focus had to be wrapping up the investigation.

He spun his glass in his hand, running through the events that had taken place and all the leads that hadn't panned out. On his own he would pursue them. Track every single one down until he found the man.

"We will hire our own investigators to pursue this," Devons said, sitting across from him.

Simon shook his head. "Before we go in that direction, I want to review everything to make sure we aren't missing anything."

Devons stayed quiet and Simon looked back at him questioningly.

"Don't become obsessed with this. You have a beautiful woman waiting to marry you. Let the investigators do the work."

Of course, what Devons proposed was the logical choice, and Simon wanted to do that, but first, he needed to look over everything. He stood and nodded. "You're right, of course. I just need some time. Clark and Collins are going to send over whatever information they have. Please make sure it is sent directly to my cottage."

He walked back to his cottage quickly. As he made his way down the path, he loosened his cravat, feeling like he couldn't breathe. He entered his home. He would give himself a week to see if he could find Walker on his own, and then he would follow Devons' advice. But first he needed to go through everything. It would only help the investigators they hired.

He made his way to the punching bag and slammed his fist into it. He took a deep breath, trying to calm his anger. He thought about Walker escaping to the Continent or living the rest of his life in some small village and the rage exploded. He pummeled the bag over and over again, letting his dark feelings consume him.

Chapter 26

The opulent Peyton townhouse dining room was filled with conversation and laughter. Her entire family, Devons, Derry, Bromley, Mrs. Walker and even Miss Markam were there to say goodbye to Clark and Collins before they left for America. The Lovely Lotus would be returned to the owners, Shell would testify about the high constable's part in exchange for a lighter sentence, and Simon's father would be cleared of his crimes with the evidence collected by Clark and Collins.

Annie should be happy, but her gaze darted to the door. Everyone was here except for Simon. Where was he? She didn't need to ask herself that. He was looking for Walker. Sadness and if she was being honest, annoyance, filled her that he had chosen to not attend this evening.

She kept her feelings hidden and forced herself to laugh at something Sophia said, not wanting to ruin the evening. Her eyes connected with Jack's. She knew he was pondering what Simon's lack of attendance meant. Shockingly, he smiled at her and that made Annie more nervous. Jack never forced himself to smile, but he did so now to reassure her.

Annie smiled back at him. Everything would be fine. No one could expect Simon to completely forget about Walker. The atrocious man had somehow skulked off, and no one, including the Peelers, could find him. Annie wasn't sure if it was his connections or lack of interest from the Peelers, but the man was proving damn hard to find.

Since Walker became wanted, Collins and Clark had done everything they could to find him, spending the better part of two weeks searching for him but it was like the man just disappeared into thin air. Annie doubted that Simon was handling the turn of events well. She wouldn't know though. The last time they were together was in her bedroom.

This morning, Simon sent word he wouldn't be able to attend dinner tonight without any further information. A vision of him leaning over documents about the case popped in her mind. She pushed it away. She wouldn't worry about it. Annie couldn't expect Simon to instantly forget about Walker. The man could still be a danger. He had done so much harm. Simon needed time.

Personally, Annie hoped Walker was long gone, somewhere on the Continent. Annie studied her brothers with their wives and a kernel of jealousy warmed her belly. Jack winked at Mercy who blushed furiously from the other end of the table. Sam, sitting by his wife, leaned into her for a private conversation. She swatted him.

For the first time she wondered if she would have that with Simon. Would he be able to move on? She would love him regardless but deep down she wanted what Jack and Sam had with their wives. Her gaze flitted to Sophia who was chatting with Devons while her husband, drinking himself into a stupor, appeared to be having an intense conversation with Derry, his cousin. She frowned. Rumors were circulating about Landers' lovers, but her sister had yet to bring it up. Instead, she was her normally cheerful self.

"I'm sorry Mr. Miller couldn't be here, my lady," Mrs. Walker said next to her.

Annie shook the confusing thoughts from her mind and turned to her with a smile. "I am as well, but we can't dwell on it. Only the most pressing issue would prevent him from attending."

"Do you think he is searching for my husband? I'm so sorry for how much pain he caused."

"Nonsense. It has nothing to do with you. I'm sorry for all you have endured, Mrs. Walker."

The petite woman smiled at her. "Please call me Leonora."

"Then you must call me Annie."

Annie thought perhaps she and Leonora could become close friends. The woman had an inner strength that Annie admired.

"Are you concerned about your husband?"

Mrs. Walker shook her head. "No, Bromley helped me find guards, and truth be told he hasn't been very far from my side. He also has made sure that Miss Markam has a guard with her wherever she goes."

Bromley, dressed in a flowery waistcoat, stopped his discussion with Miss Markam and his eyes connected with Leonora's. Affection passed over his face. Leonora flushed. Annie smiled, amused.

"He seems very protective," Annie pointed out.

Leonora's gaze flew to hers. She flushed. "We are just close family friends."

Annie didn't believe that at all. She bet her pin money that once Leonora's divorce was granted, she would wed Bromley. And it would be a shocking scandal, but Annie still thought it would happen.

Jack rose, and the table became quiet. He looked around the room and smiled. "I had hoped to have Miller speak but I will in his place." He turned to Collins and Clark. "Thank you, Mr. Collins and Mr. Clark for attending tonight and more importantly for your help. Multiple people's lives have changed because of your willingness to work this case and I and my family are incredibly grateful. I have no doubt if Miller was here he would say the same thing."

Leonora stood and raised her glass. "I would like to second that, Your Grace."

Jack nodded and everyone stood, cheering the Americans. Annie smiled looking at Clark, who absurdly was blushing. After the toast, Jack asked them all to reconvene in the drawing room.

Annie joined everyone as they wandered down the hallway to the room. Clark stopped and studied a painting of her birth father, the Duke of Peyton. She joined him.

"Both you and your brother look strikingly like your father."

She grimaced. "Agree. Manly features included."

He snorted and smiled at her. "Certainly not. You are a vision."

Annie rolled her eyes. "I wasn't fishing for a compliment."

They stood there for another moment before Clark said, "I wish we would have found Walker."

Annie nodded. "I'm sorry Miller didn't make it tonight. I'm sure he is out looking for him."

Clark frowned at the painting. "Don't let him get lost in finding Walker."

She drifted down the hallway, and he joined her. "I can't prevent that."

He stayed her with his hand, and Annie looked at him surprised. "You're right. It was a silly thing to say. The only one who can do that is himself."

She smiled at him bemused. "And you know this from personal experience."

A bitter laugh escaped Clark. "I actually do. Obsession can

destroy everything, even a relationship with a loved one."

Annie's heart thumped. Was he trying to warn her about Simon and protect her, or was that her own doubts being revealed? Trying to return the conversation to a more light-hearted banter, she said, "And did you lose a loved one over an obsession?"

He smiled tightly. "No, she lost me."

Her eyes widened in shock.

"I couldn't watch her downward spiral into it. I left," he said.

A dozen questions ran through her mind, but she didn't know Clark well enough to ask any of them. He shook his head. "Let's join the others in the drawing room. I'm not sure how we got on such a melancholy topic."

She smiled, and they continued on to the drawing room. As they made their way to the door, he glanced at her, "Again, I'm sorry for the serious conversation."

"Think nothing of it," she replied.

Annie made her way into the drawing room and sat. Her mind lingered on Clark's words. If Simon didn't move on would she be able to support him or would she walk away? She loved him but she wanted more than despair and obsession in her life.

~

Simon entered the Den, exhausted. Music blared from the theater room, and men came in and out of various cardrooms. It may be late but the evening at the Den was only getting started. His night had been a wild goose chase where the leads he hoped would take him to Walker instead turned out to be nothing.

He missed the dinner at the Peyton townhouse because of the damn lead. Guilt coursed through him. He owed Collins and

Clark so much, and instead of celebrating with them, he'd spent his evening scouting out a dodgy tavern.

He looked around, and his eyes widened with surprise. Clark was standing in the foyer, frowning at him.

"Shouldn't you be asleep? Your ship leaves early in the morning," Simon asked.

Clark shrugged. "I'm not much of a sleeper. Plus, I will have days to sleep on the ship. Why don't you join me for a drink?"

Simon followed behind him into one of the drawing rooms that served as a place for the lords to congregate and discuss the topics of the day. The room was fairly empty as the act in the theater was keeping most of them occupied.

They settled into a sitting area, and Simon requested a server bring them each a brandy. Clark leaned back in his chair, stretching.

"So, what will happen once this new system begins? Will you be promoted into one of these newly vacant high-level positions?"

Clark threw his head back and laughed. "Hell no. That is the last thing I would ever want."

Simon didn't doubt that. Some men craved power or sought out prestige, but Clark didn't strike him as that type. Still, he likely deserved such a position if he wanted it. Without him, the case would have gone in an entirely different direction. Simon would be in prison, and Walker would still be swigging brandy, happily immersed in London society.

"No interest at all?" Jack asked amused.

"Certainly not," he stated. "Any new finds on Walker?"

Nothing, Simon thought darkly. He spent every moment looking for him, and not one damn lead had panned out. How did a man so well-known in society simply disappear?

He shook his head, then took a drink of his brandy, hating that Walker was becoming an obsession. Christ, he hadn't seen Annie in almost a week. He needed to see her tomorrow. She deserved to know what he was doing. He still needed to pay Jack a visit to properly ask for her hand in marriage. The days had flown by.

"You need to allow someone else to search for him. Step away from it," Clark said quietly.

Clark was right. "I plan to," Simon said.

Clark raised a brow in disbelief. Simon bristled at his skepticism.

"You have a beautiful woman waiting for you. She deserves your attention. I'm sorry we couldn't find Walker, but you venturing out in search of him every night isn't doing you or anyone else good."

So this is why Clark had come to call on him. He was concerned about Annie. "You think you have the right to speak for her because you spent a few hours in a tavern with her?"

Clark, unperturbed by his remark, smiled. "No, I'm telling you this as someone who has seen someone they love become obsessed with something they couldn't change or fix. It will destroy your relationship."

"I'm not obsessed."

Clark scoffed. "A duke, who happens to be your friend, hosts a dinner for the men who helped prove your father's innocence and you don't attend. Likely because of a lead that didn't pan out. Most of them won't pan out."

Simon flushed. "I'm sorry. I do owe you and Collins so much."

Clark rolled his eyes, unconcerned. "My point to you is let this go. Or if you can't, hire men to do this. You don't have to be out every day looking for Walker. Focus on what you have."

Clark was right, but Simon didn't respond. As much as he wanted to walk away from the search, he wouldn't yet. He had a few more leads he needed to follow, but if they didn't prove worthwhile, he would do as Clark suggested. He just needed a little more time.

The man lecturing him rose and finished his drink. "I think I will go. As you said my ship leaves early."

"Thank you, Clark. Truly, I mean that."

Clark slapped him on the arm. "You almost lost your life here in London. Now that you have it back, don't squander it. Everyone wants Walker found but life needs to go on. You deserve to be happy after everything you have been through."

"Thank you."

Simon watched him leave the room, frowning. He finished off his brandy and pondered what he would do next. His father would want him to move on with his life and be happy. He needed to see Annie and Jack. Hire some proper investigators to investigate Walker's location.

The butler Donahue interrupted his thoughts and provided him a note. He opened it and frowned. There had been a possible sighting of Walker. He stood.

"Donahue, please have my carriage readied."

Chapter 27

A few days after sending off Clark and Collins, Annie turned her face up towards the cloudless sky. March had brought with it the sun, and she wished she was in the gardens, enjoying the weather as she read a book. Unfortunately, she had more pressing issues to worry about.

She still hadn't seen Simon. She pressed her lips together in annoyance. Annie was done waiting for him to appear. She would not sit quietly at home wondering what he was doing. Nor was she alone in her curiosity. Her family hadn't asked her directly where Simon was, but she knew it was on the tip of their tongues. The Kincaides were a nosey group.

She glanced down the street, hoping to flag a coach. If the man wouldn't come to her, she would go to him.

"Where are you headed to?"

She groaned inwardly and turned to face Jack. "I thought I would do some shopping."

Jack raised a brow. Annie bristled and pursed her lips. "Is there a problem?"

He folded his arms across his chest and frowned. "If you were going shopping, you would take a maid and our carriage. Why are you lying to me?"

She flushed. "I am going to visit Miller, if you must know."

"Walk with me," he said, holding out his arm.

Annie rolled her eyes. A lecture was imminent. "I'm practically married to Simon. Beyond that, I'm no young lady," she pointed out.

Jack stayed silent and held his arm out. They strolled along the walkway and finally he said, "Miller has not met with me about a marriage."

A light red hue covered her, but she would not be embarrassed. His focus on Walker would eventually fade.

"Regardless, I'm not a child."

"True, but for whatever stroke of luck it is, no one has discovered your adventure with Miller. I just ask that you be careful to not be seen."

He wasn't ordering her to return home. She stopped and her eyes flew to his, shocked. Jack smirked at her, enjoying her speechlessness.

"As you like to say, you are not a child, and I want you to have this conversation with Miller."

She released his arm. "You don't think it will go well."

He sighed and raked his hands through his black hair so similar to hers. "When you see him, I just really want you to think about if he will make you happy."

She scowled at him.

Jack continued, "This isn't over for Miller. It may never be over for him until he finds Walker. If you become his wife, you will never be his priority."

Fury filled her, hating Jack's harsh blunt words. But she wasn't sure if it was at him or Simon.

"He may find Walker soon," Annie pointed out.

"And if he doesn't?"

"Then I will help search for him," she snapped.

He shook his head. "What about what you want? Do you want

to spend all your time looking for a criminal? That is no way to live. I want you to live a happy life, not focused on someone else's obsession."

Annie snorted. "That's interesting coming from you."

"I almost lost everything because revenge mattered above all else. I'm not saying this to be cruel," he said quietly.

"It will be different. You will see," Annie said.

Jack nodded at her, but she knew he didn't believe her. He walked her back to the townhouse and one of the family carriages waited for her. Jack assisted her in. "Thank you, Jack."

He looked like he wanted to say more but instead pressed his lips together and shut the door. The carriage started to move, and she settled against the seat. She clasped her hands together, nervous to see him. She would do as Jack asked and think about what she wanted. Perhaps Simon wasn't obsessed with Walker but busy with the Den. He had been away from the Den for weeks.

She shook her head. No, Simon loved her. The Den would not keep him away. She looked out the window at the oddly sunny streets of London, pondering the situation she was in. She was so lost in thought, she was startled when the carriage came to a stop. The driver opened the door for her and stepped out in front of Simon's cottage.

"My lady, I will wait for you," the driver said.

She smiled. "Thank you."

Annie took a deep breath and knocked on the door. Simon didn't open, but she heard rustling, so she knocked again louder.

Simon yanked the door open. "Yes, what is it?" He froze at the sight of her, startled. "Annie?"

She brushed past him, looking around at the cottage. Paperwork was piled everywhere. She looked back at him, her eyes roaming over his frazzled state. He was dressed only in a shirt and trousers. His hair was unkempt, and his beard looked like it hadn't been trimmed in days.

"What are you doing?"

He flushed and rubbed the back of his neck. "Just looking for leads before I hand over the paperwork to investigators."

"It has been over two weeks since we've seen each other."

He had the decency to blush in embarrassment but didn't explain himself. He didn't have to. Annie could tell what he was up to. Sadness filled her. Simon was a man obsessed.

"I came to check on you. You were not at Clark and Collins going-away dinner."

He sighed. "I know. I'm sorry I missed it. That evening was a damn mess. I thought I had a decent lead, but it turned out to be nothing. Fortunately, I did run into Clark at the Den that evening, so I was able to thank him and say goodbye."

"Have you been going out to look for Walker by yourself?" she asked incredulously.

"Just the leads I think may be real."

Annie frowned at him. "You could be hurt or killed."

Simon scowled. "Not if I kill him first."

"Is that what you are hoping to accomplish?"

He clenched his jaw and said nothing.

Simon Miller wasn't a killer. "This isn't you," Annie stated.

Simon looked away from her. She walked over to him and cupped his face. "Let the investigators deal with this. No good will come from you confronting him or putting yourself in a situation where you may be harmed, or you would be forced to take his life."

"I have no other options. Nothing left but this."

She stepped away from him. Her eyes flashed. "Do you really believe that? You have me. Your friends. Your life here. Yet, instead of embracing that, you are destroying everything. For what? So you can confront him and force yourself to act?"

"He must pay."

Annie pressed her lips together in anger. "You should not be the one to make him pay. Hire investigators to find him and have them return him to America."

He was silent for a moment but eventually said, "You are right. I just need a few more days and I will do as you ask."

Annie knew he would never stop looking for Walker and if he found him, it wouldn't end well. At this point Simon was too far focused on confronting him.

"How much time do you need?"

He ran his fingers through his hair, appearing to be relieved at her question. "Not more than a week."

Liar, she thought. But she didn't argue with him. She couldn't beg or plead with him to let this go. He would have to choose on his own what mattered more, Walker or her.

She pulled him to her and kissed him deeply, wanting to feel the connection between them. She sighed as her body hummed in response to him, and when she could take no more, she stepped back.

"Thank you for understanding."

She nodded and made her way to the door. She turned back,

and he was already bent back over his documents.

"Simon."

He looked up.

"I love you."

"I love you," he said in return.

She walked out the door and into the carriage before the first tear hit her cheek. She swiped at it furiously. As much as she loved Simon Miller, she couldn't stay with him. Jack had been right. She deserved more. In disbelief, she shook her head. It was over. She brushed the tears from her face. She would not cry another single tear over him. She had done so much for the man. If in seven days he didn't come to her, she damn well wouldn't seek him out again.

~

Four weeks later

Simon sat in his office at the Den, looking over the numbers for the club. He rolled his eyes at the festivities going on downstairs. The great hall was filled with laughter and dancing. He imagined Devons was playing host tonight. They had discussed hiring someone else to allow Devons to take some time away from the club, but Devons had yet to approve anyone Simon or Derry suggested.

He rubbed his eyes, exhausted. If he wasn't doing work for the club, he was searching for Walker. Simon put his head down in shame. It had been weeks since Annie came to visit him. His mouth twisted into a grimace. She had not sought him out again. He'd broken his promise that he would hand the case over to investigators.

Instead, he spent hours hunting down leads that went nowhere. He believed he was still in the country and likely still in London, but he couldn't figure out where. Murmurs from outside his door took him away from his thoughts, and he rose to see what the commotion was. The door was thrown open and Jack and Sam Kincaide walked in.

"How can I help—"

Jack swung his fist at him, catching him in the jaw. Simon stumbled back in shock. Recovered, he glared at him and stepped forward.

"Please fight me," Jack snarled.

Sam, always the peacemaker, held up his hand. "We didn't come to fight."

"Speak for yourself," Jack snapped.

Simon took a deep breath, calming his anger. He deserved Jack's fury. He took a seat behind his desk and motioned for them to sit.

As they sat, Jack snapped. "She has not heard from you in weeks. If you are letting her go, she deserves to know."

Simon shook his head. "I'm not. I just need time."

Jack pounded his fist on Simon's desk. "You will always need time! When does this end?"

He didn't know. Annie should be what mattered not Walker, yet he had no words to defend himself. He had been consumed with finding him. It was unacceptable, but he knew he couldn't stop.

"Do you know she is leaving?" Sam said.

Simon's eyes widened in shock. "What do you mean?"

"Annie plans to travel. She decided to join a group of ladies traveling to the Continent. She plans to be gone for a year," Sam explained.

She had given up on him. Simon felt a blow to his heart that if he wasn't sitting would have brought him to his knees. He loved her like no other, but it wasn't enough. Of course, it wasn't. She deserved more in a husband than what he could offer her. She deserved more in life. Annie knew that. He thought back to her last visit when he asked her to give him a week. Did she know it was over then? He had been too wrapped up in pouring over Clark and Collins' documents to realize it.

He wanted to rush to the Peyton estate and plead with her but stopped himself. He couldn't agree to give up on finding Walker. He had to let her go. He rose and looked out the window, looking down below into the gardens. Finally, he turned to the Kincaides. "It's for the best."

Sam frowned at him disapprovingly. "You would give her up for this?"

He shook his head. "No. I would give her up, so she can be happy."

"You are a damn fool!" Jack bit out.

"You told me not to lead her down a path of misery. The only choice I can make is to let her go."

"You could choose not to go down the path you are on," Sam suggested.

How did he do that? The man destroyed his father's life and almost destroyed his. He looked at Sam. "If I tell you I will do that, I'll be lying."

Sam shook his head and Jack glared at him, but it was the truth. He was fixated on finding him and he didn't know when that would end.

"She sails in three days," Sam said, rising, followed by Jack.

"Can I see her before she leaves?" he asked.

Jack started to shake his head, but Sam said, "If she agrees to it. I hope you know what you are doing, friend. You are headed towards a very lonely life."

Simon said nothing. They left without any other words.

Simon walked over and poured himself a brandy. Both the finances for the Den and his hunt for Walker were forgotten. Moments of his time with Annie flashed in his mind. Her touch. Her willingness to always help.

He wanted to be selfish. Simon wanted to go to her and tell her he would give it all up but those lies would only lead to more heartache. He slumped back down in his chair. He could envision Annie traveling the Continent, living her life. He took solace in the fact she would not wallow in pity. That wasn't Annie. His Annie had too much strength.

He closed his eyes and pictured her in France, laughing. His hand clenched around the glass as he envisioned her being charmed by some Frenchman or being touched by one. The bile rose in his throat, but he forced it down with another swig of the brandy. He had no one to blame but himself.

Chapter 28

Annie sat with Mercy and Clara in the drawing room at the Peyton townhouse. She smiled. She was lucky to have two such amazing sisters-in-law. Clara lounged in one of the wingback chairs rubbing her tiny bump. She was starting to show, and she glowed with happiness. Annie couldn't be happier for her and Sam. Jack and Mercy didn't have any little ones yet, but they remained optimistic it would happen soon.

Life was moving along splendidly for the Kincaide family. Well, except for her and Sophia. Where was Sophia? She was supposed to spend the day with her, Mercy, and Clara.

"I'm going to check if Sophia has arrived, perhaps she went to talk to Jack before visiting us."

Annie made her way toward the foyer but was shocked to find her sister and Derry standing to the side of the corridor, arguing.

"I don't need your help or your pity, my lord," Sophia said crossly.

Derry frowned at her. What were they discussing? Landers? Annie cleared her throat, and they turned in her direction. Derry straightened and his face became shuttered.

"Excuse me, I was visiting your brother and saw your sister enter. We were just discussing—"

"The weather," Sophia bit out. "Isn't that what proper *ton* gentlemen discuss with proper ladies?"

Derry's gaze swung back to Sophia, and Annie thought he may explode, but instead he bowed elegantly to both of them and made his way to Jack's study without another word.

Sophia smoothed her dress and took deep breaths before walking towards Annie. Once in front of her, she smiled cheerfully as if the odd encounter with Derry never happened.

"Oh no, you don't get to pretend you and Derry weren't arguing. What happened?"

Sophia rolled her eyes and took Annie's arm. "Let's not talk about him. He is such a stuffy bore. I can't stand him."

"Soph—"

Her sister shook her head. "No, I don't want to discuss him."

Annie frowned at her sister. She was never angry with anyone, even people who deserved to be dressed down. Still, Annie knew she wouldn't get any information from her unless she wanted to share. She nodded, and they entered the drawing room where Clara and Mercy were halfheartedly piecing together a dissection puzzle.

Annie and Sophia joined them, taking a seat on one of the sofas.

"How is the dissection going?"

Clara sighed. "Dreadful. Sam and my brother are so good at these."

Clara's brother lived with Sam and her. He had quickly latched on to Sam and adored all things he loved. Dissection puzzles were Sam's guilty secret fun. Well, especially since becoming a married respectable man but even in his single rogue days, it wasn't strange to find him late at night in the study or drawing room fiddling with a puzzle, lost in thought.

Annie leaned over and sorted through the pieces. She sensed everyone's stares on her. She ignored them, hoping to avoid a discussion about her sudden choice to travel abroad.

"Are you sure you want to go?" Sophia asked.

Of course, with her family that was impossible. Her eyes connected with Sophia's. Her sister stared back at her pensively.

"I think it's for the best."

"He loves you," Mercy said.

Annie knew he loved her. She would never doubt that. She could feel it in the way he touched her, looked at her, and treated her. What she had learned in the last few weeks was that sometimes love wasn't enough. Sophia's romance novelettes didn't write about that. "That isn't the problem."

Sophia sighed. "You are both being foolish."

"I can't be with him, Soph. I can't watch him charge down this destructive path. It isn't just the obsession but also what he intends to do if he finds Walker."

Mercy, Clara, and Sophia stared at her questioningly.

"I think he means to do away with him."

Sophia snorted, startling Annie. "Miller would never kill anyone. Maybe in self-defense but for revenge, never."

"You don't know that part of him."

Sophia leaned back in her chair, ignoring the dissection. "Perhaps but I know the other parts of him, which far outweigh whatever darkness is consuming him. When Miller has the chance, he won't harm him. He will hand him over to the Peelers."

Annie hoped so.

"Are you sure this is the right choice for you?" Clara asked.

How many times were they going to ask her the same

question? Annie was not sure of anything, and the more they asked, the more nervous she became. Still, she forced herself to smile. "Of course, it is."

"We are worried you are making a rash decision," her sister pointed out.

Annie glared at Sophia. Her sister was the epitome of rash choices. As if reading her mind, Sophia grinned. "I know. I have no room to talk, but why don't you take a few weeks and if you still want to go to the Continent, you can."

Annie didn't want to wait. She wanted to escape London and not worry about running into Simon at a London event.

All of the Kincaide women stared at her with frowns. "Do you all truly think I'm being rash?"

They glanced at one another but before anyone could say anything, the butler entered the room.

"Lady Annabelle, you have a visitor. Mr. Miller is here."

Mercy and Clara gasped. Sophia just openly gaped at the butler. Mercy regained her composure first. "See him in, please."

Simon entered the drawing room and looked taken back to find all the Kincaide women in one room. His gaze moved to her, and her traitorous heart leaped as their eyes connected. They all rose, and Simon bowed.

An awkward silence fell over the room. Mercy, Clara, and Sophia looked at one another, a silent agreement passing between them.

"Clara, Sophia and I will go investigate if the cook has any treats we can lay out and be back momentarily," Mercy said.

Annie smiled at the women's retreating figure, knowing they left to give her and Simon a few minutes of privacy.

Her gaze turned back to the man she loved, and he watched her with a tortured expression.

The anger she had kept hidden away bubbled within her. He had chosen his obsession over her. She hated him for it. Perhaps hate was too strong of a word but it was the only one that came to mind.

They stood in the room staring at one another. Finally, Simon said, "I'm sorry that I can't let this go."

She looked away briefly. Overwhelmed by his acknowledgement of where they were at. Of the decision he had made.

"You made your choice. I won't beg you to change your mind."

He pressed his lips together as if to contain his own emotions. She wanted him to declare he changed his mind. That seeing her was enough to realize how foolish he was being, but he didn't.

"Your brothers said you were headed to the Continent for an extended trip."

She nodded. "Yes, I think it would be best under the circumstances."

"I am sorry that I couldn't give you more, Annie."

Annie refused to cry or show him how much his actions hurt her. "You made your choice, and it wasn't me."

"Perhaps, when you return—"

She interrupted him. "If I return. I won't wait for you, Simon. I can't. I don't agree with any of your choices. You could choose to be happy. You could choose us, but you won't."

He stood and paced across the room before turning around. "Do you think I don't want to be happy? I can't. It eats at me," he said, harshly.

She stood and walked to him. "I know. I understand your rage. I do, but I can't support it. When we came to London, all I wanted was revenge. It nearly destroyed my family. I can't go back to that. I refuse to. If I go down this path of revenge with you, it will destroy the love we have for each other. I would rather remember how we were than allow that."

His eyes watered, and he nodded. "I understand."

"Promise me that when you find Walker you will hand him over to the authorities. I don't want someone's murder on your conscience for the rest of your life."

He didn't promise but walked to her and leaned his forehead against hers. "I will miss you forever."

Annie's heart shattered into a million pieces. She closed her eyes and placed a kiss on his lips. Not a hungry kiss but a slow, lingering kiss that was filled with more goodbye than she ever wanted to give Simon.

"Goodbye, Simon."

He stepped back. "Goodbye, Annie."

With that he turned and strode from the room. Annie let out a strangled sob before wrapping her arms around her stomach. The sobs became louder, and they would not stop. Mercy, Clara, and Sophia rushed back into the drawing room and Sophia wrapped her arms around her.

"Shh…it will be okay."

Annie shook her head. "We're over."

Sophia pulled her closer. Annie sobbed for what seemed like an eternity before taking a seat on the sofa.

"Miller—" Clara began.

"No. I don't want to ever hear his name again. It's done."

Mercy nodded. "Let's talk about your trip then."

Sophia looked as if she wanted to disagree but instead said, "Tell me again where you will be going?"

~

Simon walked into a dingy tavern in the London Dock area known as the Lion's Tale. His latest lead on Walker indicated he had frequented this establishment more than once. His eyes roamed the room, looking for the man. If Walker did frequent the Lion's Tale, it was a far cry from what he was used to. The Lion's Tale was perhaps one of the filthiest places Simon had ever been in.

He sat down and tried his best to assess the room. His mind kept wandering to his meeting with Annie earlier in the day. He didn't think he would ever be able to forget the hurt he saw on her face. The moment he left, he regretted not sweeping her up in his arms and telling her they would figure it out.

He glared at the room in contempt. Did he really want this to be his life? Was killing Walker that important? Hell, he didn't know if he could go through with it. He had never killed anyone. Annie left tomorrow. He would lose her. Pain sliced through him and stayed lodged in his chest. Doubts swirled in his mind about the choice he made to let her go.

"What will it be, luv?"

The server smiled at him. Simon pushed his depressing thoughts away. He forced a smile and handed her a coin. "Just an ale and a question."

The woman studied the coin before tucking it in her top. "Well ask it. I don't have all day."

Simon unfolded the paper with the portrait of Walker. "I am

looking for this man. Have you seen him?"

The woman took the paper. "Not sure. For another coin, I will ask around."

Simon handed her the coin, and she took the paper. Another server deposited his ale, and he took a sip, grimacing. Even the ale was awful.

The server made her way back to the table. "Excuse me, luv, but I think I found one of the servers who has information. She doesn't want to be seen telling you nothing. If you come with me, I will take you to her."

Simon rose, anticipation coursing through him. He followed the server to a door and stepped outside into an empty alley. Dread coursed through him, and he glanced at the server who shifted nervously. Another door along the back of the brick building swung open and three large men walked out.

"Well, aren't you a fancy gent?" one of the men said with a smirk.

Simon glared at the server who escorted him outside. She shrugged and scurried back in the tavern. He turned back to the men who circled him.

"You can have any money I have," Simon said, not wanting a fight.

The man smashed his fist into his hand. "Soon enough. You think you can come in here, asking questions that are none of your business?"

"I am just looking for an associate. Do you know him?"

The man scowled. "Who enters my establishment is none of your concern. No questions allowed."

Simon nodded. "I don't want—"

The rest of his words never left him because a punch in his stomach knocked the air from him. He bent over in pain, trying to catch his breath. All the men laughed. Simon stood and jabbed the man in the face with his fist. His nose cracked with the impact. The man howled and one of the other men said, "Now you've done it."

He grabbed him, and Simon struggled against his hold. The man whose nose he broke, punched him in the face. "We don't like any of you fancy gents in our establishment. This will be a lesson for any other gents who think to come here, asking questions."

Simon took multiple punches, and his world started to go black. His legs dangled as he slumped in the man's arms. As he collapsed into darkness, it wasn't Walker he thought about but Annie. Annie and the life he would have had with her.

He made one last attempt to stand, but another punch knocked him into complete blackness. What a fool he was.

A few hours later, Simon opened his eyes, startled. His brows wrinkled in confusion. He should be waking up on the cold damp ground or worse, dead. He looked around confused. The room he was in was unfamiliar.

A hand gave his cheek a few taps, and he sat up ready to fight. He came face to face with a grinning Devons. "Good morning, Miller."

His head pounded. Groaning, he swung his feet to the ground but stayed sitting.

"Where am I?"

Derry turned to him, and Simon grimaced. The normally impeccable lord was sporting a bruise across one eye and his cravat was missing. "You are sitting in the study of Devons' new townhouse."

Still befuddled, Simon asked Devons, “You bought a townhouse?”

Devons grinned. Simon noticed he, too, had a purple bruise on his cheek and his waistcoat was ripped. “Yep, right in the heart of where the nobs live.”

“You never leave the club and if you do, you are at your tavern,” Simon said.

“Devons plans to take some time away from his businesses,” Derry said, skeptical.

Simon shook the fog in his head away. “How did I get here?”

“Well, we have been following you on your adventures. We missed you slipping away at that awful tavern, so it took us time to find you. By then you were knocked out cold. Don’t worry we finished them off for you,” Devons said with a cocky grin.

Not for the first time, Simon was humbled by how good of friends Devons and Derry really were. “Thank you.”

Derry took another sip of brandy and sat in the chair across from him. “You're welcome. Do us a favor and take some of the guards from the club with you next time. I personally have no desire to enter another tavern like the Lion’s Tale again.”

Devons chuckled at Derry’s disdainful tone. “We did speak with the server before we took you home, and she was quite terrified that you were not properly done away with by those thugs. Terrified enough to tell us that Walker does frequent that tavern.”

A thrill of victory surged through Simon, but he pushed it away. Right now, Walker wasn’t his priority. He stumbled to his feet and Derry grabbed him before he pitched forward.

“Be careful. You can’t go back there yet.”

Simon shook his head. “I’m not going back there. Can I ask you one more favor?”

Devons and Derry nodded.

“Will you hire investigators to watch the tavern for Walker?”

“So, you are done chasing Walker yourself?” Devons questioned.

“Yes, I seem to be rather awful at it. And there is something more pressing I need to attend to.”

“We will make sure they are hired today,” Derry stated.

Devons smirked at him smugly. “Does your decision have to do with a certain lady?”

“Bloody hell, you are as bad as the ladies who spend all their time reading those romance novelettes with your oohing and ahhing,” Derry grumbled.

Devons snorted. “Do any of my actions strike you as a man looking for love?”

Derry rolled his eyes and turned back to Simon. “You mumbled the lady’s name over and over again on the carriage ride back.”

He wasn’t surprised. Before his world had been pitched into blackness, it became very apparent that he was pursuing the wrong person, the wrong goal. He needed to see Annie and convince her to give him another chance. Even if Walker was never found, a life with her was what he wanted. He didn’t care what that encompassed—children, travel, or languishing in the countryside, but he wanted it.

“May I borrow your carriage?” Simon asked.

“The carriage is out front. I would advise you to go home and sleep before you go see her. In a few hours, the sun will be coming up, go to her then,” Devons suggested.

Simon glanced down at himself. His clothes were ripped and stained. He didn't care. He had to see her now. He shook his head. "I can't wait. She is planning to leave England today."

Devons stood. "We will go with you. You may need some protection from Jack."

Derry muttered something about ridiculous choices and friends but also stood.

Chapter 29

Annie tossed and turned as she laid in bed. She should be sleeping. Her ship left after breakfast, and she didn't want to be tired. Still, she frowned, worried she was making a rash decision. What other options did she have? She loved Simon, but she couldn't keep waiting for him or support his current path.

A loud pounding on the front door startled her. She sat up, wondering who could be calling at such an early hour. She told herself to go back to sleep. It didn't concern her. The pounding on the door became louder. She pushed the covers away and scrambled out of her bed. Annie was too curious to not know what was going on.

Once out of bed, she threw on a night wrap and made her way down the hallway. Jack was ahead of her rushing towards the stairs that led into the foyer. He glanced back and caught sight of her. With a frown, he said, "Stay here."

She wrinkled her nose in annoyance at his tone but slowed her walk until he was out of sight. Annie arrived at the second-floor landing that overlooked the foyer and peered over. She gasped, spotting Simon, Derry, and Devons below. What were they doing here?

Jack scowled at Simon. "Have you lost your mind? What are you doing here?"

"I want to see Annie."

Simon was here. Her heart leapt into her throat. Jack started to shake his head, and Annie rushed down the stairs. Mercy, also awakened, followed behind her.

"Simon," she said.

He turned to her, and she gasped at the sight of him. His clothes were ripped and torn. He sported two black eyes and there was dried blood at the corner of his mouth.

She moved towards him, but Jack blocked her path.

"No."

Annie glared at her brother.

"I know I have made a mess of this, Jack, but please let me speak with her," Simon said, his voice tinged with desperation.

"Jack," Mercy implored.

He scowled at Simon but reluctantly nodded.

Simon reached for her, but Jack shook his head and his hands quickly fell back to his side. Annie was too scared to wonder what he wanted. She held her breath waiting for him to speak.

"Annie, I have made a mess of this. I love you, but I know you know that. I have always loved you. I loved you in Philadelphia. I loved you the night of the Ball of Sin. And I love you now."

Jack snapped at him. "What happened at the Ball of Sin?"

Mercy swatted him. "Let him finish."

Annie silently thanked her sister-in-law.

Simon took a deep breath and continued. "I let my obsession with Walker get in the way of that. Tonight, I thought I was going to die, and my only regret was not having a life with you. That was it. It wasn't being able to see Walker dead or in prison but missing out on my chance to live life with you."

Tears rolled down Annie's cheeks, but she stayed rooted to where she was. Unsure of what to say or do. She was leaving today.

Simon continued. "My father told me once when he was in prison to move on with my life and to be happy. I couldn't fathom why he would think that was possible. I know now. He wanted me to have this, what we have. I'm done with searching for Walker. I still want him found, but I will leave it to the investigators and the police."

He stood waiting for her response. She looked around the foyer. Mercy, Jack, Devons, and Derry watched her and Simon intently.

"Can we speak privately?"

Her brother started to speak but Mercy cut him off. "Yes, of course. Please use the drawing room."

Jack scowled at her, but Mercy ignored his glare. Annie made her way to the drawing room with Simon following closely behind her.

As they entered the room, Mercy shut the door firmly behind them. They were alone. She turned and stared at him. He was a mess and possibly needed a doctor.

"Are you hurt?"

Simon shrugged. "It doesn't matter. Please don't leave today. I know I have given you every reason to leave, but I can't imagine you being gone for a year."

Anger that she had kept squashed down for weeks bubbled over. "You haven't seen me in weeks. Why do you care?"

"I care. I was a damn fool. I asked Devons and Derry to find investigators to look for Walker. You won't hear a word about him."

"I know you will still think about the case. I don't want you to keep your thoughts from me. I just don't want it to consume your life or mine. Can you say that is truly possible?"

He strode over to her, taking her hands in his. "Yes, I can. The fight I was in tonight, I thought I was done for and probably would be, if Derry and Devons hadn't interceded. At that moment all I could think about was you and how foolish I had been to let you go."

Annie wanted to believe him. She wanted to leap into his arms and tell him she loved him, but she hesitated.

"Promise me you will leave Walker's punishment to the police and the courts."

Annie expected him to argue with her or not respond but shockingly, he nodded. "I promise, Annie. I still want justice, but I don't want it to drive my life. I want a life with you. If you want to travel, we will travel the world. If you want to have five or ten babies, we will have them. I just want us to be happy. Marry me, Annie."

She cupped his face in her hands. Annie believed him. The Simon she loved was standing before her, not the man obsessed with Walker.

"Yes," she whispered.

His lips came down on hers, and Annie sighed, savoring the contact between them. She had craved his touch for weeks and his lips on hers didn't disappoint. She leaned into him, needing more of him.

"I have missed you so much," he whispered.

The door being yanked opened prevented Annie from responding. They sprang apart and a scowling Jack stood in the doorway. His gaze flitted back and forth between them. Annie smiled back at him, and Jack's eyes narrowed.

He turned back to Simon. "You will leave now and request a meeting to ask for Annie's hand the proper way. Not like some madman."

Mercy, standing behind him, peered into the room, rolling her eyes. Annie had to force back a grin.

Simon nodded. His expression became solemn. "When shall I call?"

"Request an appointment and I will get back to you. Now leave!"

Simon made his way to the foyer and Annie followed him out. Jack glared at Devons and Derry. "I can't believe you allowed him to come here."

Devons chuckled. "It seemed of great importance that he visited Lady Annabelle."

"It was," Simon said, grinning at Annie. She smiled back at him.

Jack shook his head. "All of you leave now!"

Simon, Devons, and Derry left without another word. Once the butler shut the door, Annie turned to Jack and Mercy. "I'm not leaving later today."

"I don't think either of us are shocked," Jack said, dryly.

"When will you see him?"

Jack smirked at her. "When I have time."

He stalked back upstairs, and Annie frowned at him. Mercy walked to her and squeezed her hand. "Don't worry, he will give his approval. He's just upset that Miller put you through all of this. Let him have this time to let Miller squirm a little."

Annie rolled her eyes. Brothers!

~

Simon waited in Jack's study, pacing. The man had made him wait for days for an appointment. He supposed he deserved it. Simon would do the same if he had a sister. He was prepared to take any lectures or admonishments Jack handed out as long as it ended with him giving his approval for their marriage to go forward.

In the last few days, Simon had handed over all documents related to Walker to the investigators that Devons and Derry found. The men were part of a private detective agency that had a stellar reputation. He would meet with them weekly.

Once he and Annie were wed, he would have her attend as well. He wanted no secrets between them or to give her any reason why she should be concerned. He would be lying if he said he didn't still think of Walker. The man could be anywhere, and he was dangerous.

Mrs. Walker still had guards with her in case her husband appeared back at their residence. Simon noticed that Jack had more guards and footmen around than normal as well. Clearly, no one was forgetting about him. They just weren't letting him dictate their lives.

He continued to pace, nervous about his discussion with Jack. He needed to get his approval today. Once that happened, he and Annie could marry. He hoped to marry right away but needed to procure a special license. That wouldn't happen without Jack's assistance.

Simon sighed. He'd been waiting almost an hour for Jack to appear in his study. He pushed away any annoyance he felt and grinned. He would wait on Jack all day if that is what was required to marry Annie.

The sound of loud footsteps traveled down the hallway and Simon straightened. Jack was en route. He entered and Simon bowed to him. Jack ignored him and made his way to his desk before directing Simon to sit in the chair across from him. They sat in silence for a moment and Simon had the urge to squirm like a schoolboy but refrained from doing so.

Ending his torture, Jack asked, "If I agree to this marriage, what will your priority be?"

Without thinking, Simon said. "To love your sister until my dying day."

Jack remained stone faced. "And what of Walker?"

The man sitting in front of Simon was not only Annie's brother but one of his closest friends. Or had been. He hoped someday to rebuild their friendship.

"I won't lie to you, Jack," Simon said. Jack glowered at him, and Simon added, "Your Grace."

"Continue," he bit out.

"I want Walker found but I don't want that to be my only reason for living. I want a life with Annie. Will I still check in with the investigators? Yes, but my focus will be my family, which is your sister. I will be fully transparent with Annie about anything I'm doing to find Walker."

"If you find him, will you see him properly shipped back to America?"

Previously, Simon thought he may try to end Walker's life but not anymore. He didn't care to have a person's blood on his hands, not even Walker's.

"I will. I want Walker held accountable through the courts."

"You know there was a time that all of us thought Annie would live her life as an independent lady. Well, everyone except my father. He always thought she would meet someone perfect for her. Still, if she didn't, he just wanted her to be happy. That is what Joseph wanted for all of us. Annie has suffered more than most. I have never questioned your love for her, but my doubts have been about whether you can make her happy."

"I can."

Jack quietly studied Simon and again Simon had the urge to squirm but refrained from doing so.

"I know Annie thinks I'm an overprotective brother, but I love her, and I simply want her to live a happy life."

"You're a good brother, Jack."

Jack rose and poured both him and Simon a brandy before sitting back down. "You're damn right I am. I will always be there for Annie."

The words were a warning that Jack would be there to make sure Simon made her happy. "As you should be," Simon said.

Jack rummaged around the drawers in his desk before pulling out a document. He slid it across the desk towards Simon. "You will need to sign this."

Simon didn't read it. He flipped to the last page and signed his name. Jack raised a brow at him. "You didn't look at it."

"I know what it is. It is the same document you made Landers sign for Sophia. I don't want Annie's money. Keep it in a trust. I have plenty for both of us."

Jack smiled for the first time. "You know when I had Landers sign this, albeit late, he hemmed and hawed about it."

"I love Annie. The money doesn't matter."

Jack nodded. "Have you and Annie discussed a wedding date?"

Relief washed through Simon. He didn't think all was forgiven, but they would wed. "I hope soon. I need your assistance in acquiring a special license."

"I will send the request today."

Simon nodded, delighted by his willingness to help.

"If we can procure the license, you will marry within the week. My sister has lost all interest in what is proper. Scandal hangs over both your heads."

"If she agrees to that, I would like that very much."

Jack nodded. "You can ask her now. She is waiting for you in the drawing room."

Simon rose and bowed. "Thank you. I hope someday you and I can be close again."

"Well, you will be family. We don't have much choice," Jack said begrudgingly.

Simon made his way to the door and looked back at Jack before departing. "Thank you, Your Grace."

Jack sighed. "Jack. Call me Jack."

Miller grinned and nodded, feeling optimistic that their friendship was repairable.

He made his way to the drawing room. Annie stood by a window. Her loveliness took his breath away. She was all that he wanted. He'd almost lost her, but he would spend the rest of their lives proving she was what mattered most to him.

Her eyes met his, and the connection between them filled the room. Annie Kincaide would be his wife.

She smiled at him shyly. "Hello, Simon."

He walked towards her and fell to one knee. She flushed, seemingly embarrassed by the over-the-top romantic gesture. Simon didn't care. She would get a proper proposal.

Simon took her hand and said, "I love you, Lady Annabelle. You are everything I want or need. Please do me the honor of being my wife, partner, and friend for life."

She smiled down at him with so much love that his eyes filled with tears. "Yes, you silly man. Now stand up. This is too much."

He stood and pulled her to him. "It's not nearly enough but I will do my best every day to show you how much you are loved."

Her own eyes filled with tears as she brushed his away. "And I you."

Simon brushed a kiss over her lips and stepped back. She grabbed his waistcoat and said, "What are you doing?"

He laughed. "We have done very few things properly in this courtship, but until the wedding I plan to be the most proper gentleman."

Annie rolled her eyes. "Don't be ridiculous."

"I want to do this right."

"And when do you propose we wed?" she asked, annoyed at his stance.

"Your brother said it can be in a matter of days, if that is what you want."

She pursed her lips, thinking and finally said, "Yes I would like that my oh-so-proper betrothed."

He winked at her. "Just until our wedding night."

Chapter 30

Annie walked with Simon in the gardens of the Peyton townhouse. The early spring flowers that Mercy and the gardener worked so hard on were blooming. Her sister-in-law, between spring and fall, spent hours planning and tending the gardens in London and at the Peyton estate out in the country. She was widely known for her skills and designs.

Annie smiled. They were an idyllic setting to walk with one's betrothed. Well betrothed for only one more day. Tomorrow was the wedding. She looped her arm through Simon's as they walked farther into the gardens, passing from the structured rows of tulips into the whimsical area of the gardens where the flowers grew wildly. They arrived at her favorite part of the gardens, a beautiful flower tunnel. She had always loved it since it was installed but loved it even more as a secluded spot for her and Simon.

They had only been betrothed a few days, but Simon had escorted her in the gardens every day since then, spending a few moments in this tunnel, delighting in the touch of each other. As they reached the middle of the tunnel, Simon hungrily pulled her in for a kiss. She gasped as she felt his desire pressed up against her stomach.

Her body ached for him. She leaned her body into his as he plunged his tongue into her mouth. Her own tongue teased and beckoned him. Finally, he stepped away and ran his hands through his hair.

"You are tormenting me with these walks in this tunnel. Oh, the wicked things I want to do to you."

She laughed. "Only you are preventing us from doing more than kissing."

He groaned. She loved him so much. They were to be wed tomorrow. She couldn't believe how quickly everything had come together. It would be a small wedding, but the *ton* was already talking about it. A love match for the last unmarried Kincaide. She rolled her eyes at the dramatics of it all.

Still, nothing had slipped out about her adventure with Simon. There was plenty of gossip due to Simon being the owner of a gentleman's club and his murky association with the bank theft. Well not murky. He had been cleared of wrongdoing, but the *ton* loved to speculate.

She stared at him, wishing they were already wed and alone.

"Stop staring at me like that," he murmured.

She laughed. "Like what?"

"Like you want nothing more than for me to take you right here."

She winked at him, and he shook his head. Simon sat on a bench in the beautiful tunnel. The flowers were not in bloom yet, but the greenery was lovely. She joined him, and Simon intertwined one of his hands with hers. She leaned her head on his shoulder, content.

"What are you thinking about?"

She smiled at him. "Just how wonderful this all feels."

He kissed her hand that was intertwined with his. "I couldn't say it any better."

Walker still hadn't been found. Simon had met with the investigators a handful of times but none of the leads they pursued had panned out.

"Any worries about Walker?"

Simon shook his head. "The investigators haven't been able to find a valid lead. They believe he may have fled."

"I know that isn't what you want. I'm sorry."

He kissed the top of her head. "No it isn't but in time he will pay for his crimes. When that day comes you and I will be in court to see that happen."

"Together," she affirmed.

They were quiet for a moment, and Simon eventually said, "I'm sorry it took me almost dying to realize what an ass I was."

She couldn't fault Simon for wanting to see Walker pay for his crime, but she was glad he wasn't solely fixated on revenge anymore. Still, she found it odd that no one had seen Walker fleeing England or anywhere in the country.

"Do you worry that he will try to confront us or Mrs. Walker?"

Simon nodded. "I do. We ruined his life by proving he was the real criminal. I fear he is just biding his time, waiting for us to let our guard down."

Annie shivered, hoping that wasn't true. Was Walker a vengeful man? Hopefully not. "He would be foolish to do anything. If I were him, I would leave and never come back."

"If he is still here, I doubt he is thinking rationally. Perhaps it is for the best if he did indeed flee."

Annie silently agreed.

At least his father's name would be placed on the headstone where he laid buried. They planned to travel to New York City to hold a service to honor him.

Simon stood and held his hand out to her. She smiled and placed hers in his. He pulled her up and lightly brushed a kiss on her lips. Annie grabbed his waistcoat and pulled him in for another kiss.

He groaned. "I can't wait until we are in our own home. Perhaps we will have one of these flower tunnels built with a bed in it."

Annie flushed at the thought, liking the idea. He held his arm out to her, and she wrapped hers in his before they weaved their way back through the garden to the townhouse. Annie felt such joy that Simon would be her husband, but a tiny nibble of foreboding lodged within her. Where was Walker? And was he truly gone or was he waiting for them to let down their guard?

She shivered at the thought. He stopped. "Are you all right?"

Temptation to tell him that she was worried about Walker ran through her. Fury directed at the odious man who had ruined so much in Simon's life prevented her from doing so. Walker didn't deserve another moment of her or Simon's thoughts. Walker would not ruin tomorrow. He had already ruined so much. She forced him from her mind and said, "Perfectly fine."

~

Simon paced back and forth in Devons' office as he listened to the investigators explain their concerns. They had a credible lead. Apparently, Walker was still in England, not only England but in London and was monitoring Simon and Annie's activities. A combination of fear and fury clawed at him. The damn man could be anywhere.

"Where is he?" Simon bit out.

One of the investigators shook his head. "We don't know, sir. We obtained the lead from a server at one of the taverns in the dock area, but she said it had been two days since she last saw Walker."

"Are you sure he hired a man to watch us?"

Both the investigators nodded, and one said, "Yes, she said that one night they had a rather loud conversation about your betrothed."

Part of Simon wished he would have continued to look in the dock area, but he pushed away the thoughts. That is what he hired the investigators for. There was no guarantee he would have found Walker himself.

"Put more men on this. Find him now," Simon demanded.

The investigators nodded and left the room. Simon turned to Devons and said, "We need to leave right away. I need to make sure she is protected."

Devons patted him on the back in reassurance. "Jack has the best protection and guards that any family could want. He wouldn't let any harm come to her."

"If Walker dares to touch her," Simon said darkly.

"He won't. I almost didn't have them tell you this today."

Simon glared at him. "I would have never forgiven you."

"Let the investigators do their job. Today is your wedding day. Focus on that."

Simon knew Devons was right, but the information about Walker unsettled him. He had convinced himself Walker had left England. Perhaps not convinced but hoped. He itched to track the man down himself. His old obsession rushed through him.

"Let's get to the church. You will see your bride and feel better."

Yes, he needed to see Annie. Simon made his way out the front door of the Den into a carriage. Devons climbed in with him and said, "It will be fine. Walker wouldn't dare confront Annie. I did tell the investigators to notify Bromley and Mrs. Walker in case he is also having someone watch her."

"Let's go. Bromley and Mrs. Walker will be at the wedding as well. I want to warn everyone about the new development. And I need to see Annie immediately."

The wedding was a perfect opportunity for Walker to strike. Would the man be so bold? Fear twisted in Simon's stomach.

Devon knocked on the side of the carriage, and it jerked into motion. He knew his sense of urgency wasn't logical, but he reassured himself once he saw her all would be fine.

He tried to calm himself but worry emanated from him. Devons frowned at him. "She will be fine."

Simon didn't respond, and they rode in silence the rest of the way. He impatiently tapped his foot on the floor of the carriage, cursing the slow pace at which London traffic made them move. Agitation coursed through him, but finally the carriage stopped out front of the small church they were having their ceremony in. Both he and Annie had wanted a small intimate ceremony, and the church suited perfectly.

He hopped out and glanced around. Nothing seemed out of the ordinary. A few friends and associates mingled outside waiting for the ceremony to begin. He took a deep breath, relieved at the normalcy before him.

He didn't stop to say hello but rushed into the church, looking for Jack or more importantly Annie. He breathed a sigh of relief when Simon spotted Jack and Sam standing off to one side. He made his way to them. Sam's smile grew broad as he stopped in front of them. "Are you ready?"

"Where is Annie?"

Jack studied him and finally said, "Preparing in a side room. Is everything okay?"

"The investigators have a lead on Walker."

The Kincaide brothers stiffened, waiting intently for him to continue. Simon ran his hands across his cleanly shaven face, oddly missing the scruff that used to exist.

"What is it?" Jack demanded.

"The investigators said Walker hired someone to watch Annie and me. They still don't have Walker's whereabouts, but I'm concerned he is planning something."

"Do you think he would attempt to do something at the wedding?" Sam questioned.

Simon didn't know. "I need to see Annie."

Jack shook his head. "I just left her. She is fine. You need to make your way to the altar. I will head back to be with her."

Simon didn't want to go to the damn altar. He needed to lay eyes on Annie and know that she was all right. Jack placed a reassuring hand on his shoulder. "Let me do this. Don't let Walker control this day. It's too important for you and my sister."

He took a deep breath. Jack was right. Sam said, "I will go with you, Jack."

The Kincaide brothers made their way to the side room and Simon made his way to the altar. He waited, trying his best to push his concerns away. This is exactly how Walker would want him. Jack was right. Simon couldn't let the man ruin this day. He had destroyed too much in Simon's life.

Simon took another deep breath. He was marrying the woman he had loved for years and thought he could never have. His father would be so happy with his marriage. He focused all his energy on that. His eyes darted to the door Jack and Sam left through, but it remained closed.

His body hummed with alertness. The door opened, and his body filled with relief, but it quickly disappeared when only Jack and Sam reemerged. They made their way to Simon, rushing past friends trying to greet them. Something was wrong.

Simon left his spot at the altar, meeting them halfway.

"She isn't in the room," Jack said in a hushed tone.

Simon clenched his jaw. Damn it. Walker was here. Fury and fear filled him.

"Let's take it easy. We will search the rooms down the hallway one at a time. Perhaps she is in another room," Sam said, trying to reassure both him and Jack.

Simon wasn't alone in his concerns. Jack motioned to Bromley, and he made his way towards them. Simon couldn't wait any longer. He charged towards the door that led to the side rooms. Jack and Sam were on his heels with Bromley taking up the rear.

As they reached the door, Mercy stood to the side of it. "Where are you going?"

Simon didn't answer and continued on. He heard Jack tell her in passing that they couldn't find Annie and to keep the guests in the main room of the church.

Simon stood in the hallway, unsure where to start. He threw open the first door, and the room was empty. It appeared to be the room Annie was getting ready in. Nothing was out of place except his betrothed was missing. His skin prickled with dread. Walker was here.

He turned back to Jack and Sam. "Something is wrong."

They both nodded. A handful of doors lined the hallway, and the farthest stood at the end of the hallway facing them.

It appeared to lead to another section of the church. Simon stopped a staff member walking by and asked, “Where does the door at the end lead to?”

The young man stared at him confused. “Sir, the only thing back there is the kitchen and some sleeping quarters.”

The man scurried off.

“We need to check each room,” Sam stated.

Simon frowned with impatience, but Jack nodded in agreement. “We need to be methodical about this.”

He didn’t want to be methodical. Simon wanted to tear the place apart. Still, he knew it would do them no good if he lost it. Sam’s approach was best. He nodded. Simon needed to find Annie. He hoped that her missing was a misunderstanding, but he couldn’t keep away the thoughts that Walker was here. He would kill him with his bare hands if he harmed Annie.

Chapter 31

Annie stood with Walker in the small kitchen at the back of the church. Jack had left her for a brief moment, and in that moment, Walker had squeezed his way into the room. She initially struggled with him but allowed him to usher her out of the room she was using when he started to brandish a pistol.

Her eyes ran over the unkempt man before her, so different from the charming man who seemed to maneuver so easily in ballrooms. He looked like he hadn't slept in days.

"What are you planning to do?"

Walker glared at her. "Take away what your betrothed wants more than anything, you."

Annie frowned. He pointed his pistol at her, chuckling as if this were a jolly game. She needed to make him leave or find a way to escape. Her eyes darted around the room, looking for anything to help her.

"There is nothing, my lady. I can see your brain swirling with thoughts. You are hoping there is another option, but I have nothing left. If I die here today, at least I will know that I won in the end."

"Do you think this is a game between you and Miller?" she asked, confused.

He smirked. "It has always been a game from the moment Miller and I met. Actually, from the moment he wouldn't move on in New York City. My family sent me away because he wouldn't stop investigating his father's case. Do you know how that feels to be forced away by your own family?"

"You set up another man for a crime."

Walker sulked. "How was I supposed to know they would accuse John Miller of the crime? I never saw that coming."

Annie glared at him. "Did you think you would just steal all the items from the vault, and no one would be held accountable?"

He didn't say anything. Perhaps he did. What a spoiled, entitled man, she thought.

"Regardless of my actions, your betrothed should have let it go. I thought he did until I met him at the Den. He thought I didn't know who he was, but I did. I was livid by his appearance in London. I have been nothing but respectable since arriving in England."

"What about Lemming?" Annie snapped.

Walker appeared surprised at her question but didn't answer. A coldness filled his eyes. The man was dangerous. She didn't want to be near him.

"If you leave now, you could be on a ship before Simon even knows you are here."

Walker smirked at her. "Isn't that sweet? You are already calling him Simon."

She glared at him. "Leave."

Walker moved closer to her, and her nose twitched at the smell wafting off of him.

"That is what you don't understand. I want him to know I am here. I want him to seek you out, and the moment he walks through that door, I am going to pull this trigger. Boom! Miller loses the most important thing in his life," he hissed.

Fear filled her—not for herself but for Simon. If Walker took her life, Simon would snap. Commotion in the hallway jerked her attention from Walker. Doors opened and slammed, followed by multiple footsteps getting louder. Simon and likely her brothers were making their way down the hallway.

Walker grinned at her gleefully, happy his plan was working. Simon would be the first through the door. He wouldn't wait or be cautious. He would charge in, concerned for her. Walker pointed his pistol at her as if calculating the appropriate trajectory. He really meant to do it. Annie pursed her lips together. She would be damned if she stood here and waited to get shot. Walker would not end her life. She had survived too much.

The odious man looked back at the door and Annie charged him. He tumbled backwards, falling on his posterior. She fell on top of him with a hard thud, her body holding him down. In the mayhem the pistol slid across the floor. Walker tossed her off of him, and he scrambled for the pistol. Annie grabbed his foot, preventing him from reaching it. He stared back at her, livid. He kicked at her with his other foot, but she hung on.

Eventually her arms grew tired, and his foot slipped from her hands. He let out a loud cackle before his newly released foot made contact with the side of her head. She screamed and collapsed on the floor. Pain ricocheted through her head.

She ignored it and scrambled to her knees. Walker, still crawling, scurried across the ground and grabbed the pistol. He climbed to his feet before towering over her.

"I should kill you now," he sneered.

Annie, still on the ground, held her hands up as if terrified. He chuckled and briefly looked at the door. She raised her leg and kicked one of his legs as hard as she could. He howled in pain, and she kicked the other leg, causing him to collapse in a heap. She ignored his screams and surged to her feet, almost falling as she charged towards the door. She swung it open and stumbled out. Simon, Sam, and Jack were only a few feet away.

She raced towards them. “Hide! He has a pistol.”

She looked back as Walker stumbled out of the room. He glanced between her and Simon before raising his pistol. His aim was directly at Annie. She looked at Simon as his face filled with fury. He roared by her, knocking Walker down before he had the chance to pull the trigger. Simon in a rage pummeled him with his fists. He grew tired and stopped to catch his breath. His eyes connected with the pistol lying next to them. He reached for it.

“No!” Annie screamed.

~

The fury that Simon felt for Walker was uncontrollable. He held the pistol in his hand, wanting nothing more than to kill the man. He pushed the tip of the barrel against Walker’s temple. He wanted to kill him for his father but more than anything he wanted to kill him for daring to think he could harm Annie.

The bloodied man moaned. “Do what you will, Miller. I am ready for the end.”

He pushed the pistol harder against Walker’s head. Annie gasped behind him. He looked back at her, and she remained quiet, but he could see it in her eyes. The choice he made would decide who he would be for the rest of his life. He badly wanted to end Walker’s life. The man deserved to die.

“Do it. I can’t live in prison,” Walker moaned.

He couldn’t do it. He had too much to live for. He jerked his hand away and handed the pistol to Jack. “You deserve to live the rest of your life in the hell you put my father in.”

Walker seemed to perk up with the thought of being sent back to prison in New York City. Simon leaned into him and said, “Your family isn’t in charge anymore to protect you. That is what Clark and Collins were really here for."

Walker paled considerably and collapsed either from the beating Simon just gave him or the thought of what was waiting for him.

"I had a staff member summon a constable and some of his men. They should be here shortly," Bromley said, appearing with Derry and Devons.

Simon stood and turned to Annie. She fell into his arms, placing a kiss on his mouth in front of everyone.

"You didn't choose revenge."

"He isn't worth it. Nothing is worth giving you up."

She kissed him again. Simon loved this woman so damn much.

"Enough with the kissing. You are not wed," Jack growled from further down the hallway.

Devons, Derry, and Sam laughed. Simon joined in. Annie stared at them all as if they were insane.

Once he recovered, he said, "Well today we are going to change that."

Annie's brow lifted in confusion. "You still want to marry today?"

"We aren't leaving this church until we say, 'I do.'"

She frowned. "Are you sure?"

"The moment they escort him away, I am taking my place at the altar and waiting until you meet me. I will wait all night if I must."

Annie smiled at him, and her eyes filled with devotion. "I love you."

"And I love you."

Simon pulled her in for a kiss, and Annie smiled as she heard Jack grumble in the background, "Why does no one listen to me?"

A few hours later, Simon did just as he said and stood at the altar watching Annie walk towards him. Powerful emotions filled his chest. Even after the scuffle, she was still lovely. Her black hair hung down her back in large curls, and she wore a white ball gown adorned with tiny crystals. She looked like some type of beautiful enchantress written about in books.

Their eyes connected, and she mouthed the words I love you. He mouthed them back. This would be his wife. This unapologetically bold woman that did as she pleased. And she wanted him. He would spend the rest of their lives showing her she made the right choice.

He glanced around the church and was honored to see Annie's family and their closest friends still in attendance, waiting for them to say I do. His eyes filled with tears, but he refused to let them fall.

Annie joined him. They turned towards each other, and she looked at him curiously. "Are you crying?"

"I'm just realizing how blessed I am," he whispered.

"We may have had the craziest wedding of the season."

He winked at her. She was right. There was nothing perfect about their wedding day. In truth, it was an absolute disaster, but right now all Simon could think was how lucky he was that he got to marry the woman he loved in front of his close friends.

"Ready?"

"Yes," she whispered.

Epilogue

New York City - 1845

Annie stood with Simon in the little, small neighborhood cemetery, admiring the new headstone that had been carved for his father. She stared down at the smooth rock and the inscription.

John Miller
Honorable man and loving father
1782 - 1836

It proudly declared who was buried under the previous nameless headstone. She squeezed his hand, knowing how much this moment meant to him. He wrapped his arm around her, pulling her close before placing a kiss on her forehead.

Walker's case had taken two years to wrap up and almost a year and a half before his trial started. Annie and Simon had arrived in New York City and attended every one of his days in court. In court, he cried injustice, but the evidence was too strong. Simon hung onto every word of the trial, transfixed by it. Annie sat next to him, his anchor of support. They didn't scream for joy at his guilty verdict but breathed a sigh of relief that it was over.

As Clark promised, Walker was held accountable for his crimes. Fittingly, he would serve his prison sentence on Blackwell Island, the same place Simon's father had been sent to. Justice was served. His actions and his family's had lasting ramifications in New York City.

Even before Walker's trial, the High Constable Monroe was removed from his position and the police department dismantled, replaced by a new system. The new construct was modeled after the London Peelers. For now, it seemed to be working, but Annie was skeptical if change really would happen. She hoped it would and wouldn't just be replaced by more of the same.

"A fitting headstone," Clark said from behind them.

Both Annie and Simon turned to see Clark and Collins standing at the entrance of the cemetery. Collins had been selected and persuaded to take a job as a constable while Clark said he would continue on in his current role. Annie wondered what that was exactly. She actually asked him again, and he had given her a cheeky wink, murmuring something about being better behind the scenes.

They spent a great deal of time with the men since arriving back in America. Both men had become dear friends in that time.

"So what's next?" Collins asked.

Annie and Simon glanced at each other. They hadn't talked much about what they would do after the trial. Annie wondered if a part of him wanted to stay in New York City. It was where he grew up.

Clark chuckled. "Don't ask them that. Clearly, they don't know."

Collins scowled at him. "How was I supposed to know?"

Clark rolled his eyes and clapped the other man on the back. "Let's allow them to say their goodbyes. We will meet you out front of the church."

Simon nodded and turned back to the grave. He placed his hand on the headstone, and Annie leaned against him.

"I wish I could have met him," she said.

He smiled sadly. "Me too. He would have loved you."

She smiled up at him.

He stepped back and sat on a bench at the edge of the cemetery, motioning Annie over. She smiled at her husband. He was so dashing that sometimes it made her heart hurt just to look at him. They had been through so much together.

She sat next to him, and he said, “So what is next?”

Annie looked at his side profile trying to guess what he was thinking. “What do you want?”

He smiled at her. “You have spent months with me waiting for this trial to end. I want to know what you want.”

Annie thought about it. Part of her was tempted to stay in America. Part of her would always belong here. But she would miss her family if she stayed.

Simon lifted a brow. She said, “I want to go home. To London.”

He cupped her face in his hands and gently kissed her lips. “That is what I thought you would say.”

“Is that what you want?” she asked.

He kissed her again. “You are where my home is. I am so glad we were able to do this. Not so much the trial but to make sure my father’s headstone has his name. Now, I’m ready to go home too.”

“I love you,” Annie said.

Simon stared back at her with such adoration it left her breathless. “You are my world, Annie Miller. Now and forever. We will book passage as soon as possible.”

Joy filled Annie’s heart. They were going home. She frowned thinking of Sophia. Her last letter had stated that she was casting off her widow weeds and was ready to live. She didn’t disapprove of Sophia wanting to move on. It had been two years since Landers’ death and the man had left this earth with his mistress by his side.

Two years of mourning was more than what Annie thought

Sophia should have given him but that was Sophia. Still, something in her letter made Annie nervous.

"We will make it back right when Sophia is planning to come out of mourning," Annie said.

"Christ!" Simon muttered.

Annie playfully swatted him, and he grinned ruefully at her. "What!"

This man. How she loved him.

As she turned back to the headstone, she thought about Maggie and Joseph. They would have adored Simon, especially her father. If alive, he would have gloated that he predicted she would find her match.

And he would have been right. Simon was her perfect match and more importantly the best partner in love and life. There were no secrets between them. He knew all of her flaws, even the physical ones and loved her even more for them. And she loved him just the same.

Thank You For Reading!

I hope you enjoyed Annie and Simon's story. In my mind, these two have been secretly in love since The Questionable Acts of an American Gentleman. It was so fun to put their story down in writing. Simon's past really started as an idea from reading about a bank theft that took place in New York City in 1831. Another fun fact the New York City Police Department did really model themselves after the London Police Department around this time period.

The last book in the Kincaide series will be about Sophia and her love interest. I'm so excited to write about it! If you are interested in getting updates on Sophia's story as well as other fun stuff related to historical romance, sign-up for my newsletter: https://ramonaelmes.com/?page_id=295

Lastly, as an indie author, reviews are so important. If you feel so inclined, I would love a review for The Bold Choices of a Devoted Lady.

Review: https://amazon.com/gp/product/B0B1BJZQBK

About The Author

Ramona Elmes lives in Maryland, not far from the bay with her husband, sister, two accomplished stepdaughters, one independent nine-year-old, two old French bulldogs, and one very large Chesapeake bay retriever mix. When not writing she loves to travel, hike, and peruse thrift shops and garage sales for hidden gems. To follow Ramona on her writing journey, go to her website https://ramonaelmes.com

Acknowledgements

Thanks to my awesome hubby for all of your support. 2022 has been a crazy year, but even in the chaos, you have pushed me to keep writing. 143

Thank you to Rachel Garber and Susan Keillor for your phenomenal editing skills. Rachel, I can't believe we have worked on three books together! Special thank you to always helping me enhance the story I'm trying to tell :O)

Thank you to GM Design for my book cover. Love it!

Thank you to all the beta readers and arc readers out there that provide such awesome feedback!

Made in the USA
Monee, IL
29 July 2022